AT
LARGE

Also by Lynne Murray

Larger Than Death

Large Target

AT LARGE

A JOSEPHINE FULLER MYSTERY

Lynne Murray

St. Martin's Minotaur ≈ New York

 For information, address St. Martin's Press, 175 Fifth Avenue, New York, N.Y. 10010.

www.minotaurbooks.com

Library of Congress Cataloging-in-Publication Data

Murray, Lynne.
At large : a Josephine Fuller mystery / Lynne Murray.
—1st ed.
p. cm.
ISBN 0-312-28029-7
1. Fuller, Josephine (Fictitious character)—Fiction.
2. Women private investigators—California—San Diego—Fiction. 3. San Diego (Calif.)—Fiction. 4. Overweight women—Fiction. 5. Charities—Fiction. I. Title.

PS3563.U7716 A94 2001
813'.54—dc21 2001019267

First Edition: July 2001

10 9 8 7 6 5 4 3 2 1

This book is dedicated with love to my brother Mike Murray, who put it best when he said, "We are the only two people in the world who know how lucky we are to have the parents we had."

Acknowledgments

Over the years I have counted myself very fortunate to have had the opportunity to hear wisdom on all the subtle shades and social quirks of terror from one of its foremost critics—connoisseur of horror noir Bob Stephens. May your zombies always dance on Broadway.

Thanks to both parties for the recipe for lentil soup, which was kindly shared with me by Christopher Rankin, who received it from Cees Van Aalst. I can testify that it is quite tasty when prepared without firearms.

I appreciate the energy healing insights from Gregory Booi and Jaqueline Girdner, as well as the introduction to Marilyn King, who provided invaluable information on ceremonial energy cleansing.

Robert Liebman provided useful hot tub perspectives, for which I am most appreciative.

The people whom I have thanked in acknowledgments to previous books still enrich my life beyond telling, and I offer continuing thanks for their friendship and help.

AT
LARGE

Of all the women's job skill centers in all the towns in all the Pacific Northwest, he walks into mine. It had been a rocky week already, and it wasn't Friday yet. In fact Thursday morning was moving so slowly that if I hadn't personally witnessed each second tick off on the big black schoolroom clock across from my desk, I would have sworn that time was standing still. It didn't help that no one was buying my best impersonation of a mild-mannered receptionist. As a woman who has never weighed less than two hundred pounds in my adult life, you might not guess that I can be inconspicuous, but if I keep my head down and my mouth shut, I can usually pull it off. Unfortunately the earnest blue silk pantsuit, pearls and expression of well-bred naivete weren't working.

Something about this job skill center wasn't quite right. I needed to find out what it was for Mrs. Madrone, so that my wealthy employer could decide whether to award the place a grant. Maybe I had asked too many questions.

By the time Ted showed up, I was already on Delores Patton's radar. The center director was an African-American woman who commanded respect with an attitude that could clean brass at twenty paces. She knew I wasn't your usual do-gooder. She just hadn't decided how to deal with it. Ted's arrival made up her mind, and managed to get me fired from a volunteer job—not as easy as it sounds.

Teddy Etheridge was the first male who had entered the office in the three weeks I had been volunteering there. The center was located in Bremerton, about an hour's ferry ride southwest of Seattle. I'd stayed in Bremerton during the week answering phones, helping out and nosing around. On the weekends in Seattle I saw my Persian tomcat, Raoul. Thor Mulligan took care of the cat for me during the week.

I had a crush on Mulligan, but he was still grieving over the death of Nina, his lover and my best friend. It had been three months since she died and I was mourning her too. But I was also fighting off a terrific yearning for Mulligan, who had drastically mixed feelings about getting involved with me, or maybe with anyone at this point.

We had tested this theory by spending a night together six weeks earlier. The night itself had been wonderful—right up until the emotional tidal wave of guilt and grief swept over Mulligan and left me untouched.

He had backed away from me after that. We hadn't talked about it much. I felt guilty about how I didn't feel guilty. As for what I could do next—the short answer appeared to be "not much."

For a split second when Teddy walked in the door, I thought he might be a potential employer who had strayed in without an appointment. Not that I'd ever seen an actual employer on the premises. They did call from time to time to get cheap labor. Oops—I mean to support the Women's Job Skill Center.

Then I recognized him. "Teddy!" It was always Ted or Teddy to his friends. Never Theodore, not even on his book covers. He wrote humor books for a living.

When he realized it was me, his bearded face lit up in a huge grin. "Josephine Fuller!"

"Ted Etheridge. The last of the hopeless romantics."

I came around the desk to shake hands with him, and he pulled me into a big hug. An inch or two over six feet tall and square as a teddy bear, Ted was not quite fat because he was so intensely physically active. I pulled back to take a look at him. Now in his late thirties, he would always be boyish, with a shock of red-brown hair that seemed to fall into his eyes no matter how short it was cut.

Our last conversation had lasted over a dozen hours—the night in Kathmandu when both of our marriages died.

Ted had been married to Francesca Benedict Etheridge, a gifted mountain climber. It had looked as if she might attempt an ascent on Mount Everest. That climb fell through, and she ended up ascending my husband—as he then was. Leaving Ted to entertain me in the lobby of the Everest Vista Hotel which, incidentally being quite a distance away in Nepal, does not have a view of Mt. Everest.

I had been married to Griffin Fuller, world-renowned as a photographer, and well-known (except to his wife) as a philanderer. Teddy had been playing the part of the supportive husband of a climber, helping Francesca field media coverage, and occupying himself by gathering local color in Nepal. He had a gift for mingling with serious trekkers and climbers, who sometimes mistook him for one of their own. But his appearance was deceptive. Teddy dabbled in climbing and a variety of other sports. But in everything he did, he was always looking for a punch line.

"Josephine, I haven't seen you—well, since that infamous night. Is it still Jo Fuller or did you get divorced?"

"Yes to both questions. My maiden name was O'Toole, so

I kept Griff's last name in lieu of alimony. What about you and Francesca?"

He shrugged. "It's in the works."

"Is that anything like 'the check is in the mail'? 'The divorce is in the works'?"

"You can't know what hard work that is," Ted said. "It's backbreaking labor to convince Francesca to let go of anything she once controlled. Speaking of which, she's still with Griff. Did you know that?"

"I made it a point not to know."

That night in the hotel lobby was etched in my memory. Ted and I had met a few days earlier, as both he and Griff had assignments from the same travel magazine. As we waited in the lobby, it became clearer with each hour that our respective spouses, scheduled to arrive at any moment, were both not showing up.

We adjourned to the bar, and began comparing notes. We were able to put together a pretty strong case for the suspicion that my husband and his wife were spending the night together. Ted and I had some quantity of time to reflect on the qualities we both expected in a spouse. Loyalty was high on both our lists, but the partners we were with didn't seem to feel the same way.

We got along famously. We managed to laugh quite a lot, considering the situation. The Scotch whiskey might have helped. There was never any possibility that we might have wandered up to one of the rooms together that long dark night for some mutual comfort. True, we did both have that little kink about not cheating.

But, I must also note that, as a large-sized woman, I've developed extra-sensitive radar for men who see me as a sexual being, versus men who see a surrogate mom. Ted had cried on my shoulder that night in Kathmandu. No problem, we were consenting adults crying on each other's shoulders. Now I got the sinking feeling that he viewed me as a warm, fuzzy shoulder to lay his head on, and indulge in another sympathy session.

I was in no mood. I needed to stop that in its tracks.

"So what brings you here, Ted? Are you planning a sex-change operation, and lining up future employment? I hate to tell you, but the pay cut is the most unkindest cut of all."

Teddy burst out laughing, which seemed to knock him out of what looked like a looming self-pity jag. "*Et tu*, Josephine!" he quipped with his hand over his heart. "You'll have to stand in line today—grab a knife and take a number."

"Ouch!" I chalked him up a point for quick recovery and the edgy image of Teddy as Caesar surrounded by knife-wielding, female assailants.

But there was a gasp from behind me, and I saw the center director, Delores Patton. She was the image of the Black executive woman of today from her copper-colored wool business suit with matching nails, to her short Afro hairstyle and take-charge expression. Delores had already expressed doubts about whether I should be there. My joking with Ted sent the room temperature zooming downward until I could almost hear her opinion crystallize into a solid, frozen, "No."

Ted got in a flash that I had shocked Delores, and that tickled him even more. He was amazingly good-natured for a humorist—a job that usually comes with neurotic baggage. He wrote a syndicated column, *Ted's Wide World of Bumbling,* based on his attempts to try new and daring destinations and modes of transportation, usually with hilarious results. He also wrote a series of books about adventure travel for the clueless, which had bumbled onto the bestseller list. The first one was *Bumbling Through the Jungle*—about a tourist wandering the rainforests of the world. This was succeeded by *Bumbling*

Around in Boats—about sailing boats of all sizes. In Nepal, he had been gathering material for *Bumbling Along the Roof of the World.*

Delores blinked as if she recognized Ted's name when I introduced him as a bestselling author. Ted stared at his feet and mumbled, "Aw, shucks." But Delores continued to look grim.

"Sorry, ma'am, I just bumbled into your office by mistake," Ted said, giving Delores his most boyish look. "What a wonderful surprise to find my old friend Josephine. Can you spare her for lunch?" He asked her, as if begging a parent to let their child come out to play.

"You're supposed to ask me, Teddy," I said, although Delores's reaction was interesting.

"I was getting to that, Jo. If this gracious lady can spare you for an hour."

Delores stepped past me, punched the intercom, and called one of the counselors to cover the phones. She muttered that I was free to go now if I wanted. She didn't say anything about not coming back. But it was there if I wanted to hear it.

2

So I found myself unexpectedly set free from the office, strolling with Teddy into the late morning overcast of August in Bremerton.

"Would you mind if we took the ferry to Port Orchard?" he asked. "There's a mom-and-pop restaurant here that's good, but I'm not their favorite person these days."

"What? You didn't tip?"

"It's a long story. Let me buy you a good seafood lunch, if you can spare a little more time. It's only a twenty-minute ride."

I thought about Delores, no doubt waiting to pounce when I went back to the center, and decided I would wind up that assignment, no matter what she did. "Okay."

We didn't have to wait long for the ferry. It was for foot traffic only, no cars, and it followed the waterfront all the way to Port Orchard. "You seem to know your way around this part of the world," I said.

"It's a long way from Kathmandu."

"At least we're not praying for an avalanche."

Teddy laughed a little grimly. We both watched the onshore world slip by in silence, thinking back to that night.

If we hadn't both been tortured by thoughts of what our spouses were doing together, we would have had a hilarious time. With each hour that they did not show up, the jokes got sharper and seemed immensely funnier than they could have at any other time. We decided that news of our spouses having been killed in an avalanche might be welcome or unwelcome, depending on the position of the bodies and the amount of clothing they were wearing when discovered.

As the night wore on, Ted would sneak an occasional amazed look at me. The unspoken subtext was, "What a fantastic woman. I'd go to bed with her in a minute if she weighed about a hundred pounds less."

I had a sharp reply ready. Whenever a gentleman decides to share this priceless insight with me—and an amazing number do—I am forced to cut him, and then stand back out of the way so he doesn't bleed on my rather expensive plus-sized outfit. The violence is confined to words. But it's surprising how respectful even a self-important male can become when he grasps that should he overstep the bounds of politeness, you can slice out his ego and hand it to him on a plate.

But Ted made me laugh and never ventured an insult—just those occasional cautious glances. Yep, got it right the first time, she's fat. I guess he'd never spent that much time with a large woman.

I gave him the benefit of the doubt because we were crouching on the same ledge in hell, and he was good company in hell. His face today testified that he'd managed to find a return ticket. We got off the ferry and he led the way to the Bay Street Restaurant, which had crisp white tablecloths, warm bread and a comprehensive seafood menu.

Sure enough, he ordered a double Scotch, single malt. Already planning my drive back to Seattle, I decided to stick with coffee, ordered the grilled sole lunch plate and sat back, resigned to listening.

"Okay, Ted, what's this sad story?"

"It's so incredible running into you like this, Jo. Because you really are responsible for my pathetic and heartbroken state."

"This is not about Francesca," I guessed.

"No. I've been lucky in love since Fran and I broke up. At least I thought I was lucky. I came into that center looking for the woman who was the love of my life. She just left me. But if it wasn't for you, I never would have found her to begin with."

"What's her name?"

"Lucille. How can I describe her? She was a goddess."

He was using the past tense. I sighed noiselessly. Lucille was either dead, or her goddess status had been revoked.

"That night in Kathmandu I couldn't help but kick myself for never having noticed you before. But more than anything that night, I hated Francesca. Did you know I left Nepal the next day?"

"No. I was a little preoccupied. Griff and I spent a few days fighting before I left."

"I still hear from Fran. I'm bugging her to sign the divorce papers. But she still hasn't quite accepted the fact that I didn't retire to a monastery after we broke up. But you don't care do you? You've found someone else—I can tell."

I was a little startled by his remark, but I didn't deny it. "Yes, I guess I have, but—it's complicated."

"But you're happy."

I almost said, "I am?" But I didn't want to get into my problems. Neither did he. He wanted to talk about his.

"I was as happy as you, until a couple of months ago."

A chill went down my spine for some reason. "What happened?"

"Her name was Lucille. She was a waitress at a little mom-and-pop place in Bremerton."

"The one where you're no longer welcome." I raised my eyebrows.

He managed a faint smile. "It's your fault, Jo, that I noticed her the way I did. She was bigger than you—over three hundred pounds, not that I could estimate. She told me that later. She had green eyes and the most amazing hair, like twenty-four-carat gold, with wonderful olive skin that set it off. She had this luminous cheerfulness about her. She just wore a simple white blouse and black skirt, but when she stood next to the table and I looked up, her breasts seemed to go on forever. We chatted a bit, and I guess I just basked in her simple friendliness. When she brought my order, I told her about my book and she seemed thrilled—which got my attention." He smiled.

"So you're telling me she gave signs of sharing your enthusiasm for yourself?"

"Yes, I love that in a woman." This time he came up with his most winning smile but then stared back into the middle distance and conjured up the past. "When she went to get me more coffee, I told myself here was a warm, charming, lovely woman whom I once would never have given the time of day to. So I flirted a bit, she flirted back, and that was the end of it. I told her I was about to bumble across the country on my motorcycle, and I'd see her in a few months. That was when I was writing *Bumbling and the Art of Motorcycle Maintenance*."

"Right. I read it. Great stuff."

"Thanks. Anyway, Lucille told me that sounded like a lot more fun than slinging hash, but she guessed she'd still be doing that when I returned. It was fun to talk to her. I told myself I must be over Francesca, because what could be more unlike her than this unpretentious waitress? Fran was always—well, you remember Fran."

"Oh, yeah." Fran was petite but muscular, the kind of woman who looks like she's wearing an elegant designer outfit when she's sprawled on a sofa in jeans and a thermal undershirt. I had spent lots of time successfully not thinking about her, and I wasn't about to start dwelling on her now.

"I don't know why, but somehow just flirting with Lucille, I felt pleased with myself," Ted continued. "As if I had tried some exotic dish I'd heard rumors about."

"You sampled her dish?"

"No, no. We just talked, but I thought about it."

"And?"

He sighed. "Once I got on the road I started to get this obsession with her. That hair, those eyes, those breasts."

"Okay, okay, I get it. Turn your motor off."

"Sorry. Anyway by the time I'd got my material, and was settling down to write, I told myself I was creating an ideal woman out of a wild fantasy. Still, I could write anywhere, so why not down here on the peninsula near that charming mom-and-pop restaurant?"

"So you came back here."

"I found a place, and started writing. I took my meals at the restaurant. Lucille was still there. She seemed glad to see me, but I noticed she was nice to everyone. It was like I was a kid again. She wasn't wearing a ring. She didn't seem to be going out with anyone. But I just couldn't get up the nerve to ask her out."

"What happened?"

"It came to the point where I couldn't stand it anymore. I found out when she got off, and rode over there on my motorcycle just before quitting time. I asked if we could talk. I told her how I felt, and she agreed to go out with me."

I sighed. "Well, that's good, Ted, what happened then?"

"We were great together, amazing. One thing led to another." He smiled in a way that made me distinctly uncomfortable. "I sampled her dish, as you put it. We were so happy." I nodded. Ted leaned forward, gazing past me into that earlier time. "I was writing; we moved in together. We even talked about her maybe taking some night classes. She was fascinated with my work. She was a great reader. But her family owned the diner where she had worked since junior high school. No one ever told her she could go to college. I would have been delighted to support her in anything she wanted to do. It turned out what she wanted to do was lose weight."

"That wasn't your idea?"

"I believe on that memorable night when you and I talked, I got an earful of your views on that subject." He looked up at the ceiling and recited, " 'Long-term studies show that all but a tiny fraction of the people who do lose weight gain back every pound, some gain back more,' et cetera, et cetera."

I blinked at him. "Gosh, I don't even remember telling you any of that. It's true, but I can't imagine how the subject came up."

"You can't remember how you told me off?" He stared at me, incredulous.

"Sorry. Don't take it personally. That was a crazy night. I gave you a hard time, huh?"

"I was pompous, I deserved it." He looked a little sheepish. "I made some casual remark about losing weight, and you told me in a rather dramatic fashion what an ignorant ass I was."

I shrugged. "Okay, I can imagine my saying something like that. A lot of the details of our conversation were driven out of my mind by the sight of Griff giving Francesca a pelvic exam along with a farewell kiss in the lobby."

"That was a shocker, wasn't it? But I got the impression you were more surprised at what Griff did than I was at Fran.

It just confirmed what I'd been suspecting for months. She was always looking for a higher mountain and Griff was it. Poor bastard." He shook his head. "Anyway, I told Lucille what you said about the futility of dieting. Maybe it lost something in the translation. She said it sounded like sour grapes to her. All I could say was I loved her, and I would still love her no matter what. I went on an assignment for a travel magazine to Costa Rica. I was gone for a month, did some book promotion along the way. When I got back to Bremerton, Lucille had lost forty pounds. In the next year she lost another sixty. I had never been around anyone on a serious diet before. It was like she had PMS for a bloody year. Both of us were nervous wrecks."

"And?" I was wondering if I should even bother to go back to the center. We had finished our lunches and I'd had a refill on the coffee. It was getting late.

"The more weight Lucille lost, the more hyper she got. Her doctor had her on some prescription diet pills. She lost a hundred and fifty pounds in a year and a half. I scarcely recognized her, but I still loved her. I was worried that she was having some kind of breakdown, she was so anxious. Then she just disappeared. I think she left town. Her family refused to tell me where she had gone."

He pulled a piece of pale blue stationery from his pocket. The handwriting on it was large and rounded but very clear:

> *Dear Ted,*
>
> *It's not that I don't love you, because I do. I always will. But I have to love myself more and try to be the best Lucille I can. Maybe it's because of my weight that you haven't gotten divorced even though you said you loved me.*

"Ted!" I looked at him.

He gazed at me sadly, "I don't know what to do."

"Well, how about getting a divorce, Ted? I'm with her on that one."

"I know, I know!" He threw up his hands. "The web around Francesca is harder to untangle than it should be. We've got some small property that I should get half of. Maybe I should just let it go, but I think I've persuaded her. If only I could contact Lucille, I could explain what I'm doing."

"Ted." I reached out and patted his hand. "I like you. We suffered together on a very dark night of the soul, but you can't expect a sensible woman to stay with a married man, even if he is separated and working on a divorce."

"You're right. But I'm married in name only, and even that will be over soon. I love Lucille. Losing her is driving me crazy. She told me she was getting so much male attention nowadays that she was afraid there was too much temptation there. Maybe she already had another man." He looked so miserable that I put aside my exasperation.

"Were you guys getting along otherwise?"

"I thought we were. I adored her. We made love several times a week, and she came like a freight train. Is that what you wanted to ask?"

"Gosh, Teddy, mince me some words, would you?" I laughed, but now he was making me very nervous.

"Well, you wanted to ask didn't you?"

"Um, well—anyway, thanks for sharing." I knew in his way, he was paying me back for the crack about the sex change operation. Fair enough. That was another thing I remembered about Teddy—he kept track of who made fun of what. I could almost see him mentally chalking one up for himself.

I had felt so comfortable with him during that long night of suffering. It took a minute to see what was different. He wasn't shy about looking at me now.

I decided to try the man-to-man approach. "You need to clean up that unfinished business, Ted. That might go a long way toward mending things with Lucille. Otherwise—how shall I say this? If you have broadened your tastes to include large women, there are even more wonderful ladies out there than you ever imagined."

He sighed. "You think I'm not serious about finding Lucille."

"It's not that. But she doesn't seem to want to be found right now."

"I was a sucker for an ambitious woman. Again."

He looked so stricken that I reached out to offer another comforting pat, but he captured my hand and squeezed it. I pulled free as soon as I could without being rude. I didn't know much about Francesca Benedict Etheridge. I had purposely kept it that way. Now Teddy told me she was still married to him, even though she was living with my ex-husband. I didn't waste any energy feeling sorry for Griff. Francesca might be a black widow spider, but I suspected my very resourceful ex kept a packed suitcase in the closet for those sudden escapes.

I started gathering my things to go. Teddy gestured for the check. "I'm begging you to trust me here, Jo. You know I'm harmless, and I am worried about Lucille. Even if she never wants to see me again. If you have any way of getting a message to her to let her know that I need to talk to her, just for a few minutes, just to make sure she's all right."

"I can't give you any information about the center's clients, Teddy. Even if I had access to it, which I don't, it would be a breach of ethics. But I'm just a receptionist and you saw the way Delores looked at me before we left. I think today's my last day."

"I'm sorry if I contributed to you losing your job." Teddy looked at the floor like a bad puppy.

"It was only a matter of time anyway. Now I have a long weekend."

We walked out of the restaurant and I took the ferry back to Bremerton. Ted said he wanted to walk around Port Orchard and think about things. We parted with an exchange of phone numbers.

I was almost looking forward to being fired.

3

Delores did not disappoint me. When I came back from lunch, which had lasted over two hours, she hustled me into her office, motioned me to sit and regarded me with the serene expression of someone who is soon to be rid of a minor irritant.

"I'm sorry Josephine," she said in tones of less-than-infinite regret. "I realize this is only a volunteer position for you, and we do appreciate your donating your time here. The work may not always be fun, but we just can't have volunteers bringing their boyfriends to work. It's too disruptive. Your visitor and the way that you just disappeared for two hours threw off our whole schedule. I'm afraid we'll have to ask you to leave."

She probably couldn't figure out why I was looking at her with such a joyful grin. "I understand, Delores. But, I haven't been totally forthcoming with you about my aims in volunteering here."

She examined me carefully, sensing that the sands of control were shifting under her feet. "What do you mean?"

"To be totally frank, I've been assigned to evaluate your facility on behalf of a major charitable foundation that is considering it for a grant. It was thought best to simply volunteer, and get a sense of your day-to-day operation. As far as my old friend Ted dropping by, that was totally coincidental. He was trying to trace a woman who is missing, and he had no idea I would be here at all."

She made a little strangling sound, but no actual words came out. I took that as an "uh-huh" and proceeded.

"As you said, it's probably time I left. I certainly have quite a lot of information for our purposes."

"Well, um, sure, anything you want. But couldn't you have told us—"

"Sorry. In this case it was deemed wiser to observe. I can finish out my report from other sources. There is just one question I wanted to ask, and I'll be on my way."

I had to admire how quickly she could shift gears, her face slipped into a bland mask to hide whatever she was feeling. I had never warmed to her but I could sympathize with her situation. "What's your question?"

"Well, it's just a coincidence that Ted Etheridge came in here." As I said that, I realized I wasn't so sure it was true. He had gotten to me a little bit though with all his talk of love, so I thought I'd at least give a try to get a message to his girlfriend. "He was looking for a Lucille Meeker—"

"That little tramp!" Delores leaped up, instantly and totally irate. I sat back in the chair in alarm. "That's where I heard the name Etheridge! Is he related to Francesca Etheridge?"

That stopped me cold. But Delores was striding back toward her office so fast that I had to get up in a hurry and hustle to catch up with her. Once in her office, she plucked the top item out of her in-box, didn't even have to look at it, and slammed it down on the desk top. "Look at that!"

I edged over, wanting to read the letter but not sure whether Delores was angry enough to hit me instead of the table. She stood back to let me at the letter, but was too angry to watch in silence.

"You want to see damage? You want to destroy all our work here? Lucille Meeker may well get us closed down."

I looked up from reading. "Wow," was all I could say.

She nodded grimly. "We received this via fax totally out of the blue this week. We don't often get complaint letters and never have we gotten a letter from someone complaining about an applicant whom we didn't even recommend."

It wasn't an eloquent letter, I was pleased to note that Francesca made spelling and grammatical errors, but her accusations were clear enough. In the course of an afternoon's temporary assignment, Lucille Meeker had stolen a laptop computer, the expensive carrying case it was stored in and miscellaneous personal items in the case including unspecified financial information. Francesca threatened to press criminal charges and she was holding the Women's Job Skill Center responsible for the stolen property's immediate return. I also noted that, as irate as she was, Francesca made no mention of having already reported the theft to the police, which was interesting.

I couldn't see rhyme or reason in any of this. "How did the center get involved?"

"Clearly she used our name without permission." Delores snatched the letter back.

I asked if anyone else on the staff remembered Lucille Meeker.

Delores urged me to wait while she asked the other staff members. All anyone could remember was that Lucille was tall, blond and a little heavyset—this with nervous glances at me. She had been around for a few weeks, done well on all the tests, brushed up her high school computer skills with workshops and gone out on a few interviews. A couple of weeks back she disappeared. She stopped calling and no one could reach her.

Then there was the faxed letter of complaint. Only no one at the center had heard of Francesca. They hadn't recommended Lucille to her and it took a few days to get straight just exactly what Fran was talking about. Delores had talked to their legal counsel. She sighed when she told me that the center didn't have much money for legal matters and she was not looking forward to getting the bill for the consultation.

I left soon after, taking the literature they pressed upon me—I already had copies of most of it. But turning down an extra copy might make it seem like I was voting against a grant for them. I truly wasn't sure at this point. I promised Delores that someone would be in touch.

I thought about it all the way back to Seattle.

No one had a current address or phone number for Lucille Meeker, although Delores didn't blink when I wrote down every address in the file including that of Francesca Etheridge in Seattle. No one challenged my credentials to get any of this information or even asked the name of the charitable institution considering the grant. That bothered me a little. Suppose instead I had been stalking Lucille Meeker or someone whose information was in the file I had looked at? Suppose I had been a jealous rival of Francesca Etheridge? Wait a minute, I *had been* a jealous rival of Francesca Etheridge. I just wasn't anymore.

4

I got to Seattle before the real rush hour started. I knocked at Mulligan's door. I didn't expect him to be home; it was the cat I was after. I had a key to his basement apartment. In fact, I could have had the keys to the whole building, having inherited a half interest in the place, but I hadn't quite gotten used to that fact. The owner of the other half was not available to make any decisions but part of the terms of the inheritance had been to continue to employ the manager, Maxine Gamble. She was highly capable, so I just tried to stay out of her way. Lately she had been badgering me to make some decisions about the place.

The only decision I had made so far was to leave my cat with Mulligan during the week when I went out of town. He invited me to come get the cat whenever I got in. At this hour he was probably at work. Still I knocked a few times, and called out his name—I felt awkward letting myself into his apartment. We had spent one night together, but somewhere between sex and dawn, our relationship took a wrong turn. My affair with Thor Mulligan appeared to have stalled before it had properly begun. My problem was that it hadn't ended either—at least on my part. I looked through his small one-bedroom apartment, and found no sign of feline occupation.

I climbed the stairs up to Apartment One. Maxine answered the door. She was a short, full-breasted woman in her sixties with wildly cut gray hair. Today she wore a mauve sweatsuit and hoop earrings.

"Hi Jo. You're back early."

"I finished up. Thought I'd come home. You don't know where that silly cat is, do you?"

"Mulligan probably let him out. He might be in the backyard or he might have gone up the back stairs to get into Nina's place."

"Okay, I'll go look. Where's the bird? He's awfully quiet. Is he okay?" Groucho, her green Military macaw had a shriek that could be heard blocks away and he usually made some sort of preparatory shrieks when he saw that Maxine's attention was focused into the hallway, rather than on him where it properly belonged.

I blinked in surprise when a face popped up behind her shoulder. A man squeezed in behind Maxine and wrapped his arm around her substantial middle so that her breasts flowed over his forearm, nearly but not quite covering the crude tattoo that snaked up from his wrist to curl around his elbow. Without meaning to, I took a step backward into the hall.

"I've been threatening to put him on a spit for dinner, but Maxine won't let me. Her daughter took him down to her place, the noise was driving me apeshit," the man said with a gravelly voice. "Don't worry—Bird lives!"

"Can you believe I've hooked up with a literate jazz buff?" Maxine said in tones more appropriate for baby talk.

"*Hope* took in Groucho?" I said in disbelief.

"Oh, she was glad to take him." Maxine's new friend grinned broadly. "She hustled that cage outta here in ten minutes flat, once I told her I liked him a lot and I'd like him even better fried with biscuits and gravy."

"He is such a kidder," Maxine said with a chuckle, not exactly a girlish giggle, but her voice was normally so husky that I guess it counted as a giggle. I gazed at her in astonishment. If I hadn't just seen it, I could never have imagined Maxine allowing that kind of threat-in-joke's-clothing about her beloved and fragile, if totally cantankerous, Groucho.

"Josephine Fuller, meet Dick Slattery," she said fondly, running her fingers along his muscular forearm.

I murmured hello, still wondering at Maxine's new incarnation as sixty-going-on-sixteen. The guy had a certain muscular resemblance to Popeye the Sailor, although I'd eat a can of spinach on the spot if he turned out to be a hard-working, good-natured type. Dick Slattery was not tall. Maxine was short, and his chin dug into her shoulder. His hair was brown, shot with gray and thinning. His face was carved down to a leanness that reminded me of a coyote, maybe it was the predatory yellow eyes. Maxine would be the rabbit in that scenario. She looked totally dazed and blissful. If she was a rabbit, she was a happy rabbit.

I turned to go as Slattery pulled Maxine back into the apartment. He reached across her to pull the door closed, but as he did, he looked at me one more time and winked. I shook myself, realizing I was standing on the stairwell like—well, like a hypnotized small mammal. Not good. The guy gave me an anxious feeling in the pit of my stomach that was the opposite of erotic.

I went upstairs. The apartment below Nina's was vacant. The door was open, and a couple of men in white coveralls were just finishing after a day of painting the place. It was time to rent that apartment again.

On the next floor I paused a moment outside the door to what had been my friend Nina West's apartment. Something about the place frightened me. But the strident cries of a hungry cat on the other side of the door forced me to take a deep breath, open it, and go in. The big gray tomcat twined around my legs, meowing. He had been Nina's cat and when she had introduced him to me, as a small fluffy kitten, she told me he could say his own name. He was doing that now. "Hi, Raoul." Whatever it was that frightened me didn't appear to scare him, but it did seem to me that sometimes he was looking for Nina. Maybe I thought that because I found myself looking for her. Mulligan had indicated that he did too. I didn't know if we humans were better off knowing that Nina's ashes were in Puget Sound, or if we would have felt better like the cat, only knowing that she was gone, hoping against hope she might come back. It hurt my heart.

I reached down and petted Raoul, who rubbed against me, purring. "So, did you come in the back window?" I asked him, as we headed for the kitchen. I closed the window. I decided to talk to Mulligan about letting Raoul out for long stretches. Maxine's new boyfriend made me nervous with all his talk about pets for dinner.

Opening the cat food, I kept having the feeling that something had changed while I was gone. I could have sworn that I had left that stack of mail on the kitchen table rather than the counter, but Mulligan might have moved it if he had sat down at the table when he was coming in to feed Raoul during the week. A couple of kitchen cupboard doors were open, but that might have been the cat's doing. I felt guilty about leaving him alone for so long. Mulligan came up to tend to the cat's needs and Maxine had looked in from time to time, but with her new boyfriend she clearly didn't have time even for her own pets. I didn't like to think about Maxine coming up here and maybe bringing along Dick Slattery.

I sat down with the mail and a glass of water while the big Persian polished off a can of cat food and commenced his post-meal grooming ritual. I found his brush, and settled down on the sofa with him to brush some potential mats out of his soft coat, a process that he found quite enjoyable as long as I didn't stray into any sensitive areas. He notified me of forbidden areas, which changed from day to day, by trapping the hand holding the brush, and extending his claws enough to signal not to go there.

For some reason I felt all right in the living room of Nina's apartment, but the rest of the place made me very anxious. I had been camping out on the sofa on the weekends when I stayed here. It made sense that the big back bedroom at the end of the hall would scare me—that was where I had found Nina's body. The room had been thoroughly cleaned by a professional agency specializing in crime scenes. It had even been painted and recarpeted. Most of the furniture had been cleared out, claimed by some of Nina's friends. Her women's group had been in here about a month earlier, and taken things that they wanted.

Maxine had sat me down and suggested in her forthright way that it made sense that the apartment would bother me, and perhaps I should consider using it for some nonresidential purpose or renting it out to someone who had no connection with Nina. She was probably right, but I couldn't do any of those things.

I didn't tell her just how much it actually frightened me. I felt embarrassed about that. But I also couldn't seem to leave it. I was frozen, frightened and oddly trapped. Mulligan had offered to rent it. On the one crazy night when we consoled each other in bed, I even had a fleeting fantasy of living here with him. But thoughts of Nina had cut short our time together, and now he kept a certain friendly distance. As much as anything I was keeping the apartment because of Raoul. The cat's companionship was the primary emotional thread by which my connection with the world was anchored. It was a lot to ask of a cat, but he purred when I brushed him in the preferred manner, and that was more than Mulligan offered. At least I could set some small part of the world right. Raoul raised his head and stared at the door, and a moment later there was a knock.

Raoul hopped up, and followed me to answer it, which gave me an idea of who was knocking, and indeed it was Mulligan. He was a big man with longish blond hair and calm, brown eyes in a rugged face like a discontented bulldog. For some odd reason the very sight of him set off this nearly electrical shock effect in all my pulses.

"I got your note, you came back a day early."

"I got fired."

"From a volunteer job?"

"Long story. I was thinking of ordering a pizza, would you like to share one?"

"Sure. You want to eat up here?" he asked. I hadn't confided to him in words my fear of the apartment, but he must have realized I was sleeping on the sofa rather than in one of the bedrooms, because I folded the sheets and blankets but didn't always put them away.

"That's fine. I think there's some wine in the kitchen." For all I knew, he had bought it for Nina a few months earlier. The kitchen didn't bother me too much; although I hadn't done a lot of cooking in my life, Nina and I had spent some good times there together when I visited her.

Mulligan and I ordered pizza, and while we sat in Nina's kitchen, slightly depopulated by things her friends had taken, we drank wine. He told me about the latest bureaucratic insanity in the telephone security division where he worked, and I told him about my day, Teddy Etheridge and the unpleasantness at the Women's Job Skill Center.

"So you spent the night in a hotel with this Etheridge guy but he never made a move on you?"

"Well, to be totally accurate, we started in the lobby, moved on to the dining room, then to the bar. We even walked out into the streets to watch the sun come up."

"Uh-huh."

"I did give him an earful of my views on women and self-acceptance and how diets destroy self-confidence and our health."

"Uh-huh."

"Today at lunch he explained that he'd never thought of a large woman as a sex object before."

"And now that you've converted him to an appreciation of abundance in a woman, he's ready to drag you under the table and have his way with you?"

"Uh . . ." I didn't know what to say. We still hadn't sorted out whether Mulligan just needed a while to mourn, whether he was worried that I might find someone else, or even what the heck was going on with us. For the moment my mind went blank, and Mulligan started to blush, which fascinated me in a man so blond. It was like watching a sunburn spread in quick time. I looked at the pizza. "Do you want to split that last piece?"

"Okay."

As I cut the piece in half I had a minute to think, then I answered, "Teddy did look at me a little differently now, and I have to admit, it made me very nervous to be around him."

"I'm not real crazy about it myself," Mulligan said gruffly.

I had to laugh at that. "That's very sweet of you, I think."

"Are you going to stay here tonight?" he asked, then quickly added, "I mean you're not going back to Bremerton?"

"No. I'm done there. I guess I'll camp out here."

"You really are camping out—on the sofa, aren't you?"

"Yeah." He had noticed all right.

"Why? This is a two-bedroom apartment, you could sleep

in the front bedroom." He didn't suggest the back bedroom. He hadn't actually seen Nina's body, but he knew I had. "Are you afraid to be here?"

"I don't sleep too well, but I'm not exactly scared." That was a lie.

"That's not good, Jo. I don't want you to be anxious. Would you like to come down to my place? I would have offered before, but it feels awkward, after what happened in San Diego."

I sighed. His saying it like that made it even worse. As if that night we spent together had been an unavoidable accident. "No, but thanks."

"Would you like me to stay up here with you?"

I had to laugh, from nerves rather than amusement. I was starting to feel the sexual tension build between us, and I had never been more confused in my life. "I don't think either of us would sleep much if you did."

Mulligan looked at me for several seconds. "I've got to work tomorrow but I worry about you."

"I—I don't know what it is. But I've got to get past this."

"For tonight, why don't you keep your phone near you? We've both been through some tough times the last few months. Call me if you feel strange."

"Thanks, Mulligan." We hugged—a consoling bear hug. It was the first time we had embraced since our encounter in San Diego. I walked him to the door.

"You need to talk to someone about this, Jo. I'm always here for you, but you need to talk to someone who's further away from it."

"I know." It wasn't until after I'd locked the door behind him that I realized I'd forgotten to ask about the mail being moved and the cupboard doors opened. It sounded silly the minute I thought of it, so I put it out of my head and prepared for another anxious night.

5

Whether it was the wine, the hug from Mulligan or Raoul's purring presence, I slept better than usual in the apartment, and I woke up feeling that I really did need to talk it out. Maxine was the logical person. I hesitated to call her. Dick Slattery was probably still there. But it was a weekday—he might be at work.

I cast around for an excuse and decided to bring a notebook and a question about the painters who had just finished in the apartment below me. After all, Maxine had knocked on my door unannounced several times since I had been living in the apartment. Sometimes she had brought a coffee cake or a package the mail carrier had left, but I suspected those were excuses to chat because she always came in, sat down and talked awhile. It wasn't even a faint echo of the intimacy I had felt with Nina, but it was a start. I cast around for something to bring. Fortunately I had bought a pastry for breakfast that was unopened. I felt silly running around the halls with a pastry on a plate, so I put it in a bag and went downstairs.

But just as I rounded the stairwell, Dick Slattery came out and padded barefoot over to retrieve Maxine's newspaper from the building's front steps. He was wearing her lavender terry cloth robe. When he turned to go back to the apartment, he purposefully let the robe fall open. You couldn't call it flashing—it was more of an intentional exhibition. He met my eye with a raffish grin, making no move to close his robe as he strolled back to the apartment, swaggering a bit at the opportunity to display his natural endowments. So much for the theory that he might have a job.

I had to shake my head in amazement. Slattery was trouble and proud of it. He worked hard to give off a strong aura that in the short run he might be worth it. I was immune to his particular brand of pheromones, but frustration with my own social life made it easier to sympathize with Maxine.

I gave up on the idea of a cozy chat with her and went back upstairs. Raoul looked at me hopefully when I came back in. He tried to squeeze through the door, but I didn't want him around the building or the yard if Dick Slattery was around. This was ridiculous, I was acting as if the man was literally a predatory animal—in fact my gut level reaction told me he was. I had been so anxious with no obvious reason lately that I didn't totally trust my instincts, but I was taking no chances with Raoul's safety, just in case.

I sat down with my pastry and some orange juice. By the time I put the leftovers in the fridge, I was restless. I needed to get out of the building.

I didn't know where I was going, but it wasn't anywhere fancy. After spending day after day in a business suit, I was happy to be able to go out in rose-colored leggings and a matching long cotton shirt with a batik design. Maybe the bright colors would raise my mood. I did bring a jacket. It was in the mid sixties outside and just slightly overcast with no sign of rain or fog, but even in August, this was Seattle, and the weather could change. When I got to my car, I sat for a moment trying to figure out just where I intended to go. While I sat, Dick Slattery came out of the building. If he saw me, he didn't acknowledge my presence. He walked past the car to where Maxine's old Dodge Dart was parked. He started the Dart, drove around the corner and was gone. I started my engine.

For a moment I considered going back into the building, and having that heart-to-heart talk with Maxine. Then I decided to forget about talking to her at all. Lust might have clouded her judgment overall. Worse yet, if she was conjuring up romantic fantasies about Slattery I might end up having to listen to them. I didn't even want to chance it.

I started to drive with the idea of going down by the water, but I wasn't really surprised when I found myself in a neighborhood that bordered on the address on the letter I had read the day before. The letter from Francesca Etheridge.

I didn't admit to myself until I parked across the street that I was going to try to contact her. Francesca's building bore a stylized logo of a killer whale and the words Orca Harbor Townhomes. I wasn't so sure that that it was in fact reasonable to investigate Francesca's complaint. I hadn't seen her since that morning when she was pasted up against Griff in the hotel lobby in Kathmandu. I couldn't very well pretend to be someone else because she might easily remember me from the time we met briefly in Nepal—even though there was also the possibility that she wouldn't recognize me if I wasn't sitting next to Griff and wearing a wedding ring. My memory was that she had examined me with some calculation, as she might have considered a steep but not insurmountable stretch of glacial ice. Then she set her sights, with a total lack of pretense, on Griff.

This was probably not the best frame of mind to talk to the woman who was now living with my ex-husband. For all I knew, Griff would be there. I hadn't seen him since I left Kathmandu. Our divorce had been a formality of papers that hadn't involved more than a few phone conversations. I was so frustrated on so many fronts at this point that it would almost be a relief to talk to Griff and Francesca. If my coming around and asking questions made them uncomfortable, well good. Let somebody else squirm for awhile.

Standing on the doorstep, I toyed with an opening line such as, "Remember me? You stole my husband. And speaking of theft, what's all this about a missing laptop?"

It never occurred to me that Francesca might refuse to see me until I buzzed the number labeled Etheridge, and got no answer. Of course, she could be out. I felt a flush of embarrassment wondering if Griff might answer the door. But as I stood and rang the buzzer yet again, I looked more closely at the hand-lettered card underneath. At one point it had read Benedict Etheridge/Fuller. But "Fuller" had been inked through. Had Griff left or been kicked out?

That was when I noticed that the door was slightly ajar, which was highly unwise in a city the size of Seattle. I was reaching out to push it inward, when it was yanked open, and I was literally shouldered out of the way by a tall blond woman who left the door wide open.

She paused at the bottom of the steps long enough to turn back and call out, "Don't go in there! Call the cops, she's dead!" She turned and ran across the street.

"Wait!" For a stunned second, I watched her get into a faded blue Volkswagen bug that was definitely older than she was. It started up promptly and took her down the street and around the corner.

I turned back to confront the polished stairs leading up into the townhouse. I took out my cell phone. The top autodial button was programmed for 911. I didn't press the button, but I did keep the phone in my hand as I cautiously went up the stairs. Confronting me at the top of the stairway was a larger-than-life, beautifully framed print of a color photograph of Francesca. It dominated the entry. It was clearly Griff's work, and he had done her justice. It showed her hanging from a wall of sapphire ice, supported by two ice axes and the crampons attached to her boots. Her hair had been short in that picture, and the hood of her parka had fallen back a little to show a spiky halo around her determined face. The sun that illuminated the blue ice reflected in her blue eyes. She looked great. It was easy to see why Griff had fallen for her. She looked like a snow goddess—the petite version.

At the top of the stairs I saw a series of huge prints of Griff's pictures hanging along the back wall. Every one showed Francesca in climbing gear. From the massive peaks in the background, I guessed that these were taken during the early days of their relationship in Nepal.

The condo had high ceilings and hardwood floors. The cathedral effect was heightened by the sparse furniture, which gave the room a cavernous, empty quality. The place seemed deserted except for the persistent buzz of a fly. The main room was blocked from view as you rounded the top of the stairs by a glass cabinet that must have been seven feet tall, filled with sports trophies and climbing memorabilia.

I went around the trophy display, and tripped over a black leather case that had been unceremoniously dropped at the edge. I went down sprawling on the hardwood floor, cursing myself for awkwardness. I lay for a second, assessing any damage, cringing in expectation of laughter and expecting to look up and see the petite and athletic Francesca sneering at my huge awkward self, complaining that I had scuffed the waxed floor.

Instead, cautiously getting to my feet, I saw a long oak table with a new canvas tarp half pulled off it, and what appeared to be a dummy, submerged in a welter of climber's gear—harnesses and rope, caribiners, crampons, pitons. I had never climbed a day in my life but I'd watched enough people pack and unpack their gear to easily commit it to memory. I didn't see any ice axes, although I saw the harness with the holster from which most climbers hung a couple of axes with their claw-like heads for climbing ice, the way Francesca had in that huge photo.

I went a little closer, puzzled. Mountaineers are usually very particular about their gear. After all, their lives depend on it. Someone had scattered Francesca's stacks of pitons like matchsticks. Her ropes were tangled into a spider's nest, hanging half off the table.

This was a cruel joke surely. I went a little closer, my steps echoing on the hardwood. The tarp had been partially pulled off the gleaming oak table. The climbing gear made a disorderly still life.

My stomach lurched when I realized that the totally still figure at the center of the disorder was no dummy. Francesca Etheridge, a rope around her neck, her red face distorted, lay among her gear, one of her ice axes planted in the soft base of her throat. The bloodied rips and tears in her thermal undershirt showed where she had been hacked before dying. She was clearly lifeless, the blood long clotted. Twisted where she had fallen like a broken doll, her arms were trapped by the ropes and frozen at an awkward angle, not by cold but by death.

I forced myself to take a breath. For a moment I thought I was going to black out. I don't know how I got back down the stairs. It wasn't till I got out in the fresh air and took several more deep breaths that I pressed the button to dial 911.

6

I stood on the front steps, breathing deeply and consciously. I wasn't sure I wanted to sit, so I half-leaned against the outside wall of the building. Across the street, I heard an elderly car engine start and looked up to see a Dodge Dart drive past. For a moment I wondered if it could be Maxine's. Dick Slattery had driven off before I did. He could have doubled back and followed me. But why? Maxine didn't know Francesca, and Slattery wasn't the sort of person Fran would have bothered with—unless she wanted to contract out some sort of crime. I shuddered and told myself that there were probably many aged Dodge sedans in a city the size of Seattle.

I expected to see the police at any moment. What I saw instead was Teddy Etheridge walking briskly up the steps to the front door of the condo. He was getting out a key when he saw me, and stopped dead, his hand with the key in it frozen in midair.

"Josephine! What are you doing here?"

"Teddy, there's been a—" I don't know what I would have called it. That had clearly been no accident, and murder—which must be accurate—seemed a cruel thing to say to someone who had been close to Francesca.

Before I could say more, I was cut off by a yell from across the street, "Teddy! Can you let me in?"

The young woman who came sprinting toward us was a little below average in height but very lean. She moved with an athletic grace. Her dark brown hair was sheared into a short brush cut that, together with a certain defiantly mannish body language proclaimed her sexual identity without need for the pink triangle on the shoulder of her jacket.

"Isadora, this is Josephine Fuller, she used to be married to Griff. Jo, this is Fran's sister, Isadora Benedict."

"Ted! Don't do that." The woman socked him hard on the arm, which he immediately began to rub with a sheepish expression. "I told you not to use my slave name. I'm Isadora Freechild," she said holding out her hand and firmly shaking mine.

"Uh, look, something has happened. You'd better not go up there. I called the police, there's nothing we can do."

"What do you mean? Is my sister all right?" Isadora said fiercely.

Teddy met my eyes and grasped immediately that it wouldn't be wise to let her go in. He put a protective arm around her.

"Did you hurt my sister?" Isadora demanded.

A siren announced the paramedics, and a police car arrived at the same time. Two uniformed Seattle PD officers got out. "Did one of you call in about discovering a possible homicide victim?" one asked.

"My sister lives up there!" Isadora shrieked. She tried to escape from Teddy's grip, but he held her firmly. I was surprised to see how lucid he was in a crisis.

The policemen sized up the situation. One of them shoved past us, and went quickly up the stairs while the other barred the door. "Let us check that out ma'am. The paramedics will be here any second. You should all wait down here while we see if there's something we can do." An emergency response truck drove up to double-park in front of the unit and a couple of paramedics hustled past us up the front steps. Teddy and Isadora had moved back onto the sidewalk, conferring in low tones and watching the doorway anxiously. I knew there was no good news coming out that door.

When I got back home, it was mid-afternoon. Dick Slattery was lounging in the front hallway, watching the postal carrier fill the mailboxes. She was young and blond and seeing the way he followed her every move made me nervous. I swept past him with a curt nod. With Nina dead and Maxine—preoccupied, to put it kindly—I couldn't think of anyone I did trust to talk to. Mulligan had patiently listened to me the night before, but how long he would continue to put up with my disordered life and fears? Not to mention that a major heading on my worry list was whatever the hell was or wasn't happening between us.

I went straight up to Nina's apartment and found Raoul, stretched out in one of those boneless, totally relaxed feline positions on the sofa. I pulled him into an embrace. "Will you listen to my problems, kitty?" I nuzzled his large, soft, furry head. He let me pet him for a moment, then squirmed free, and led me through the kitchen to the back door that let out onto the fire stairs. He looked at me expectantly. I let him out. He swarmed down to the backyard, and paused in a patch of sunlight near a rose bush to survey his small empire. Certainly the cat wasn't interested in my problems.

I turned back to the apartment. I was too jittery to concentrate on my report for Mrs. Madrone. There were still gaps in the information, but I decided to start filling them tomorrow. I turned my attention to tidying up the apartment—never my first choice, and a pretty good indicator of how much nervous energy I was trying to defuse. For the first time in weeks, I picked up the flat stack of unassembled boxes that had been leaning against the wall near the back door. I hauled them into the living room, and sat on the sofa to assemble the first one. I could start here.

So many of Nina's belongings had already been given away. Her clothes, patterns and sewing equipment went to the women she had known who could use them. The bookshelves had been partly emptied of the books that interested her friends. Many of the art objects she collected and the little clay statues she sculpted herself had found homes with people who admired them. As I looked at what was left, I was surprised to find that without Nina to enjoy them, these things didn't mean much to me.

I folded down the last cardboard segment of the first box and stabilized it. I decided I would put the things I didn't want into boxes and see how I felt about what was left when more space was cleared.

A few hours later I got up to turn on the lights. The gray afternoon had darkened into early evening. I had worked my way across the living room and into the hallway that led to the bedroom. I looked at the bedroom.

Like the shock of pain from touching your tongue to a sore tooth, the inexplicable fear that the apartment sometimes harbored gripped me. I was not going in the bedroom today—I wondered if I'd ever be able to face it again. But I did decide to move the narrow shelves Nina had put up in an alcove near the bedroom door. She had used them to hold small plaster and fired clay statues. I would never have put that many small plaster statutes on a shelf near a doorway. Nina moved through her life gracefully and purposefully, while I barreled along in fits and starts. If I ever did get up the courage to go in that bedroom, I might easily come through in a hurry, and accidentally knock the whole lot into pieces on the floor. It seemed less of a betrayal to disagree with Nina's decorating choices after I had been putting discards in boxes for a few hours.

I was sitting on the floor putting another cardboard carton together when the buzzer rang. I stood up, a little stiff from hours of crawling around on the floor. I looked through the peephole before I opened the door, half expecting Mulligan or Maxine, and just a little worried that it might be Dick Slattery. I found myself looking into the roguish green eyes of Griffin Fuller, my ex-husband. I opened the door.

"Griff. Hi." We stood for an awkward moment. I hadn't seen him in over two years. "You could have called."

"I thought maybe you'd refuse to see me."

"No." Feeling awkward, I stepped back and he walked into the apartment. I sat back on the floor next to the last few unassembled boxes. The growing pile of boxes I had filled with Nina's things were labeled, and stacked across the room. Griff sat down on the sofa next to where I sat on the floor. He was a little closer than I would have liked.

Griffin Fuller was not conventionally handsome. He had lost more hair since the last time I saw him and shaved the beard that he had cultivated in Nepal, but his craggy, wind-wrinkled face was sun-baked and as usual he looked as if he was about to smile or laugh. He had the most amazing light green eyes, the color of Japanese celadon, a paler, bluer green than jade. Women were always getting lost looking into those eyes.

"You're looking good, Jo."

"Thanks—you too." I didn't know what else to say so I

picked up the box again and started to assemble it. "You know about Francesca." I wasn't asking, it probably had something to do with why he was here.

"The police made it a point to tell me. They said you found her, Jo. I am so sorry you had to get mixed up in this mess. If I hadn't gotten involved with her, we might still be married—"

"Unless I caught you with one of your other lovers. It would have happened eventually, Griff, you know that. I could only stay young and stupid for so long. Francesca was just the most dramatic choice."

Griff burst out laughing, "So honest! God, I've missed you, Josie."

I was tempted to ask just whose fault that was, but then I met his eyes, which were sad. "Well, there's lots of things about you that I miss too, Griff," I said, trying to keep away from dangerous topics.

When I trusted myself to look again, he had looked away. He seemed serious and exhausted—perhaps a little lost himself. I turned my attention back to the box in my hands, which had stalled, half-assembled.

"Did you know Ted Etheridge has a key to Fran's condo?"

"No. But it wouldn't surprise me. I know he called from time to time. How did you find out he had a key?"

"He came up with a key in his hand while I was waiting for the police. Fran's sister showed up at about the same time. A woman with a crew cut." I finished the box and picked up its lid.

"That would be Isadora."

"Right, Ted did tell me her name—I totally forgot."

"She calls herself Isadora Freechild. She's a lesbian activist. She and Fran were quarrelling off and on the whole time I knew them. Dora would come around every few weeks or so, and they'd start a new fight. They were close, but they never agreed about anything. Both of her parents are in town this week. There may be some family business in the air—although I have to admit, I didn't smell any brimstone."

"I never thought of Francesca as having a family."

"Technically speaking they are a family. I used to call them a nest of snakes, but they seldom all show up in the same room, so it's more like an occasional snake sighting. You know that their mother is Brenda Benedict, the actress?"

"The name is familiar."

"Their father, Don Benedict, was in the first two Hanged Man pictures, but he retired early, and Brenda pretty much left the kids for him to raise. He was a big outdoorsman, and now he's building ski resorts, almost franchises really, aimed at family skiers and snowboarders. You might have heard of them, they're called Snowcones."

"I really don't follow the ski resort business."

Griff laughed again. I finished folding the box lid, risked a glance, and saw that he had stretched his feet out on a box to lounge on the sofa. "That's what I miss most about you," he said with warmth that reached me in spite of myself. "You can make me really laugh. It's like fresh air after the reptile house."

I favored him with an eyebrow-raised look but said nothing. If he was trying out his "the-woman-I-left-you-for-doesn't-understand-me" speech, it was no sale.

"After her movie career fizzled, Brenda embarked on a career of serial marriage," Griff continued. "She's on husband number four, the politician. She still has business ties to Fran and Dora's father."

"The resort guy?"

"Right. They both have a piece of the Hanged Man series. You've heard of it?"

"Who hasn't?" I asked. "They're teen slasher epics, right?"

"I think the first one was halfway artsy. Wolf Lambert, the

director, was Don Benedict's college roommate, fresh out of film school."

"Didn't they make about twenty of those?"

"They were cult classics. Brenda and Don Benedict were among the original investors, so their finances are all tangled up together. They might be in town on business about that. Or they might have dropped in because little Miss Francesca has written a book about them."

"She climbs mountains and writes, huh?"

"I didn't say it was a good book. She didn't show it to me. But judging by some of the horror stories she's told me about her childhood, I get the feeling her family doesn't want to see it on every morning talk show in America."

"Are you in the book?"

"I doubt that I'll merit a footnote. The last time we spoke, she told me I was both washed up and dried up."

"Lucky you."

He shrugged, although there was pain in his face. "I think when she met me, she was under the impression that I had enough money to finance her climbing."

I had to laugh at that, but I managed to stop as soon as possible because I could see Griff really was hurt. Women of all ages had always thrown themselves at him, simply for his charm. It must hurt a lot to think that a woman might have wanted his money as well—not that he had any. He looked like a million dollars, but he lived like a college student. Griff was a good ten years older than me—in his early forties—but he looked older than that at this moment.

I felt sorry for him, but all I said was, "Could her book do you any real harm?"

"Hey, don't worry about me. As long as she spells my name right, eh?" He cleared his throat, as if anxious to change the subject. "What were you doing over at Fran's?"

"A woman connected with one of Mrs. Madrone's charities seems to have stolen a laptop computer that had a copy of Francesca's book on it."

"I hadn't heard that. Poor Fran. She felt the world was against her, and sometimes she was right." He cleared his throat again. Could he be crying? He seemed just a little choked up. Maybe he had genuinely cared for her.

"Are you okay, Griff? I mean, it was a shock to me, and I hardly knew her, and certainly never liked her."

He sighed. "You know how I am, Josie—a moving target. I'm just not moving as fast as I used to. Francesca and I were breaking up, so I made it a point not to be around that much. The only way we could tell it was over was to notice that the absences just weren't making the heart grow fonder anymore."

I didn't say anything. He used to do that to me too, when we were fighting, or he was prowling after fresh conquests. At the time I hadn't realized what he was doing. Now it was ancient history.

Our eyes met, but I looked away first.

"She wasn't like you." Griff said. "She didn't follow me around. I guess I really blew that one, didn't I? Sometimes I look back on the time we were married, and it seems like the best time in my life."

I didn't know what to say. After a several seconds he cleared his throat. "I noticed coming up the stairs that there was an apartment being painted, do you think I could rent it?"

"Oh, Griff, that would be a really bad idea. I'm going to be moving into this apartment and, uh—" I didn't realize until I said it that I had decided I could live with whatever sorrowful memories the apartment might bring up. "The last thing I need is an ex-husband in the building."

"I understand."

"Besides, you never stay anywhere long enough to finish out a lease. Most of the time we were married, we didn't even have an apartment."

"Maybe I'm getting soft in my old age. I've been taking some pictures here in the area, I thought maybe I'd travel a little less."

There was a knock at the door. For a moment I was seized with a dread that it would be Mulligan. Not that he wouldn't understand, I just didn't feel up to explaining it. I opened the door to reveal two policemen in plain clothes. I knew they were policemen because I had met one of them before. His name was Gonick. He was tall, stout, sunburned and red-haired, and he worked in Seattle Homicide.

Gonick seemed surprised to see me. "The manager downstairs told us Griffin Fuller would be here," he said.

I introduced Griff to Detective Gonick.

"Mr. Fuller, your answering service had the manager's number, and she sent us up here," Gonick said, then he turned to me. "I thought your boyfriend was that guy downstairs called Mulligan," he said, irritably.

I let the boyfriend part of the remark go. "Griff is my ex-husband."

"Which explains why you have the same last name."

"What happened to your partner? Lasker, wasn't it?" I asked.

Gonick looked over at the short, dark-haired, olive-skinned man next to him, as if he had just remembered the man was there. I could see he preferred asking to answering questions. "Lasker's on vacation. This is Tarrasch," he muttered. Tarrasch nodded but said nothing. Lasker had been equally silent, and I wondered if Gonick always drew silent partners.

Gonick continued. "Mr. Fuller, you spoke with Officer Chambers early this afternoon, and he told you about the death of Mrs. Etheridge, the woman you had been living with."

"He told me about Francesca's death, yes."

"And you came right over here to talk to your ex-wife?"

"I heard that Jo had found the—uh, found Francesca. I was worried about her."

"The woman you were living with is murdered, and you suddenly get the urge to see your ex-wife?"

"Well, first off, I hadn't been living with Francesca for several weeks."

"That's right, you informed Chambers that you were no longer living with Mrs. Etheridge. Are you living here, Mr. Fuller?" He cast a glance around the place, took in the boxes and the air of disarray.

"No."

"When was the last time you saw Mrs. Etheridge?"

"Last weekend. We went to that film festival." Griff sat down abruptly on the sofa as if his knees had given way. He ran his hands over his face and hair. It made me nervous to see how guilty he looked. Not that I for one moment suspected he was guilty of anything. Other than, well—feeling guilty.

"When I heard what happened to Fran, all I could think was, maybe, I don't know, I should have protected Fran. Jo might be next."

"Why?"

"They said she left the door unlocked. Even though Fran and I weren't together, I kept thinking if only I'd been there, I might have been able to protect her."

"Was she in the habit of leaving the door unlocked?"

"She might have unlocked it if she was expecting someone."

"So you came over here to tell Ms. Fuller to keep her doors locked?"

"I needed to talk to someone sensible and clear-headed. Jo is the most sensible person I know."

They all turned to look at me, and Gonick shook his head sadly as if bemoaning the fact that Griff didn't have a wider circle of sane acquaintances.

Griff ignored him, and continued, "The minute I thought about Jo, especially after Officer Chambers told me she discovered the b—that she found Francesca—I started to think about Jo's safety. I mean what if this was somehow aimed at me? I worried that Jo might be in danger."

Gonick's eyes lit up a little at that. "Do you have any enemies, Mr. Fuller?"

"Not that I know of. Some people might not like me, but no one I can think of who would harm Fran."

Gonick sighed loudly. "Let me get this straight. You worried about the safety of your ex-wife here, Ms. Fuller—who even though she kept your surname after the divorce, has been on her own, and presumably unhurt for years since you separated."

"I'm not saying it was rational. I just wanted to see Jo. And hearing that she had been at Fran's today made me wonder if somehow I had put her in harm's way," Griff said, steadfastly not looking at me. I could see it cost him something to say this.

"From my acquaintance with Ms. Fuller here, I would say she doesn't need any help to put her in harm's way. She'll do it on her own."

Griff shrugged, and opened his arms in a gesture of helplessness. For some reason this seemed to mollify Gonick just slightly, although his next question was, "Mr. Fuller, do you know anyone, aside from your ex-wife, who might have wanted to harm Mrs. Etheridge?"

Griff sighed. "I don't know, I don't know who could do such a terrible thing to Fran. It just doesn't make sense."

"So you can't think of any enemies she might have had?"

"Fran was a strong, opinionated woman. She thought she was indestructible. That's why she could take the kind of risks she did in mountaineering. She could be insensitive and she was very ambitious, but I never knew her to consort with violent people."

Gonick took me by the arm. "Tarrasch, why don't you go over Mr. Fuller's account of where he was Thursday night. Ms. Fuller, could we speak in the other room please?"

Tarrasch, still silent, sat down across from Griff. He didn't seem to be about to ask him anything. Maybe his assignment was to stare at Griff until he cracked and started babbling. Maybe he was waiting for me to leave the room so I couldn't coordinate my alibi with Griff's. No danger there—I didn't have an alibi. I led the way into the kitchen.

Gonick looked around, "How long have you been living here?"

"I'm in the process of moving in, but I've been traveling on business, so it's taking a little while."

Gonick nodded without comment. He had been in the apartment after Nina's murder. He knew more about me than I really wanted a policeman to know. I offered to make coffee and he declined. I sat at the kitchen table and he sat across from me. "You're on pretty good terms with your ex-husband," he remarked.

"Yes and no. It's the first time I've seen him in over two years."

"But there must have been some bad blood between you and Mrs. Etheridge. After all, she broke up your marriage, right?"

I felt stung in spite of myself. "I don't think it would be accurate to say she caused the breakup. I just caught her with Griff and it became crystal clear that she wasn't the first woman he cheated with. She probably wouldn't have been the last, either, if we'd stayed married, which was what he wanted at the time. Francesca and I never exchanged more than a few words." I shut up, suddenly realizing I'd said more than I ought to.

"And yet you visited her this morning at her townhouse.

About what time was this?" He took out a little notebook and wrote something as he spoke—probably noting something incriminating I had just said.

"Just before noon. I was looking into a women's job skill center for my employer." I gave him the address, thinking that Delores Patton was going to be even more irritated with me now. "They showed me a letter that Francesca had written complaining that someone from the center had come to do some work and stolen her laptop computer. I certainly recognized the name, and I was just curious what her story was."

"That's interesting. Did you see a laptop computer on the premises?"

"No."

He leafed back through his earlier notes. "You told the uniformed officer on the scene that you tripped over something heavy in a leather case at the head of the stairs."

"Yes. I fell, and then I looked up, and saw—saw her. I pretty much didn't notice anything else."

"Would it surprise you to know that there was a laptop computer in the case?"

"I didn't look, but there could have been."

"So then you saw Mrs. Etheridge."

"Right. With climbing rope around her neck and that ice axe," I gulped.

"Did you touch the body or anything near it?"

"She was so clearly dead, I didn't go near her. I got up, and went out."

"And you're sure that you don't want to tell me about having some words with her before she died? After all, she stole your husband."

"No. I hadn't spoken to her since I first met her nearly three years ago in Nepal."

"Okay." He made a very brief note. "How did you get into the apartment again?"

"The door was open, and a tall blond woman pushed past me. She yelled at me to call the police, that there was a body up there."

"That's right, this tall blond woman you told the police about," Gonick said skeptically. "How tall was she—taller than you?"

"I'm five eight, and she was a couple of inches taller, at least five ten."

"Had you ever seen her before?"

"No."

"Then what did she do?"

"She went down the front steps, ran down the block to a parked car. Jumped in and drove off."

"You didn't happen to get the license plate of her car, did you?"

"No, sorry. It was an old blue Volkswagen bug. I didn't even think of memorizing the license plate till the uniformed officer asked me the same question, and then it was too late."

"Why did you go on upstairs rather than calling the police immediately?"

"I didn't take it for granted that someone was dead. I wondered if maybe someone was up there and needed medical attention."

"And you were going to give her medical attention?"

"No. Maybe it didn't make sense, but I wanted to see what the situation really was before I called for help."

"So you went up and found her?" I nodded. "Aside from Mrs. Etheridge's body, did you notice anything about the scene that struck you as unusual?"

I tried to think back to the room, and not focus on the body. "It looked as if someone had attacked her after she had laid out her climbing gear on the tarp on the table. The gear was all messed up."

"You know a lot about that sort of mountaineering equipment, Ms. Fuller?"

"I've seen a lot of it. This was the usual stuff, rope, harness, caribiners—those are ascension devices that clip to the rope to keep the climber from sliding down—crampons, you know, spikes to go on the boots. And a couple of ice axes."

"Two ice axes you say?"

"Climbers on ice sometimes use one axe in each hand."

"I wouldn't have figured you for a climber, Ms. Fuller." He gave my plus-sized body a cynical look.

I let it go by. "I've been with Griff when he did some climbing to get pictures. I sorted and packed that equipment many times along with the photographic gear. I'm not a photographer either, but I can tell a light meter from a camera body."

"We saw those pictures of Mrs. Etheridge, hanging off the ice with an axe in each hand. But there was only one ice axe found in the apartment—the one you saw in her throat."

I gulped as the image returned to me. "I don't remember seeing a second one, but I wasn't inventorying her gear."

"Would you mind if we looked around?"

"Should I be calling my lawyer?"

"Not at the moment."

"Well, I would want to talk to my lawyer before letting anyone search my property without a warrant."

He stood up and sighed silently but visibly. "Sit here for a minute, Ms. Fuller. I'll be right back."

I sat at the kitchen table, and contemplated the knife rack hanging on the wall. At least I wouldn't have to go in and provide fingerprints. They had a set of my prints from before.

He came back a few minutes later, and without commenting further, asked me to describe my trip to visit Francesca again in detail.

"So then you say you called 911, and before the response team arrived, the victim's estranged husband, Theodore Etheridge, arrived along with the victim's sister, Isadora Benedict?"

"Right, except she called herself Freechild—she snapped at Teddy when he introduced her as Benedict. She told him Benedict was her slave name."

"Her—what?" he noted the name down in his notebook.

"I think it's a feminist thing," I said, resisting the temptation to say more.

"Go figure," Gonick said with a shrug. "You keep your ex's name, so does the victim, Mrs. Etheridge."

"That one kind of makes sense because Francesca and Teddy Etheridge weren't divorced."

Gonick looked up from his notebook, "And you know this how?"

"Teddy Etheridge told me that."

"You keep in touch with this guy?"

"I just happened to run into him in Bremerton."

"And this coincidence happened the day before his wife was murdered?"

"Yes."

"Tell me about it."

I explained the women's job skill center and Ted's search for Lucille. I left out the weight loss part—Gonick started nodding when he heard about the note.

"So she kept waiting for the guy to get a divorce and he never did, and finally she just dropped him."

"That's what it sounded like."

Gonick flipped his notebook shut. "Looks like he won't need that divorce now. I think I do want to talk to this blond woman after all. Unfortunately there happens to be quite a few husky blond women in Seattle. Now all we have to do is narrow it down bit more," Gonick said with a sardonic leer. "Now just for the record, where did you go when you came back from Bremerton?"

"I was here last night and early this morning until I decided to drive over to Francesca's."

"You were here alone?"

"Except for the cat."

"We're checking to see if anyone can confirm where your husband—sorry, ex-husband was Thursday night. Now, you say you didn't see anyone aside from the cat?" Gonick raised his eyebrows. The cat might count as far as I was concerned, but he had a point. Raoul wouldn't be testifying in court as to my whereabouts. "Did you see or talk to anyone here or on the way to Mrs. Etheridge's apartment?"

I thought of Maxine's boyfriend, and gave Gonick his name. I was sure that Dick Slattery would be none too pleased to talk to the police—or maybe he would get a kick out of remembering that he had exposed himself to me. I didn't mention that to Gonick, although I did tell him that I'd seen Slattery in a bathrobe in the foyer and a little later driving off in Maxine's car.

"What made you decide to go over to Mrs. Etheridge's condo? Why not just call?"

"I wanted to ask her about the theft of her laptop. But visiting her was an impulse. I wasn't far away, so I thought I'd drop by and try to talk to her."

"But you never got the chance because she was already dead."

"Right."

"There's a lesson in there somewhere for you, Ms. Fuller. And your ex-husband showed up here at about four o'clock?"

"Right. It looked as if Francesca had been dead awhile when I saw her; do you know when she was killed?"

Gonick looked at me narrowly. "You were helpful to us once, and by some miracle we didn't end up investigating your death. Just let us do our job. The Medical Examiner's job will be to determine time and cause of death."

I shrugged and said nothing. Gonick relented enough to sigh and close his notebook. "Unfortunately Mrs. Etheridge had some rather well-known relatives."

"Right, her mother was a movie star."

"And her stepfather is a candidate for congressional office in Orange County, California. You narrowly missed making your television debut on the evening news, Ms. Fuller. Brenda Benedict is in town with Matt Gunther. They've got reporters trailing them most of the time. Once they realized that Mrs. Etheridge was Brenda Benedict's daughter they were all over that condo."

"Can't say I'm sorry I missed that."

"I wish I could say I'd missed it." He allowed himself a grim smile. "We expect to be working under a lot of press scrutiny here. Anything else you can remember will be helpful."

They left and took Griff with them. They didn't say anything about arresting him. I hugged him good-bye, and whispered to him to call me.

8

After they left I went looking for Raoul. He was down in the garden behind the building. When I called, he came strolling up to the back stairs and bounded up them cheerfully enough. I was glad to bring him in and close the window. When I got back, I saw my phone message light was blinking. I retrieved the messages. The first was from Thor Mulligan telling me that he was going to have to postpone our dinner date because he had to work a few hours overtime. The other message was from Ambrose Terrell wanting to know just when I would be able to make a report on the Women's Job Skill Center.

I called Ambrose immediately. To paraphrase a SWAT team member I once heard speak, it's never wise to keep a sniper waiting—especially if they've got you in their sights. Mrs. Madrone's assistant was impatient with both delay and imprecision. I envisioned him, tall, lean and red-haired, listening to my explanation while he sharpened his sardonic wit and examined the information for flaws that needed correction. Before I realized he was notoriously soft-hearted, I had been a little intimidated by Ambrose. Even now, knowing that, I was careful to respect his demands for efficiency. I told him about the murder, and explained that I had expected to finish my report by the weekend, but it seemed prudent to see just how the Women's Job Skill Center was involved, if at all, before making any recommendations. "Unless you want me to assume that they aren't involved."

There was a brief pause. "Assume" was a dirty word in Ambrose's dictionary. "If you took a few more days to look into it, you wouldn't be doing anything that would put you in danger, would you?"

He had a point. I had done that before. "I can't see how it would."

"As I recall, that was what you said the last time you got in trouble. Bear in mind, these are the sort of lovely people who just happened to have an axe and ropes handy in their urban apartments."

"Come on, Ambrose, Francesca was a mountain climber. Of course she'd have climbing gear."

"Oh, wait, Francesca Benedict—daughter of Brenda Benedict. She has a sister named Isadora who lives here in town, doesn't she?"

"That's right. I ran into Isadora on the doorstep with her brother-in-law immediately after I found Francesca. Isadora did indicate rather strongly that she preferred to be called Freechild, what's with that?"

"Freechild, one of those gender-neutral made-up names. She's a lesbian poster child for outdoor life, raw foods and rocks, the kind you climb. There's a picture of her on top of a mountain with her African-American girlfriend at the Yellow Brick Road Bookstore."

"Oh. Griff said they were an unusual family." Neither of us spoke for a moment. I took a deep breath. "The police didn't exactly say why, but they were most interested in Francesca's ice axe, which they didn't find on the scene. They wanted to search this apartment."

Ambrose was silent for a moment. "You've still got the number I gave you for that criminal attorney?"

"Yes."

"Let me know if you get in any more trouble, it could really put a dent in our schedule on this end."

"One other thing," I hesitated, not wishing to offend Ambrose, which was like opening a large container of dry ice in the middle of any conversation I would have with him for several weeks. "Uh, this Isadora Freechild, I was wondering if you, uh, might know someone—"

"If I knew her because she's a famous lesbian? Honey, I can't know everyone in Seattle who's gay."

"Oh, gee, and here I was thinking that, between the gay grapevine and your formidable intelligence connections, you knew everything."

"Well, you're right that I usually know someone who does know whatever it is I don't know," Ambrose said, mollified by my awkward compliment. "In point of fact, both of us know someone who took her course."

"She's got a course? In what?"

"You're not going to like it."

I sighed. "Go ahead, what is it?"

"As I said she climbs mountains, eats raw things and writes lesbian erotic fables. She's put most of those things together into a body-mind fitness workshop. I think it's called Digesting Your Inner Child. No. That's not it. Depriving Your Inner Child? Something like that."

"What?"

"It's some sensitive new age diet-fitness-empowerment thing. Val took one of her workshops. Now he's got all her books. Well, he probably doesn't have the lesbian erotic poetry. You remember Val?"

"Of course. He lives here in the building. But why should he take a diet course? I remember Val as on the thin side."

"Yes. But his inner child was quite chubby until Isadora got hold of him. Now the poor thing is absolutely skeletal."

"Val is?"

"No, the amusing thing about it all is that Val hasn't changed outwardly at all. But he feels Isadora has changed his life. Maybe I should let him tell you. I was planning to have brunch with him at his place this weekend. He's going through one of his vegetarian phases, so I can't vouch for the food, but I'll ask if he'd mind if you came along. Seeing as how you've got some inside gossip on the divine Ms. Freechild, I'm sure he'd be glad to talk. That is unless you have other plans for the weekend." Ambrose had observed my off-again-on-again relationship with Mulligan, although I was embarrassed to confide the depth of my confusion.

"I'm free," I said, and agreed to join them on Saturday.

"Jo, I'll tell Mrs. Madrone that you'll be late with the report, but I'll have to tell her why," Ambrose warned. "If I were you, I'd start putting what you do know about the Women's Job Skill Center together in case she wants a progress report."

I gave Raoul a little snack. I was certain his inner kitten was as round and bouncy as he was. I realized I wouldn't be hungry myself for awhile. Finding Francesca like that, and then seeing Griff and the police had riled me up so that I couldn't sit still. It was impossible to return to sorting. I decided to take some of the boxes of Nina's things down to the basement and bring up some of my own belongings that had been sitting patiently for years waiting for me to settle down. A little heavy lifting would probably calm my nerves, or at the very least exhaust me so I could collapse.

The storage room occupied the end of the building, and

took some space away from Mulligan's apartment and Maxine's daughter Hope's apartment which faced it across the hall. As I came down the stairs into the basement, I could hear Groucho, the macaw, warming up with some preparatory shrill cries. It must be intolerable when he let loose a major shriek in Hope's small, windowless apartment.

I put the boxes down and opened the storage room door, feeling around for the string that would turn on the overhead light bulb. The room was crowded with some furniture that Nina had stored there. A table and three stacked chairs pressed up against the stacks of boxes that held all my earthly possessions. Nina had kindly stored them for me, at first when I was following Griff around the world and lately since I'd been traveling on the job for Mrs. Madrone.

An oddly angled shadow sprang into view when the light bulb went on. I realized with a sinking feeling at the pit of my stomach what it was.

The cardboard packing box just inside my door had my name in black felt marker with the word "BOOKS" below it. An ice axe, its leather harness trailing, was embedded in the front of the box right below the label, its claw end half buried in the corrugated cardboard, and a thin layer of dried blood coating the edges of the point of penetration.

I screamed and backed out of the storage room, slamming the door, which promptly hit the door frame and flew open again. Hope's apartment door opened, and a bleached platinum head peered into the hall.

"Are you okay?" Since she was now doing the prison visits to her boyfriend, Maxine's daughter had abandoned the rainbow hair for a platinum blond look with dark roots. She saw me staring into the storage room, and came out of her apartment. "What is it, mice? You'd think that good-for-nothing cat would—" Her words trailed off in a gasp.

She stood next to me, and stared.

"Close it! Close it! Lock the door. We've got to call the police." She kicked the door closed, and I locked it, and followed her back to her apartment. I was too shocked to say a word. Not that Hope would have heard me. "It's him." She said, pacing back and forth. "I told her she was crazy to let him stay here."

I went to Hope's phone, and pulled the fresh business card Gonick had given me out of my pocket. Groucho's cage had been installed in one corner of the small front room. He craned his white-masked green-feathered head sideways to fix me with a glare from beady black eyes. As I walked past to get to the phone, he spread iridescent green wings wide in alarm.

While I was talking to the man who answered the phone in Homicide, Groucho let loose a shriek so deafening that the man asked if I was in immediate danger.

"No, it's somebody's pet macaw. But I do need to talk to Gonick, tell him it's about the ice axe."

Hope paced back and forth muttering to herself. I had never seen her so agitated. I wondered if Gonick had even had time to get down to Police Headquarters with Griff. After I hung up the phone I meditated briefly on my little talk with Gonick about searching Nina's apartment. I put a call in to the local lawyer Ambrose had suggested. I got her answering machine. I looked at my watch. It was 6:30.

"It's that slimy creature that's living with Mom," Hope said heatedly. "He's killed before you know."

"You mean Dick Slattery?"

"Of course I mean Dick Slattery, you know of any other career criminals shacking up with my mother?"

"I didn't realize he was a criminal."

"He's a convicted murderer. But you know how it is, he only served seven years."

"You know, Hope, you've done a few prison visits yourself this past year."

"How dare you compare my William to that—that—that criminal upstairs!" She stopped pacing, and put her face up to mine like a small but very hostile dog, threatening a larger animal. "That bastard somehow found out about William and he was threatening to make contact with him through his prison connections. It was a threat to me. He knows I don't like him, but he was acting as if he and William had some sort of prison brotherhood thing. Well, they don't. William's crime was manslaughter—he was defending himself and his family. He had never been in trouble before, not even a parking ticket. Dick Slattery was a criminal who killed the woman he was living with. The only reason they didn't send him up for longer—I don't even know how he got out, insanity or something. It sounds like he's been in jail most of his adult life. Believe me, it doesn't make me feel any better to have him living upstairs with Mom when I hear that he got off for good behavior."

"How did Maxine meet him?"

"He had some half-assed delivery job and he brought flowers to Mom by accident. He wouldn't let her turn them back, he insisted she keep them because they matched her pretty blue eyes. She thought he was soooo romantic. Of course, he lost his delivery job and he hasn't worked a day since he moved in. She actually thinks they have so much in common because he goes on about how much he loves jazz and what a great reader he is. Well, I haven't seen him touch a book. I know he's not paying rent or buying groceries. I took in this horrible bird because he was threatening its life."

"Yeah, he made the same joke when I met him."

"Well, it's not funny, it's scary. Mom says she thinks he's joking but I noticed she let me take Groucho out of harm's way. That jerk has been living off her now for two weeks. He walks around in the hallway wearing nothing but a bathrobe, and hits up every woman who walks through the foyer including the postal carrier. I told that to Mom but she never listens."

"I'm sorry, Hope. I've been preoccupied with my own situation, and I guess I just haven't been paying attention to the rest of the world." I sat down, momentarily distracted from the thought of the bloody axe sticking out of a box with my name written on it. "You say Slattery's been living with Maxine for two weeks?"

"Just about. She's acting like a damn teenager. I tell you one of these mornings she's going to wake up dead with her apartment ransacked."

I managed not to laugh at the idea of waking up dead. If it hadn't been a serious and possibly dangerous situation, I would have found Hope's reaction amusing. Under normal circumstances, it was her job to shock her eccentric mother, which was no easy task. Maxine might scandalize the world at large simply by owning a large attack bird, cussing like a sailor, and admitting to having a sex life in her sixties. But Hope had grown up with Maxine's excesses. Now, for all her piercings and changeable hair color, Hope sounded like a disapproving chaperone.

There was a knock at the door. "Oh, my god, it's Mom. Look and see who it is."

I looked through the peephole. It was Detective Gonick. "It's the police."

"Good. You talk to him. Give me the phone." While I talked to Gonick, Hope called her mother, and told her briefly to stay inside because the police might have found the murder weapon in the storage room. "Is *he* there?" she asked. Both Gonick and I looked at her but Hope turned away.

"Mother-daughter stuff," I explained.

"She's got a point," Gonick said. "Her mom has latched on to a real piece of work."

Hope slammed down the phone and looked at Gonick. "You talked to him?"

Gonick just looked at her. He turned to me. "Let's see what you found."

I led him out into the hallway and unlocked the door.

"Is there a light in there?"

"It's a string that hangs just inside the door." I reached past him and pulled the string. The interior of the storage room sprang into glaring illumination. For what seemed a very long time Gonick, Hope and I stood staring at the ice axe with that drizzle of dark red rimming the gash in the cardboard. Then

Gonick pulled out a cell phone and dialed without taking his eyes from the axe.

Mulligan arrived home from work about the same time that the police technicians arrived to begin to search the storage closet. I hadn't ever thought of it before, but it was very forcibly brought home to me how few possessions I'd managed to accumulate. Except for my work and traveling necessities, which were in the upstairs apartment, everything I owned was in that storage room, labeled, neatly sealed and now being examined by a police evidence team.

Mulligan took me aside, and surprisingly hugged me hello. "Would you like to explain why there are evidence technicians and homicide detectives in our hallway?" he asked softly, making no move to take off his coat or go into his apartment.

I laughed a little hysterically, and told him it had been a very long day.

"If the police can spare you, would you like to go to Chester's for dinner?"

Gonick dryly suggested that he would be in touch, and as long as he knew where to reach me, my presence was not required.

Chester's Grill was a short walk away through the overcast but not rainy August evening. We were among the first customers there. Chester was a tall man, and nearly as broad as he was tall, with gingerbread-colored hair and cheeks reddened by slaving over a hot stove. He wore a white shirt and trousers with a white apron tied round him, and welcomed us as if we were long-lost kinfolk. A waiter and waitress, who seemed small and childlike next to their super-sized boss, were setting tables in the background. In another hour the place would be packed, and Chester would be sailing among the tables with wine and special orders, birthday cakes and a few words of conversation for the regulars.

"If it isn't Thor Mulligan," Chester said as we came in the door. I liked Chester, but he made me nervous.

"Your lady friend—it's Josephine, isn't it?"

I blinked a little at that. When we sat at the table I touched Mulligan's arm. "He knows your first name? I had to practically sleep with you to find out your first name," I said only half in jest.

Mulligan looked at me in surprise. "It's on my credit card."

In fact, what got my attention was that that the restaurant owner would remember my name. I had been to the grill a few times. The first time Chester had expressed his condolences about Nina's death, and offered us free wine and desserts. Mulligan seemed pleased by the attention. If the rest of the day hadn't exhausted me past caring, I might have felt uncomfortable. From my earliest childhood when my father's military intelligence work called for us to move every year or so, I had almost a knee-jerk reaction that once clerks in stores started to know our names, it was time to start packing.

After the day I had had, I took a long swallow of wine, and decided to indulge in Chester's high-rent version of chicken pot pie, while Mulligan had the equally excellent shrimp pasta. I waited until we'd drunk most of the wine and laid waste to the entrée before telling him about Griff's visit, and how the police seemed to suspect him.

Mulligan didn't seem surprised or concerned. "They've got the odds in favor of it being a boyfriend or husband. You've met her, and you were married to him, what do you think?"

"I never knew, or ever wanted to know much about Francesca," I told him. "But from my experience with Griff, I'd say it's more his style to run away than to strike out at someone."

"Maybe he's never been rejected like that before."

"Probably not," I said thoughtfully, remembering the weary sadness on Griff's face.

"You said the book she was writing was supposed to be extremely nasty."

"That's the rumor."

"It is odd that a blood-covered axe should show up in your storage area around the time he visits you," Mulligan said.

"I can't see Griff trying to incriminate me," I said. Mulligan didn't answer.

The subject was a little touchy for both of us, so we gossiped about Maxine's new boyfriend and Hope's violent reaction. As we walked back home after dinner my cell phone rang. It was Teddy Etheridge.

"Jo, you've got to come over here. It's Lucille. She's here, I just don't know how to help her."

"Teddy, it's late, can we talk tomorrow?"

"She can't stay. I've begged her to stay. Would you talk to her?

"I don't see what I—"

"Hello, is this Josephine?" The woman on the other end of the line sounded doubtful.

"Yes. Lucille? How are you doing?"

"Not good. I came by your house but you weren't there."

"When was this?"

"Earlier today. Teddy told me you were a good person to talk to. I went to your apartment building, but the police were there. I got scared and left."

I couldn't help wondering if she knew something about the blood-covered axe in the storage room. "Lucille, when you—hello . . ." I took the phone away from my ear, then turned it off. "The phone went dead," I told Mulligan. We were just reaching the apartment building. "I've got to go over there. Could you come with me?"

"You don't think you should call the police to do that?"

"You think the police will drop everything to go see if those people are okay? We could call the police from there if it looks bad."

Mulligan sighed.

"I could just check, and come right back."

"Let's take my truck. The whole thing could be some kind of setup. I don't think you should go alone, but mainly I want to get a look at this Teddy character."

We took Mulligan's truck, and drove over to the South Tacoma address Teddy had given me. It was a small dark-gray house that would have disappeared into the growing darkness if the window sills and roof trim hadn't been painted white. A trash can the same gray as the house sat off to one side of the door on the front porch. Two motorcycles were parked in the driveway.

Mulligan gave me a look that made me realize no further information on this subject was welcome.

Both motorcycles were Harley-Davidsons—one considerably smaller than the other. I wondered if Lucille rode a motorcycle. If so that was a side of her personality Teddy hadn't mentioned. I rang the doorbell and Teddy threw the door open and stepped back to let us in. He looked as if he had thrown on the first things he found—a chambray shirt with the collar half folded under the neck over a Wile E. Coyote T-shirt and blue jeans that looked like yesterday's wash. His anguished expression and general air of mute distress made me want to reach out and fix his collar and give him a big hug. But Mulligan was radiating a palpable air of disapproval. I smelled the whiskey on Teddy's breath as I said hello. "We came as soon as we could."

The room was tidy but I recognized the neatness of someone who travels light. The faded sofa and chairs—tropical flowers on a green background, matched the green carpet, but the place had the air of space rented out furnished to people who hardly noticed their surroundings. In one corner of the room a standing lamp cast a spotlight on a card table with a laptop computer and a small portable printer on it. An ergonomic task chair was pulled up to the table, and a neat file of typed pages were stacked up next to the printer. A folding chair next to the table held a pile of books, papers and magazines. Teddy stood near the flower-splashed sofa in front of the blinds, which were drawn. Outside of the circle of light illuminating the card table the room was dim. It was like entering a cave, and Teddy had the look of a bear dazed from hibernation.

It was only because of her closely trimmed hair and the distinctive jacket that I recognized Isadora Freechild sitting in an armchair near the window. She lay in the chair almost as if she had fallen there, staring at the closed shades without really seeing them.

She looked up without much interest when we came in. I had stood next to her on her sister's doorstep that morning, and although it seemed an age ago, I was once again struck by her resemblance to her sister. Even the way she lay in the chair was a less extreme version of how her sister's body had lain amidst the welter of climbing rope. Noticing that gave me a chill up the spine.

"Where's Lucille?" I asked, seeing no sign of another person. Isadora ignored me as totally as if I had not spoken.

"She left," Teddy said dully. "Jo, you met my sister-in-law."

I said I remembered from earlier. "I am so sorry for your loss." I introduced Mulligan who murmured a few words of condolence also. Teddy shook hands with Mulligan. Isadora nodded faintly, and returned to her contemplation of the closed blinds.

"Lucille is gone," Teddy said. "I'm sorry she hung up on you. She got hysterical, and left just a few minutes before Isadora arrived. But she has your phone number and address. She tried to reach you before." His voice trailed off.

"Before?" I repeated. "When exactly did she try to reach me?"

"I'm not sure. She just stopped by here briefly." His face showed anguish. "She wouldn't stay. She was very upset." He shook his head. "I think she'll try to contact you again, Jo. She needs to talk to someone."

"She was at Fran's apartment, wasn't she? She's the tall blonde who came running out and told me to call the police."

"Yes." Teddy nodded. "She said she went back to return the laptop. I am so sorry you had to get involved in all this, Jo."

I heard Mulligan make a faint sound that might have been a snort of disgust, but when I glanced at him, he was looking around the room.

"I don't understand why Lucille had to take that laptop, Teddy. If she wanted to read the book, why not wait a few months and buy a copy?"

"I think she wanted to see if there was something on that computer that would show her whether Francesca and I were still involved. I blame myself for not having pursued the divorce long ago." He shrugged. "You know how women are."

"Yeah, well, knowing how women are doesn't explain why she set up the whole thing to begin with. The Women's Job Skill Center is taking the heat and they say they didn't even recommend her. She set it up all on her own using their name."

"I don't know why she did that either," Teddy said, rubbing

his eyes. "If she calls, please talk to her. Tell her to get in touch with me. I think she's in trouble and I can help." Teddy moved in close to me as if to exclude Mulligan.

Suddenly the image came to me of the ice axe embedded in my storage box. "Sit down, Teddy, we need to talk."

He sat on the sofa, almost as far away as he could get from the computer in its circle of light. I passed it on my way to the armchair at the end of the sofa. The laptop screen was open but dark. I sat in the armchair near Teddy. Mulligan followed me, and sat on a straight wooden chair nearby. Teddy regarded him a little uneasily, which made sense because Mulligan's frown radiated disapproval.

"When did you give Lucille my name and address?"

"Yesterday."

"How did you get it?"

"I beg your pardon?"

"I gave you my phone number but not my address. How did you get it?"

"Griff's Rolodex. The day we had lunch I went to see Fran but she wasn't home. I left her a note I'd be back the next day but it was too late. She was dead the next morning. Anyway, Griff's Rolodex was sitting on the desk, so I looked up your address."

"Oh." That made sense. Griff's Rolodex was Army surplus green metal—old, battered and legendary. It was like an encyclopedia of his travels. It had outlasted most of his wives and girlfriends, and probably still contained all their current names and addresses.

"Lucille called me. I tried to get her to call you. She said no, but she did want to talk to you. I told her all about you, I'm afraid you're kind of a—I don't know, a symbol of something she wants to believe in but can't. When she came here, all she would say about Francesca is that she returned her laptop, found the body and ran away. I'm worried about her." All at once, I realized he was dazed with shock.

I patted his hand. "I'm so sorry, Teddy."

A knock at the door interrupted us. Teddy got up to answer it. "Brenda, Matt, come in." He stepped back with the same weary tread that he had when he let me in. A small, delicate woman and a man of about the same height came in. They were both in their late fifties, and they shone with the sort of polish reserved for the rich and frequently photographed.

Brenda Benedict was just a shade over five feet tall and slender, with a few artful platinum streaks in her gorgeously cut blond hair. Teddy took her fur jacket and hastily hung it behind the door with an anxious glance at Isadora. Brenda's sinuous shape, revealed in a cowl-necked sweater and slacks, had a coiled steel tension that reminded me of a rampant cobra.

She embraced Teddy, who patted her back while she choked out a ladylike sob or two, and then composed herself. Matt Gunther, her politician consort, bent toward her as if to shelter her, and handed her an immaculate white handkerchief, which she used to dab her eyes. Her eye makeup was starting to smudge already, so I didn't doubt that her tears were real. He let her keep the handkerchief.

Gunther grasped both of Teddy's hands in his. He was tanned and dapper, with light hazel eyes, even features, silver hair and mustache, and an extraordinarily well-cut suit. He had the aura of power that comes with the search for high public office, but on him it flickered like a bad fluorescent light bulb. There was something more anxious under his glossy exterior. I examined him and realized it was a deep-seated nervousness that he had under excellent control except for his eyebrows, that twitched from time to time like a squirrel's tail.

For all his nerves, he radiated concern in a way that his wife couldn't quite manage. He shook Teddy's hand earnestly, and paused only a heartbeat when introduced to me, before giving me an equally warm and encouraging handshake.

Having met other politicians, I gave the couple high marks for traveling without an entourage. "This was personal," they were saying in political language. "We are simple people, sharing our grief."

Brenda swept past me to get to her daughter. I am incurably heterosexual, but I had to fight off the urge to stroke her blue-gray angora sweater. The only thing stopping me was the reptilian glint in her deep blue eyes. She was an odd combination of cuddly and cold-blooded. Perhaps it was that predatory quality that raised the specter of Dick Slattery unbidden in my mind.

Isadora wearily rose, met her mother and embraced her. After a moment Brenda held her off at arm's length, contemplating the crew cut, pierced ears, eyebrow. "The tattoo is new," she said in a throaty dramatic voice, running a luminescent pink fingernail to trace without touching a writhing serpent that ran from behind Isadora's ear around the front of her neck and into her white T-shirt just at the V where her collar bones met.

"It goes down around my nipple and back up again. It has my girlfriend's name at the center. Want to see?"

"Later, darling."

"Perhaps at the funeral home," Isadora muttered. "I'll be there." She turned back to the chair by the window, shrugged into her jacket and walked out the door before anyone said another word.

The slam of the door was immediately followed by a yowl of pain. Mulligan, who was closest to the door, went to open it and I followed him, contemplating an exit strategy. A tall, lean, deeply tanned man in a neon blue and orange ski jacket was standing on one foot on the front porch, holding his other foot in his hand and massaging his shin.

"The little bitch nearly kicked my knee!" he exclaimed to all of us, as if we were responsible.

"You were in my way," Isadora yelled, just before she kick-started the smaller Harley-Davidson in the driveway and roared off past the black Mercedes, around which a couple of dark-suited, beefy men stood, enjoying the show. Those must be Matt Gunther's bodyguards.

The man in the ski jacket looked us over. "Brenda," he said, with a tight smile. He put his foot down, and dusted off his hand. "That was my bad knee too."

"I'm sure she knew that, dear," Brenda Benedict said serenely.

"I don't believe we've met," said Matt Gunther, stepping out onto the porch and introducing himself, which caused a slight ripple effect among the bodyguards, who were clearly torn between protecting their charge and respecting a family moment.

"I'm Don Benedict, Francesca's father."

"Donny, you bad boy," Brenda stepped out onto the porch as well, and allowed her ex-husband to bend down to sketch a kiss in the air somewhere in the general vicinity of her face. "Dora is your daughter too—"

"Days like today I wonder about that," he said, reaching down to rub his knee again.

"She's even more like you than Franny was."

Don Benedict turned away from her, and clapped his son-in-law on the shoulder. "How you holding up, Teddy?"

Teddy mumbled something that was too soft to hear.

I followed Mulligan out to the porch. We didn't even have to signal to each other that it was time to leave.

"Who are all these people?" Don Benedict asked, as if reluctant to turn back to his ex-wife and her new husband.

Teddy introduced me, and I, in turn, introduced Mulligan. Benedict seemed to lose interest after hearing our names and wandered into the house muttering, "You got anything to drink, Teddy?"

Matt Gunther watched as Mulligan and I prepared to leave. His serious but unruffled expression seemed appropriate, but his eyebrows still twitched. He wasn't quite done with us. This was not a man who did well in poker games. "So, Ms. Fuller and Mr. Mulligan, do you know Teddy from back East?"

Teddy interrupted, "No, Matt, I met Josephine when we were in Nepal. She was married to Griffin Fuller."

Gunther did the math. Didn't like it. Pushed it aside.

"Griffin Fuller," Brenda folded the handkerchief into a tight square. "I never liked him. If you ask me, he's the one who's responsible for this whole tragedy."

"Now Brenda, we've never heard any evidence that Fuller was a violent man," Matt said, patting her shoulder. "Have we?" He looked at me appealingly.

I shook my head. "Griff had a lot of trouble resisting the temptation to sleep with every woman he met, but he was always a very gentle man." I suddenly realized that we were speaking of Griff in the past tense, as if he were dead along with Francesca.

"I heard she was breaking up with that photographer. You were always my favorite of Francesca's men," Brenda said to Teddy, grasping his arm before he could move away. "I was hoping you would get back together again. I think she wanted that too."

"We'd better be going," I said into the sudden silence. "I'm sorry to have met you under these circumstances."

Brenda nodded regally and Matt twitched his eyebrows cordially.

As the door closed I heard Brenda ask, "Teddy, have you found the book?"

I wanted to stay to hear the answer to that question, but I suspected she wouldn't have asked it if I hadn't been gone so far as she was concerned. The door flew open, and Teddy came out before we could leave the porch. He leaned close so that the bodyguard at the foot of the walkway, who was pointedly examining the roof for snipers, could not hear. "Call me, and if you hear from her, tell Lucille to call me," he hissed.

"Okay."

He turned his head unwillingly to the house and went back in. Mulligan and I escaped. We walked past the black Mercedes waiting at the curb, and nodded to the two bodyguards trying to look inconspicuous with security radio earpieces, and nothing to do but stand in their impeccable suits tailored to conceal their guns until the couple emerged from their visit. I was almost tempted to stay to watch Brenda and Matt resume their campaign personas, but it probably wasn't worth the wait.

Mulligan was already starting the truck. I got in, and looked at him. He hadn't said much beyond hello to each of the people we had just met. "So what do you think?" I asked, wondering if he was angry at me for some reason.

He let the engine idle and turned to me. "You didn't mention that you don't find Teddy attractive."

I stared at him, and realized it was true. "I'll be damned." I started to laugh. "You noticed it before I did." He didn't laugh, but he smiled. "How could you tell, I mean what made you—?" I stopped, a little confused.

He reached out and traced his finger from the side of my face down my shoulder, under the still-unbuttoned jacket and down the side of my body to my hip. It was a surprisingly sensuous gesture that brought up a flood of emotion. "I can't help paying attention to what turns you on."

"I don't know if that's good or bad," I said with an unavoidable catch in my voice. "It's very confusing." I put a hand on his chest. I didn't mean to unbutton his jacket and attract the attention of Matt Gunther's bodyguards. He didn't indicate that I should move my hand, and he left his where it was.

"But you didn't even notice that you weren't attracted to Teddy. Why is that?"

I pulled back just before slipping into a deep crevasse of arousal. "Come to think of it, I was so busy being irked by how astounded he was at the novelty of looking on me with lust that I didn't pay much attention to what I might or might not feel for him. My affections are already engaged."

"Even after the past couple of months?" Mulligan turned back to face the steering wheel, and slid his hand away from my hip. I took my hand off his chest a little regretfully.

I sighed, "I don't know what inspired me to feel this way about you. But I have trouble turning my feelings on and off. So why shouldn't you?"

"Yeah." He started the engine.

What I wanted to say was, "Make up your damn mind whether you want me or not." If my track history with men was anything to go by, I'd probably end up saying that or something very much like it pretty soon, which was bound to effectively end the romance. But I didn't want to add to either of our suffering at the moment. I really did feel sorry for his grief—and guilty that my grief didn't seem to be quite as great. He was hurting and I was terrified. He didn't know how to stop his pain and I didn't even know what I was afraid of. Great.

"What made you think I was interested in Teddy?"

"Are you kidding? You were raving about how smart and

funny he was. I couldn't help being curious. Now I've seen him. Somehow I can tell I haven't heard the last of him either."

A cream-colored limousine pulled up to hover just behind the truck. Mulligan had managed to snare the closest parking space to Teddy's house and the limo driver appeared to want it. Mulligan pulled the truck out of the space and glanced back to see the limousine pull into it. It was dark, but I turned back and watched the limo driver go around to open the door. We were out of visual range before I could see who got out.

"More Hollywood folk, I'll bet," Mulligan said.

"No argument there."

When we got back to the apartment building the police had left, and the storage room door was locked without any seal. "I'll look at my stored stuff over the weekend," I muttered. "I guess I'd better go see how the cat is doing."

Mulligan nodded. "Would you like to have lunch tomorrow?"

"I would but I'm getting together with Ambrose and Val."

"Okay." He turned to go.

"I am free for breakfast."

"Come down when you're ready, I have onion bagels and coffee, but I don't have any cream."

"I'll bring some down."

The blinking light on the message machine up in the apartment signaled that Detective Gonick had called and asked me to call him back. The second message was from Mrs. Madrone—herself, not Ambrose calling to tell me to call her. It was too late to return either call and it was a toss-up which one worried me more.

I must have been tired, because I slept, even with the irrational anxiousness the apartment inspired in me and the all-too-rational anxiousness of the phone calls I had to return. Mulligan woke me up at eight o'clock and I tried calling Ambrose before I went downstairs. Of course, Ambrose was out, but I told his machine about the call from Mrs. Madrone, and that I would return her call at a little more civilized hour. I decided that if they could wait, so could Gonick, and I went down to Mulligan's. He had very good coffee and I brought some half-and-half. Over bagels and scrambled eggs I told him about Isadora's books.

"All these athletic writers—I thought writers were couch potatoes who never budged from their keyboards," Mulligan said, sipping his coffee.

"Most of the writers I've met were photographers who dabbled in writing articles to get money to travel," I confessed. "So they were pretty antsy characters. I'm going to borrow Isadora's books from Val this afternoon. I'll let you know what I think, or you can read them too, if you want."

"I don't care what they're about, I'd probably like them better than that Teddy guy. We've seen Isadora in action, and I'd stay out of her way if I were you. What's her book about, martial arts?"

"I'll have to ask Val. All Ambrose could do was make jokes about some kind of 'Inner Child Diet.'"

"Wait, she must be the one teaching the 'Finding Your Vegetarian Inner Child' cooking class at the Seattle Center."

I stared at him. "You're taking cooking classes?"

He laughed at my astonishment. "Hey, you got a problem with that?"

"No. You just never mentioned it."

"Well, to be honest, I went to a seminar on electronic surveillance over there, and when I looked at the other events at the Seattle Center I saw that Vegetarian Inner Child thing. It stuck in my mind."

"And when was this?"

"It was a few months back. I didn't pay a lot of attention but 'Finding Your Vegetarian Inner Child' has got to be the sappiest name for a cooking class I've ever seen."

"Vegetables have sap—there's no way around it."

"And that motorcycle boot-stomping terrorist we saw last night writes books on vegetarianism?"

"Ambrose said Val swears by her. So I should be able to find out more over lunch."

"Have a good time. I've got errands all day."

"If you'd like to come up for dinner, I could make spaghetti," I said, a little surprised at my own offer.

Mulligan seemed surprised as well, but he said, "Sure."

"Vegetarian or not?"

"Not."

"Okay." Spaghetti, vegetarian or not, was one of the few things I knew how to cook from scratch.

Back in my apartment, Raoul was standing by the back door and softly but relentlessly stating his name, in a clear effort to be released upon the backyard. I relented and let him out, but I brought my cell phone and called Mrs. Madrone from a vantage point where I could keep an eye on the cat. Ambrose answered and put me through to her without comment.

"What's this about your being involved in another murder, Josephine?" she said by way of introduction.

"Well." I couldn't really argue that I wasn't involved, the police seemed interested in me as a suspect. "It's complicated, Mrs. Madrone, I'm sure Ambrose told you the particulars, but it's the woman my ex-husband was involved with."

"Yes, I believe I told you that Griffin Fuller took a portrait of me, some years ago, when my late husband was alive. Of course we'd heard of his reputation before we met him."

I only wish I could have said the same. But I held my tongue.

"My husband rather subtly made sure I was never alone with him during the photo session."

I had to laugh, and I could imagine Mrs. Madrone smiling, thin as a whippet, probably with Prince the lilac point Siamese on her lap.

"Rather amusing in retrospect," she continued. "This was more than a dozen years ago. He did excellent work, you'll have to see it sometime. It's at the house in San Francisco."

"I didn't realize that Griff did portraits."

"I believe he might have given it up because it got him in trouble. Portraits were an indulgence that might have proved dangerous for your ex-husband, my dear. He's much better off photographing mountains and wildlife. The man is too charming for his own good."

"No argument there. But I don't think he killed the woman he was living with. As you said, he's charming, and he has kind of a short attention span when it comes to women."

Mrs. Madrone chuckled, "Aptly put."

"But he's not vindictive or violent. I just couldn't imagine him killing someone."

"You know him better than most, Josephine, and I suppose it says something that you're not anxious to help put your ex-husband behind bars. But it will greatly inconvenience me if you end up in trouble yourself. So try not to do too much meddling. For my sake."

"I'll try."

"And I do expect the report on the Women's Job Skill Center next week."

"Yes, ma'am."

She hung up without saying good-bye, moving on to the next thing on her crowded agenda. If I had been in her presence, she would have simply directed her wheelchair and her attention in another direction and banished me as if I had vaporized the moment the conversation concluded. And yet she had cared enough to call. Or worried enough.

After talking to my multi-billionaire boss, a chat with Gonick in Homicide was a picnic. He didn't have any new requests, but asked if I'd heard from Griff since we last spoke. I said I had last seen Griff departing for the police station.

"I haven't been able to reach him at the number he gave me."

"He stays with friends a lot."

"Next time he calls, tell him to keep in touch. I'm betting he'll call you." We ended the conversation on that note. The skeptical tone in Gonick's voice made me uneasy. Well, I was already uneasy. I guess it made me uneasier. It was that kind of morning.

I had heard that Val had redecorated, and I was interested to see if he had replaced the yellow stripes and sharp-edged African sculpture. He was in the interior design business so

I expected that his apartment would demonstrate the latest thinking in decorating. I wondered if, for the first time in my life, I was starting to feel a nest-building urge stirring.

Val and Ambrose met me at the door carrying several shopping bags with handles bearing the elegant logo of a local gourmet delicatessen. Ambrose was all in black, which made a startling contrast with his pale skin and bright red hair. Val was equally subdued in a gray wool jacket over a charcoal turtleneck. Val lacked Ambrose's commanding height and dramatic coloring, but he had an exotic, distinguished look with his black beard and its artful white streak.

Ambrose took Val's shopping bags, and handed them to me. "Hold these, Josie, while Val goes in to get the books for you. I'm sorry to cancel on such short notice, but Val and I have been called on a mission of mercy." Ambrose leaned into the apartment, "Get your cutting board and bread knife too," he called to Val. Looking past him, I was rewarded with a glimpse of green wall and some curious lamp-like furniture that looked like luminous amber tree trunks. I turned back to the hallway.

I looked down into the shopping bag I suddenly found myself holding. "What kind of mission of mercy requires paté foie gras?"

"That's mushroom paté, and everything in these bags is strictly vegan. It's for Isadora Freechild. Her loyal cooking and camping followers are providing some food at her home as a kind of wake. For her sister."

Val came back out, and locked the door behind him. He pushed two slim volumes into my hands. One was entitled *Iron Maiden, Stainless Steel Mother, Chromium Crone*.

"Thanks." I glanced through it. "Politically correct fairy tales—hasn't that been done?"

"Only five or ten times before," Ambrose said, stowing the cutting board and bread knife in a cloth compartment of his carrying bag.

"Not with her name on it," Val said. "Besides they were funny."

"Funny on purpose, or funny by accident?" I asked

Val appeared not to have heard the question. "They're even reasonably faithful to the original."

"Oh, please," Ambrose said with an elegant wave of dismissal, "there was no Beppo the necrophiliac groundskeeper in the original Sleeping Beauty. She took all the grotesque beauty of the old fairy tales, and replaced it with grotesque dogma."

"Ambrose, are you telling me you've read this woman's work?" I asked in astonishment.

Ambrose hesitated. "Oh, all right, I read it. I wanted to see what all the fuss was about. Besides it's a quick read, and the message is clear enough. Although I must say it's not my idea of a charming fable to be told that my gender has become redundant, and is going the way of the dinosaur."

"It's just a metaphor, Ambrose," Val said.

"Uh-huh." Ambrose sounded unconvinced.

"May I borrow them overnight?" I asked, turning the books over in my hand. "I can return them tomorrow. Oh, this one is a cookbook."

"It's called *Finding Your Vegetarian Inner Child,*" Val said, "and yes, you may borrow it. There are some lovely recipes in there. I lost five pounds following her recipes."

"When was this?"

"It was two years ago. And, yes, I have gained it back. But I stopped following her program."

"I'd appreciate borrowing both books," I said, sidestepping the whole five-pound-weight loss pitfall with the air of one trying not to step in a puddle of unknown depth on a rainy day.

"Well, since you live upstairs, bring them back whenever you get the chance."

"Come on, we don't have a lot of time," Ambrose said impatiently.

"Can I come? I met Isadora yesterday, and I had met Francesca." I didn't elaborate on the circumstances. Ambrose may have known just exactly under what circumstances I originally met Francesca but he was tactfully silent. "I can make myself useful."

Ambrose and Val looked at me a little oddly.

"That does strain the imagination somewhat," Ambrose remarked, examining me doubtfully, "but it's up to Val. This is Val's friend we're talking about."

"This doesn't have anything to do with that blood-covered hammer they found in the storage room downstairs, does it?" Val asked.

"It was an ice axe, and I'm not supposed to talk about it." Of course, I just had.

"An ice axe," Val said.

"Like mountain climbers use?" Ambrose asked.

"I think so," I said.

"You know Isadora is a mountain climber too," Val said. "She'd done some easy climbs for women only and the girls in the cooking class say they're quite empowering."

"I dare you to call them girls to their faces." Ambrose smiled and turned to head downstairs. "Come on, let's go."

We passed Maxine's apartment and went through the foyer. Dick Slattery was lounging on the steps, lowering the tone of the neighborhood all by himself. For some reason his eyes fastened on Val, who took a deep breath and kept his eyes averted.

"What was that?" Ambrose asked softly after we passed out of earshot.

"Maxine's new boyfriend," I said.

"I love Maxine," Val said, "but she has deplorable taste in men."

"Hope says he's an ex-convict," I added helpfully. "He made threats to Groucho, so Hope took the parrot down to her place."

"You mean the macaw," Val corrected.

"Okay, okay, the macaw."

"What is this paragon's name?" Ambrose asked.

I told him. He took out a small leather notebook and wrote it down. Then we reached his black Ford Taurus and took a moment settling in with all the assorted shopping bags.

"Where does Isadora live?" I asked, fastening my seat belt.

"Not too far away. We could even walk, but these bags are heavy, and we've got work to do. We really need to make this look nice," Val said, a little plaintively.

We were silent for a moment, and Val added, "Dora really hasn't been the same since Sandy died."

"I wonder if that's the girlfriend whose name is tattooed on her breast," I said.

"Josephine!" Ambrose glanced back at me in surprise, "You're shocking Val."

"Speak for yourself, sweetie, I'm fascinated," Val said, putting an arm over the seat and twisting back to look at me. "I had no idea you were such a fast worker, Josephine. And you only met her yesterday."

"Guys, come on. This was at Francesca's husband's place. She told her mother she had this tattoo. She didn't show it to us. Well, she offered, but her mother asked her not to."

Ambrose said nothing.

Val turned back, reluctantly, "Okay, so you're a fast worker in a little different way than I originally meant. You invited yourself today and I never even thought anything of it."

"Josephine sneaks up on you, but she can be quite effective," Ambrose said. I was honored—sort of. But I couldn't think of a word to say. There was a short silence.

"Dora used to hold her cooking classes at the Seattle Center," Val said at last. "But she's been forced to move them to her home. She just got no support at all from the mainstream people. Her work was too advanced."

"So she does cooking classes, mountain climbing and writes revisionist fairy tales," I said.

"A woman for the new Renaissance," Ambrose remarked dryly.

Val looked from one of us to the other as if unsure whether we were mocking his mentor. "It's a lifestyle book. Isadora is very serious about health, vegan cooking, mental housecleaning, nurturing your better self."

"So you got to know her when you were taking her cooking class?" I asked.

"Our group was kind of a continuation of the class. Of course, since we're meeting in her home, we all got to know each other—it became like a gathering of friends."

"A gathering of friends who pay their hostess every time they come over," Ambrose remarked.

Val gave him a reprimanding look. "She was very conscientious about teaching us new recipes. The people who went on treks with her said it was life-altering. She's serious about her teaching, but in person she's, well, a little brusque, but very vulnerable. Whenever I managed to follow her plan, I've been much healthier. You know I needed healing after what I went through with K.C.—"

Ambrose held up a hand, "No one appreciates more than I do the fact that you're feeling better."

"Dora was very sympathetic to my problems with K.C. leaving me. She's been through tremendous loss herself with Sandy's death. It was so tragic."

Ambrose had stopped at a traffic light. He turned to look Val in the eyes. "What happened?"

"It was a climbing accident. In fact, it was a climb with Francesca. Dora was injured and Sandy died up on Mount McKinley."

I was suddenly much more keen to see Isadora again.

Isadora Freechild's apartment was a two-bedroom in a high-rise at the edge of Capitol Hill near the University District. We were met at the door by a woman so thin that her plain gray wool jacket hung off her shoulders in an A-line. Her hair was gathered in a knot at the back of her head. Silver and jet earrings were her only adornment. She clasped each of our hands in turn despite the shopping bags we held. "I'm Iris Quinn," she said softly. "Call me Quinn."

"Where shall we put these?" Ambrose asked, holding up the bags.

"Follow me," Quinn said, and led the way to a surprisingly large kitchen where several women in their thirties and forties were putting food on serving platters. Quinn made a space on the counter for the bags, and began to inspect the contents for organic and political pedigree. The eggs barely passed muster.

"Some of us eat eggs," Quinn said. "But Val, couldn't you have bought organic—from cage-free hens? I believe I told you last time about factory farming."

"Please don't show me the pictures again, Quinn. It was a weak moment," Val protested in an aggrieved tone. "Besides, the only other alternative was fertile eggs, and I know how some of you women feel about ingesting sperm."

This brought him a moment of silence. I could feel Ambrose suppressing a laugh, and I didn't dare look at him.

"Speaking of roosters," said a young woman in a tank top that displayed impressively muscled arms. "Isadora hasn't arrived yet, but her father is sitting in the study offending people right and left. He's very upset that there's no alcohol here. He keeps drinking out of a flask he brought, and trying to hit on my girlfriend. He challenged her to arm wrestle and she's actually going to do it."

"This looks like a job for Josephine," Ambrose said.

Quinn nodded, and went back to inspecting the food items from Val's bag. Ambrose and I followed the woman in the tank top down a hallway into a room not much bigger than an alcove with a day bed separated by an end table from a ladderback rocking chair.

Ambrose stood back to let me enter, and then disappeared down the hall. Don Benedict sat on the day bed, and a young woman with boyishly cut hair, wearing a long-sleeved blue blouse with a bolo tie and blue jeans had pulled the rocking chair up to the end table so she could put her right elbow on the table and grip Benedict's right hand in hers. They were about to arm wrestle.

The participants looked up, but only Benedict acknowledged my presence with a cordial nod. The woman in the tank top had followed me into the room, which suddenly seemed very crowded.

"Go!" said the woman with the bolo tie. The two wrestlers strained for a moment, and then she handily pinned Benedict's wrist to the table.

"Too strong for me," he said good-naturedly.

"You got that right," his opponent said a little gruffly. Then she rose to her feet and pushed the rocker back slightly as if to let the next competitor sit down. The woman in the tank top nudged her and she let herself be pulled away, whispering down the hall. Don Benedict and I were alone in the room. I pulled the rocker back several inches and sat down.

"So, do you want to arm wrestle?" Benedict asked, rubbing his arm.

"No, thanks."

"I let her win you know," he said with a wink. "I've found that it pays to let the ladies win. I usually end up winning in oh, so many ways."

"Okay."

"Usually I would read their tarot cards. Women love that. But Dora took my tarot deck away from me this morning at the funeral home. Just because I was doing a reading for a mourner from another family."

"This was while your family was arranging the funeral?"

"Well, we can't really arrange it till they release Franny's body, but we were just—well, I guess we were arranging it. I don't know why those girls all went away. I'm not going to hurt them," he remarked, half to me and half to himself. "You look familiar."

"We met last night at Teddy Etheridge's place," I told him. "How is your knee?"

He rubbed his knee, and regarded me thoughtfully. "I'll ice it when I get to the hotel. You're related to Griffin Fuller, right?"

"In a manner of speaking."

"I always liked him. Brenda thinks he might have hurt Fran, but she's looking for a quick answer that won't rub off on her precious Matt."

"The police don't seem to think Griff did it—or at least they haven't arrested him so far."

"Are you sure about that?"

"So far as I know." I hadn't checked on Griff recently, perhaps they had. "Did you hear differently?"

"I heard something about finding a murder weapon at his ex-wife's house."

I let that one go. Don Benedict didn't remember that I was Griff's ex. "But Griff had no reason to kill Francesca. They were breaking up."

He shrugged. "Maybe he didn't want to let go. Fran's like her mother, she keeps getting better offers. That's why Brenda dumped me. I was a big deal in the Hanged Man movies when we met. We married, and she took my name. Then her career started to take off just when mine went down the toilet for good. Brenda had this idea that she could become a big-time movie star so she left me with two little girls to raise. They were okay, they were both outdoor kids—serious athletes, took after me that way. But Fran turned out ambitious just like her mother. She didn't only climb mountains, she climbed right over the bodies of everyone she ever knew."

He shook his head sadly, and pulled a small flask out of his pocket. He poured a liberal shot into the glass on the table next to him, which appeared to contain some kind of fruit juice. He offered me the bottle, and when I shook my head he offered me the glass before shrugging, and swallowing most of it. "You didn't even know I was in movies, did you?"

"Someone told me you were in a very popular horror series."

"Correction. I was the inspiration for a very popular horror movie."

I had to laugh before I realized he hadn't said it on purpose, but he laughed too. "That doesn't sound right," he said, shaking his head and dismissing it. "Anyway. I was in college when I discovered that reading the tarot was very popular with girls. I was a nice-looking kid, which got me in the door. But reading a girl's cards would put her at ease—made her feel I was interested in her. Wolf Lambert and I shared an apartment in West LA. I was on an athletic scholarship—he was in film school at UCLA. We had very different tastes in women, but between the jock groupies and the film groupies we made out like bandits. When he decided to make his artsy little horror movie, I came up with the Hanged Man. I got screen credit for creating the idea. I even played the part in the first two. Of course, I had a hood over my head the whole time, so I was easy to replace."

"Wow," I said, not being able to think of another comment.

"They made a dozen films. They might even make another—lucky thirteen." Benedict judiciously poured more vodka in his glass, which by now had very little fruit juice remaining.

"Have you seen Dora since this morning at the funeral parlor?" I asked.

"No. She mentioned that her friends were cooking so I came over. She told the rest of the family too, but I don't guess they'll come."

"Aren't you worried your daughter will attack you again?"

"Oh, that's just her way. Isadora's like me, she's real physical, but she doesn't hold a grudge. I would have expected her to be the serious climber, but Francesca had this raw determination. Maybe I'll go home with one of these pretty ladies. She sure does have a lot of nice-looking women friends."

"You do know that most of them are lesbians?"

"That's what they say. I think half of them just haven't met the right man yet."

I stared at him in silent shock for several seconds. I decided his time at this gathering was limited, and I had better get what information I could out of him while he was here, and more or less coherent.

So tell me about these resorts you operate," I said, leaning forward. He actually spoke for several minutes about Snowcones Family Resort Villages, snowboarding, ski lessons for toddlers, and malls for non-sports-minded family members or guests.

He was just getting to the summer season mountain events when he fell silent, and stared at the doorway behind me. I turned to see what had riveted his attention. It was a delicately built Asian temptress in a black satin, high-necked dress with a slit up the side of the tight skirt. She was so pale, and the dress was such a cliché, that she looked like a black and white still from a Hollywood Asian intrigue film where an inscrutable seductress extracts state secrets or cash from an unwary traveler.

"Well, hello there, Dragon Lady. Are you looking for the bar? There ain't no liquor in there, but I've got some right here." He held up his flask.

I moved out of the way so that Miss Asian Menace could slink past me to perch on the arm of Don Benedict's chair. While he poured some vodka into her glass of juice her eyes met mine over his head, and she winked. As I turned to leave, I noticed that she was running elegantly manicured fingers through his thinning hair. He was gazing up at her in fascination.

I met Ambrose in the hallway. "I don't think he has quite got that his daughter is a lesbian, and I would bet money he doesn't know that that Asian bombshell in there is a transvestite."

Ambrose smiled, "And your point was?"

"Never mind."

He went back into the living room and I went into the kitchen where Quinn and her younger friend were dishing what looked like meatballs into a hot pan of sauce. "You have non-vegetarian dishes?" I asked, more out of curiosity than hunger.

"Never," Quinn said, giving me a suspicious look. "You didn't bring anything like that, did you?" She cast a baleful eye on me as if I might be smuggling veal in my pockets.

"You know I would never do that or allow someone I brought to do it," Val protested.

Quinn rolled her eyes. "Well, you know how sometimes people who are new to the class bring fish or even chicken because they think vegetarian means no red meat."

"I just wondered what vegetarian cooking had to do with your inner child," I said, hoping to turn the conversation toward Isadora Benedict.

"You haven't read Isadora's book, have you?"

"Not yet."

"Her book explains it better than I can, but it's all about reversing bad nurturing and bad nourishing."

"No one could argue with that."

"But you were arguing with it. You thought we were serving meatballs."

"Darling, don't go menopausal on the poor thing," Val said.

"She hasn't read the book yet. Her inner child may be drowning in a toxic pool."

"Yes, Quinn, it's a long process," a much younger girl in overalls piped up. It was the first time she had spoken, and her voice had the precision of a young child unused to speaking around grown-ups. "Not everyone is ready to grow their own vegetables and get their grains wholesale."

"They would be if they had any idea—" I managed to escape from the kitchen while she was warming up to her lecture.

The living room was small but the sparse furnishings made it seem larger. The woman in the bolo tie was hovering as her companion in the tank top tried out an elaborate weight machine that occupied one corner. Several men and women sat on large pillows strewn around the floor, with one cluster sitting in easy reach of a table made of a door resting on four concrete blocks. A small feast had been laid out there.

Near the fireplace at the other end of the room a higher table held a hotplate with herbal teas and slices of lemon on a plate. Three wicker chairs ringed the table. Ambrose sat in one, and across the table from him sat an African-American man with startlingly gray hair against cocoa-colored skin that set off his dangling gold earring. The chair next to him held a large, pink-faced woman with copper red hair that was probably a distant echo of the color that once was her own. She wore an impressive turquoise and silver necklace over a brightly woven Guatemalan blouse.

"He wanted to make sure there was no cheese in the dip," the black man was saying. "He described to me in some detail exactly what would happen if he ate cheese, and once I'd heard that, *I* wanted to make sure there wasn't any cheese in anything that came near him. I mean that apartment only had one bathroom."

"Josephine," Ambrose said, "here, have a chair." He stood, and gave me his chair over my murmured protest. "Allow me to introduce Darryl Franklin and Juno—just Juno, no surname."

"Yes, ma'am, no surname," I said after shaking hands with both.

"I create jewelry," Juno said. "In another lifetime, Darryl and I were married, before we discovered our true natures."

"Before she discovered me with my boyfriend," Darryl said with a tremendously good-natured laugh.

I noticed that Juno did not laugh, but simply smiled benevolently.

"Now don't shock Josephine," Ambrose said gently. "She's our token heterosexual at this gathering."

"What about the bereaved father," I asked. "He looked rather assertively heterosexual to me."

Ambrose smiled. "We were just talking about that. I think Miss Anna May Wrong can handle him."

Juno gave another one of her enigmatic smiles, and Darryl laughed.

"Do all of you know Isadora from her cooking classes?" I asked.

For some reason this question cast a shadow of sorrow over both. Darryl reached out, and took Juno's hand.

Ambrose said softly, "Their daughter was Isadora's partner—the one who . . ."

He didn't say, "died," but I remembered that I had heard that. "I am so sorry," I said, "I didn't know."

"You must not have seen Sandy's picture when you came in," said Juno, pointing to the mantelpiece just above us. There was indeed a sort of shrine there, with pictures of a tall, strong-looking young woman with skin the color of golden toast, and a short cropped frizz of reddish hair, embracing

Isadora Freechild. The two of them were wearing matching shorts and Hawaiian shirts. Both had garlands of flowers around their necks. I got up and examined the pictures—another showed Sandy wearing a cap and gown just after a college graduation, also hugging Isadora.

"What a beautiful young woman."

Juno was clasping Darryl's hand. "I guess we did something right, babe."

Darryl wiped his eyes with his free hand. "Poor little girl, you'd think she'd have been all confused—didn't know if she was black or white, didn't know if her parents were straight or gay. Her own momma didn't even have but one name."

Juno freed her hand and swatted him gently on the shoulder, but the mood lightened a little. "She knew we loved her, no matter what else happened."

"That's right, and she just grew up strong as a little sunflower. She always knew what she wanted. She was in love with Isadora from the day they met."

"How long were they together?"

"Since college—three years," Juno said. "They would have gotten married, if they could have, legally. They did a ceremony on the beach in Hawaii. We all attended. It was beautiful. That's where that picture was taken."

Darryl and Juno were holding hands again, and I hated to ask them, but the thought of that blood-covered axe in my storage area made me press ahead. "When did Sandy . . . ?" I hesitated, not quite bold enough to say the word.

Ambrose had gone to get a box of tissues, which he put between Darryl and Juno. They both helped themselves. In the silence that followed I looked around, and realized that the women who had been messing with the weight machine had come over, and several others in the room had either fallen silent to listen or actually gravitated over so that I was standing in a half-circle of people who were protectively grouped around Darryl and Juno. "It's been six months since the accident," Juno said.

"It was no accident." Everyone in that half-circle turned to look. Isadora Freechild had come home. Her face was expressionless but her fists were clenched at her sides. "My sister killed Sandy," she said grimly.

Darryl and Juno both stood, and swooped down on Isadora, hugging her between them. She returned their embrace.

She turned to speak to me, although she kept her arms around them. "I should never have listened to Fran. It was another one of her crazy publicity things. Everything was always about her. Sandy never should have gone with us. She wasn't ready for Denali. Fran wasn't capable of leading."

Her face was flushed, the room was totally still as she remembered. "I got injured, pulled a hamstring. Fran was showboating, somewhere up ahead. One of the other women was taking her damn picture. Sandy tried to help me. She shouldn't have. It was more than she could handle. She slipped into a crevasse. I saw her fall. She died up there. Her body still is up there. I should have died that day. Fran should have died up there, but not Sandy. She was the best thing that ever happened to me." Isadora dissolved in tears.

Juno led her off to comfort her, looking back at me as if I had committed a major crime. Darryl gave Isadora one last pat, turned, and headed for the kitchen, giving me a wide berth. The small crowd that had gathered around Isadora all turned to look at me. Their expressions were not cordial. I really didn't blame them. Making the hostess cry at a wake after she has just suffered two major bereavements is a surefire ticket to unpopularity.

Silver-haired Quinn came out of the kitchen, and took charge. "Come on, I'll walk you to the door."

Ambrose followed along. "I'll drive you." He stuck his head in the kitchen as we went past. "Val, are you coming now or staying?"

"I'll stay a bit longer, and maybe walk home," Val said.

Quinn held the door open for Ambrose and me to exit. "Be careful on the road," she said solemnly to Ambrose. "There are people out there driving under the influence of meat and caffeine."

As Ambrose and I walked down the block to where he had parked his Taurus, the front door to the apartment slammed, and Don Benedict walked down the stairs, arm in arm with Anna May Wrong. I wondered if his daughter had kicked him out on sight, or if he had forgotten that he ever wanted to talk to her. As Ambrose and I got into the car, I noticed Darryl coming out the front door and closing it quietly. He set off down the block, looking for all the world as if he were following Don Benedict and his exotic companion.

I asked Ambrose if he would drop me at the market, but he had some shopping to do as well.

"Sorry I caused a scene back there," I said, a little ruefully.

"You rubbed salt in some wounds, Josie. But let's keep it in perspective. You didn't cause the wounds."

"It was interesting to see what a following Isadora has in the community. Is she making a living from that, or does she still have a day job?"

"She seems to get by doing just that, though for all I know she might get something from her parents. I know she's got a master's degree in social work, and before she got into the inner child diet cookbook thing, she wrote lesbian porn, and those fairy tales."

I glanced at the book in my shoulder bag, *Iron Maiden, Stone Mother, Chromium Crone*. I could wait till later to read that, my consciousness had been raised to the point of severe cramping already today.

With my own brand of perversity I headed for the meat counter, and purchased ground round while Ambrose headed for the produce area. I met him there when I was getting mushrooms, green peppers and onions. Ambrose had sun-dried tomatoes, lentils and spinach. "Is that a vegetarian thing?" I asked.

"Well, it does have beef bouillon, but as long as I don't admit that to whoever I'm cooking for, it could pass for vegetarian."

"I'll ask you for the recipe later," I said, surprising myself.

"It's simple enough, you should be able to make it," Ambrose said graciously. "You can start by buying these ingredients."

I dutifully put them into my basket. Ambrose has that effect on me. "Shall I add gourmet cook to your list of accomplishments?"

"Nothing so official," he said with a smile. "But I dabble in the culinary arts; I'll meet you at the checkout."

I enjoyed the cozy feeling of cooking for Mulligan, but I had nearly exhausted my repertoire of salad, steak, and baked potato, toasted cheese sandwiches, and tonight the spaghetti. If I kept up this domesticated lifestyle much longer, I was going to have to start studying some cookbooks. I remembered all the cookbooks on Nina's shelves, and decided that I should take another look at them.

About the only other thing I could make offhand was

scrambled eggs. Under the influence of the food police at Isadora's apartment, I had bought the brown, organic hens eggs. If Mulligan suddenly decided to stay over, I could cook him breakfast. I cursed myself for this irritating yearning mindset, and bought several extra cans of cat food for the male whom I no doubt would end up sleeping with—Raoul.

Back at the apartment, Raoul greeted me from the sofa with such a cordial meow that I felt guilty for thinking his company was inadequate. Home is where the cat is. He followed me into the kitchen and watched with interest as I put away the cat food, and opened up the refrigerator—a mysterious realm that intrigued him so much that I always double-checked to make sure he hadn't sneaked in when I shut the door. There didn't appear to be enough room anywhere in the fridge for a cat of his bulk, but he had crept into some pretty small places before, so I wasn't taking any chances.

The Olympic Peninsula Organic Hens Eggs came with an enclosed note. Judging by the calligraphy-style font, it was not from the hens, unless they had progressed beyond chicken scratchings. I sat down at the table to read the note. "Our Olympic Organic Hens eat a vegetarian diet without antibiotic stimulants, and live in a barnyard environment, free to preen themselves, run, scratch, and sleep when they please, with a resident rooster for every twelve hens." For the first time in my life I was living at least as well as the free-ranging hens—except that they appeared to have a better sex life. Although the rooster-to-hen ratio left something to be desired by my lights. I noticed that the hens also had a website. I envisioned them having virtual hen sessions on nest-top computers pecking out postings to mailing lists complaining about the rooster's latest antics.

I chopped the onions, mushrooms and green pepper, and sautéed them with the hamburger. I put the whole thing in a pot with tomato sauce to simmer on the back burner. Raoul sauntered past to go out the back window and hesitated. He heard the trouble before I did. A door slammed in the back somewhere on another level and there was a heavy thumping sound. A woman's voice down in the yard below yelled, "Hey! What are you doing? Let him alone!"

Raoul prudently decided to wait and watch on the window sill. I opened up the back door and went out on the landing. As I leaned over the railing I heard a swish of bushes and the garden gate click. I looked down and across the building to see Val standing, clutching the railing, half supported by a robust blonde, probably taller than my five-foot-eight inches but sturdy rather than fat. I recognized her. It was the woman who had come running down Francesca's steps and warned me there was a dead body up there. She recognized me too, but we both immediately looked at Val.

His face was covered with blood.

Val!" I called, starting down the stairs, and then realizing I might need to get my cell phone. "Are you okay? Shall I call the police?"

"No!" He looked up at me. "May I come up? I don't want to go back in there. Would you close that?" he said to the blonde, and she reached out and firmly shut the back door to Val's apartment. She followed him solicitously down the stairs to the backyard at his end of the building, across the rear of the building and up the stairs to the back of my apartment. I held the door open and they came into the kitchen. I pulled out kitchen chairs and went to get some towels and a washcloth. But in the few seconds that that took, the blonde had wet some paper towels and was sitting on the kitchen chair next to Val, dabbing at his face.

"I couldn't believe the way that guy was just hammering on you," she said to Val. "Who is he anyway?"

"One of our neighbors," Val said, through a split lip. "Who are you?"

"You don't know each other?" I was puzzled.

"No, but she scared off Dick Slattery," Val said. "Thank you for yelling," he said to her. She put down the bloody paper towel and I handed him a wet washcloth that he used to gingerly pat his split lip.

"What was Dick doing in your apartment?"

"Robbing it, I guess. He was going through my desk when I came in. I asked him what the hell he was doing and he came charging over and started cursing me out. He said I made a pass at him." Val turned to me. "You saw how that guy looked at us when we were leaving. He's crazy. Then he started hitting me."

"Wait, how the hell did he get in? Was the door—oh my God, Maxine's keys." I went to the phone and dialed.

"I asked you not to call the police." Val started to get up.

"Sit down, I'm calling Ambrose on his cell phone." Ambrose answered and I told him briefly what had happened. He said he would be right over.

I turned back to Val and the blonde, who was still standing next to him. Her hair was the color of twenty-four-carat gold, and her eyes were pale green, and beautifully set off by olive skin.

"You're Lucille Meeker," I said with total certainty.

"Yes," she said.

"I'm Josephine Fuller."

Val looked up at both of us. "You know her?

"We've never been formally introduced. Please to meet you," I said holding out a hand to Lucille, who shook it with a wan smile.

The downstairs buzzer rang. "That must be Ambrose." All three of us went to answer the door. "That was quick," I said, when I let him in.

"I was in the neighborhood," Ambrose said. He went over and hugged Val. "Come over to the light and sit. Let me look at your face." I had never seen Ambrose so grave. "Tell me what happened." His voice was tight and I realized he was very, very angry.

Val explained again about finding Slattery in his apartment

and having to escape out the back door from an attack that only ceased when Lucille started yelling.

"Then where did Slattery go?" Ambrose asked Lucille.

"He ran down the stairs past me and out the back gate," she said.

"Val, would you like to stay at my place for the night?" Ambrose asked gently.

Val nodded.

Ambrose turned to me. "Jo, you'd better talk to Maxine about her key situation. Val is going to get new locks and I'd advise you to do the same. Whether you keep copies at Maxine's is up to you. We'll call later. Come on, Val."

Val turned to Lucille and hugged her. "I don't know you, but thank you for helping me."

Lucille patted his shoulder. "Take care of that lip. You may need a steak for the eye."

Ambrose sketched a smile. "Don't say that. This one's a vegetarian. We'll have to make do with cold compresses. Come on now, let's get out of here. I have some very nice sherry that will help immensely."

Val heaved a shaky sigh and left with Ambrose.

I gulped. "Lucille, I don't have any sherry, but I have some wine, or tea or maybe some soda. We should talk."

"I can stay for a minute. I wanted to talk to you anyway. That's why I was hiding out in your garden getting up the nerve to knock on your door."

We went back to the kitchen. "I notice that we all seem to be unanimous about not calling the police about this attack on Val," I said, getting out a glass for each of us.

Lucille accepted a glass of red wine and drank a hearty sip before speaking. "I guess that gay guy isn't sure how well he'd be treated," she said, glancing toward the door.

"That's a beautiful scarf," I said.

She ducked out of the scarf and held it out to show me the rain cloud and rainbow embroidery. "Teddy bought it for me at a crafts fair," she said. I checked the spaghetti sauce, feeling very domestic, and pulled a step stool up to the counter so I could sit and talk while I peeled and crushed garlic for the garlic bread.

"So you decided to see Teddy after staying away from him for a while," I said, looking for the most harmless part of the situation. "He really seems to be crazy about you."

"What's that supposed to mean?" Lucille bristled. So much for the harmless opener.

"When I ran into Teddy at the Women's Job Skill Center, he asked me to help him get in touch with you."

"I don't see how you could do that."

"You're right, I couldn't. I told him I couldn't try to reach someone who didn't want to see him. Teddy seemed to care about you a lot, but I don't know him well enough to know what he was like behind closed doors."

Lucille was examining her closely-trimmed fingernails.

"He wasn't abusive or anything, was he?"

"Or anything," she said at last.

"I don't understand."

"My mother just said I could do better now that I've lost weight, okay? It really bugged me that he didn't get a divorce."

"That makes sense to me."

"Anyway," she looked down at the kitchen table, "I wondered if it was something about me that stopped him from getting a divorce. That's why I agreed to go meet his wife. I wondered if he was still in love with her."

"So what did you think of her?"

"I thought she was a total bitch."

I had to laugh. "I'd agree with that. But she ran off with my husband back in Kathmandu, so I can't be objective. It was a couple of years before I realized she did me a favor. Maybe she did Ted a favor too. He got to meet you."

"Teddy told me he never would have looked at me if you hadn't opened his eyes to the joys of larger women."

I sighed. "All I can say is I never put it like that."

"I never heard of any man liking a woman my size. I mean, as big as I used to be. Every boyfriend I had till Teddy treated me like they were doing me a favor sleeping with me. I just gave up trying. But Teddy was different—or so I thought."

"And what do you think now?"

"Even if whatever moonshine you fed him never did wear off, everybody else in this world still treated me like garbage. Now men notice me on the street and go out of their way to talk to me."

"Just because more men approach you, doesn't mean better men approach you."

She sighed. "Yeah. I met a wonderful guy a little while back, and he still thought I was too big. It's always—*just lose another forty pounds*. The thing is—" She looked at me with tremendous pain in her eyes. "I can't lose any more. I'm starting to gain it back, even if I starve, I can't help it." She looked at me defiantly, as if expecting me to argue with her.

"That's what happens to most people who diet. It's an open secret. Nobody wants to admit it's true because so many people think being fat is a fate worse than death."

"Isn't it?"

"No. Not everybody has the same body type."

"What?"

"Lucille, considering all the garbage we get thrown at us,

no one these days would choose to be fat. No one would choose to be short either, but we don't seem to have any choice."

"Don't say that. I can't stand putting up with people treating me like dirt again."

"Then throw it back in their face every time they try."

Lucille shook her head and finished off her glass of wine. I poured her another. "I don't know what to believe," she said. "Dating a married man was bad enough. Now I'm running from the police."

"But you didn't have anything to do with that murder. Did you?"

"No." She looked me steadily in the eye. "I really didn't."

I believed her. Of course, there are con artists who can do that all day long while they're picking your pocket. "Then why are you afraid?"

"I set up that job with that woman. It never even went through the Women's Job Skill Center."

"That much I know. Delores was pretty adamant on that score."

"Right. Delores. I bet she had a few things to say."

"Oh, yeah." We both smiled at that and, as if in agreement, both of us drank a little more wine. "How did all that happen?" I asked.

"Teddy set it up."

"Why?"

"Teddy just told me she would be expecting me to call and say I was from the Women's Job Skill Center."

"So Ted knew about that place."

"Sure, I told him about it." She looked away shyly. "See, I moved out of the place I was sharing with him and I meant never to speak to Teddy again. But I couldn't help calling to talk to him sometimes. I kind of missed him."

"So he asked you to do him a favor?"

"Right. He said to tell her I could do the job for her right there in her apartment—cheap. He said she'd jump at the chance, and she did."

"You knew how to do that? I thought you were a waitress."

Lucille glared at me, "I took computer classes in high school, okay? I know how to mark documents for an index. But I can pick my own hours and make a lot more in tips waiting on tables than I could typing."

"What happened?"

Lucille lowered her voice, along with her eyes. "Teddy wanted me to steal the bag she kept her laptop in. Not just the computer. The whole bag—it was one of those shoulder bag things like a briefcase."

"If he wanted something stolen, why didn't he do it himself? He had the key to her apartment."

"He said whenever she went out, she took that shoulder bag thing with her, and if he went to her place when she was there, she watched him the whole time. He told me that there was something in that bag that would stop her from holding up the divorce. He said if I went in there and started doing secretarial work, she would lose interest and go do something else. He was right about that. The minute I started typing, she went in the other room." She pushed her hair back. "It was wrong, but . . ." She fell silent for a moment.

"But?"

"I didn't bring it to Teddy right away, once I found out what was in it. He said something in there was holding up the divorce and I wanted to see what it was, like if she was blackmailing him or something, I just wanted to know. I skimmed through her book. She gave me a list of people to index and it looked like she was going to send pages to people who were mentioned, and maybe get them to pay her to take them out of the book. There was really nasty gossip about her parents and every person on that list."

I wanted to ask what stuff, but I was afraid to derail her. "So the book was very critical of her parents; what about Teddy?"

"I expected her to write that he was the great love of her life. Or maybe she had some big secret she was holding over his head. Okay, I left Teddy, but I—I still wanted to know."

"You still care about him?"

She shrugged. "I guess. But her book barely mentioned him. Then I saw what else was in that leather case."

"Which was what?"

"A bankbook from someplace in the Cayman Islands, with three million dollars in the account, just deposited the week before. She even inked in the password for the account—her mother's maiden name—everything was right on the bankbook. God, they say I'm a dumb blonde. I could have transferred that money out of her account and started one of my own real easy."

"What did you do?"

"I just drove around for a while. I was so afraid. Finally I called Teddy and he was so angry. He wanted me to bring it right over. Said it was his money. That didn't seem right. Nothing seemed right. I even wanted to talk to you, but I didn't know how to reach you till the next time I called Teddy and he told me."

"When was that?"

"The day before . . . before she died."

"That must have been when Teddy contacted me, in case I heard from you."

"Yeah. Well, finally I decided to take it all back to Francesca's house. I thought by then, she might have even changed the password on the account. I expected her to yell at me. I was just going to leave it inside the door, and run."

"Anyway, the door wasn't locked. So I thought I'd sneak

in and put it up at the top of the stairs. I didn't want someone stealing it from inside the door and then I'd get blamed. So I went upstairs, and that was as far as I got." Lucille twisted her hands together in anguish.

"I know it was horrible."

"You went up there? After what I said?"

"Okay, it wasn't too bright. I had some idea about checking to see if she might be alive."

The doorbell rang. "Are you expecting company?"

"Not this early, go ahead." I wasn't sure I'd get another chance to talk to Lucille. "What did you do?"

She swallowed and I felt my own throat constrict. I offered to refill her wine glass, but she shook head, emptied it and pushed it aside. "I dropped that briefcase and ran like hell."

The doorbell rang again.

"You sure you don't want to answer that?"

"In a second—go ahead."

"I just drove till I got to the Canadian border, then I turned around and came back. I went to Teddy's. I didn't know where else to go, but I couldn't stand to stay with him. I know he's in love with me, but—I just don't know what to do."

"Did you leave the bankbook in the case or—?"

"Are you okay?" I turned around to see Mulligan standing in the doorway. Lucille looked up at him, half dazed by what she had been talking about, and a little startled by his huge presence. Mulligan has that effect on women, I should know.

Hi Mulligan, I'm sorry, we were talking. I didn't expect you for another hour. I'd forgotten you had a key."

"Sorry, but after all the craziness lately, when you didn't answer the door I got concerned."

"Lucille, this is my good friend Mulligan. And this is Lucille, the woman Teddy Etheridge told me about."

Lucille smiled at Mulligan in a way I hadn't seen before. I could imagine how she snared Teddy when she turned on the charm.

The doorbell rang again. "I'll get it," Mulligan said, giving us another careful look.

"You're entertaining. I should go," Lucille said, shifting uneasily in her chair.

"Teddy said you wanted to talk to me. What was it about?"

Lucille leaned forward as if to impart a great secret. "After meeting you, I understand how Teddy was so impressed by you, but I don't—" She broke off as Mulligan appeared in the doorway again.

"Josephine, you'd better come in here."

"Just a minute." I turned back to Lucille. "You didn't tell me what you did with the bankbook."

"Go answer the door." She sat back in her chair and gestured for me to go.

"If you'd like to stay for dinner, I've made enough for everybody." The instant I said it I realized food might be a sore point for her.

"Jo, come in here!" It was Mulligan in the front room.

"You better get in there," Lucille said, waving me off.

"I'll be right back."

Detectives Gonick and Tarrasch were standing in the front room. "We'd like you to come down, and answer a few questions, Ms. Fuller," Gonick said, a bit formally.

"Can you hang on just one minute, I've got a guest in the kitchen who—" I went back to the kitchen. They followed me. But the back door was open, and Lucille had vanished.

Gonick just stared at me in silence when I pointed to the open back door and told him that the woman I had seen running out of the murder scene had been sitting in my kitchen. I didn't mention the attack on Val. I didn't know why Val was afraid of police attention, but it seemed that he had suffered enough for one evening. I did say that Lucille had seen Dick Slattery coming out of one of the tenant's apartments, and that I wanted to get my locks changed before I left the place again. I got a reprieve from Gonick. He agreed that I could come in, and make a statement very soon. I promised to do that in the next day or so.

"I guess I can leave you at large for another day or so without a major risk to the citizens of Seattle," Gonick said grudgingly.

He asked a few more questions about what he called "your dispute with the deceased" which sounded like a very unequal contest. I refrained from asking how you could argue with someone, if that person was no longer breathing. I didn't want to seem overly jocular and it occurred to me that he might counter that one of the parties might have been breathing when the argument began.

Gonick might have been using a police tactic when he glared at me as if his patience was wearing thin. He appeared to be taking the position that my visit from Lucille Meeker had been a figment of my imagination. Even when Mulligan confirmed that he had met the woman, Gonick nodded skeptically as if he expected Mulligan to support me, even in a lie. If this was all part of a strategy to make me nervous, it was working.

"I have a question for you before you go," I said, when Gonick rose to leave.

He didn't bother to sit back down at the table. "Yeah, what?"

"I'm assuming you found the missing laptop in the bag I tripped over."

"What? You want to know if you broke it? Don't worry, no one's gonna sue you, if you did."

"Was that all that you found in there? No ID or anything?"

"As a matter of fact, we don't release that kind of information. Why do you ask? Do you have Mrs. Etheridge's ID?"

"No." I refrained from saying that he appeared to have just disclosed that he did not have her ID. "But are you sure the laptop even belonged to Francesca to begin with?"

"Oh, it was hers. That much we checked. A pretty spicy story on there too. That book she wrote about her parents. Sin and sex in Hollywood—I guess their mother liked all kinds of weird stuff. I have to keep it under lock and key or it would leak in a hot second."

"Just curious."

"You and everybody else. I'm getting calls from every trashy publication in the world, and lots of major media too. Just let me know immediately if you find anything that doesn't belong to you. That goes for laptops, wallets, axes, anything. You're in this deep enough for anyone. Call me when you're coming in to make your statement. I want to be there."

His attitude didn't seem to bother Mulligan, but it scared

me. Even though I was relieved not to have to go down to the police station this evening to spend several hours answering questions, the prospect loomed like an upcoming dental appointment.

"He's got lots of public pressure on this one," Mulligan said, clearing off the table, and setting up some dishes. "Shall I boil some pasta for that sauce?"

"Sure."

The wine helped us get through dinner. I explained to Mulligan how Lucille had interrupted Slattery's attack on Val.

"Maybe you should have told Gonick about that."

"Val asked us not to call the police. He was scared to go back to his apartment, but if we'd called the police, he was ready to bolt out of here."

"Talk to Ambrose tomorrow," he said. "These are homicide cops. Dick Slattery has already killed one person. This is nothing to fool around with. The man was burglarizing his apartment, for crissake. Just because he muddied the water by yelling that Val was making a pass at him, doesn't mean that he deserves to be robbed. I'm going to go get a new lock from the hardware store. That's the one bit of common sense you've uttered this evening. Talk to Ambrose, but stay here and call the cops if you hear anything—if Slattery has Maxine's keys, he could get into any of these apartments—so I'm getting locks for both of us and for Hope. You should get a locksmith in for the rest of the tenants too."

"I can pay you for the hardware."

"Cook me another couple dinners and we'll call it even. I'll be back in an hour or so to install it. In the meantime, keep the chain on the door and don't let in anyone you don't trust a hundred percent."

I agreed with that one. I did the dishes and sat down on the sofa. I didn't relish calling Maxine and explaining what had happened with Slattery. But, as it turned out, I got Maxine's answering machine. I told her I needed her to call, and before I knew it, I had fallen asleep. I woke vaguely at one point when Mulligan put a blanket over me, and picked up some tools to go. "I left a note and two keys tacked inside the door," he said. "I haven't been able to rouse anyone at Maxine's."

"I know, I got her answering machine when I called earlier."

"It's late but we should talk to Maxine tomorrow. That guy Slattery is a danger to the whole building. Call me if you need me, I'll be downstairs."

I muttered something, and fell back to sleep. A cry from the kitchen awoke me well before dawn. I leaped off the sofa, terrified by the idea that there might be an intruder here. I got up, and went to the kitchen where I discovered that Mulligan had cleaned up and installed a gleaming chain latch on the inside of the back door.

The crying was accompanied by a loud scratching at the outside of the door. "Oh, my God!" In all the excitement, we had closed the window and I had gone to sleep with Raoul locked outside.

I let him in and hastily locked and chained the door again, cursing myself for forgetting. Raoul rubbed up against my legs, cold, damp and protesting furiously. I got a towel and dried his long coat, while he rubbed his head against me and voiced his distress in his soft but urgent tones. "I am so sorry, Raoul," I said. "Out there with scary people prowling around." I opened a can of trout cat food, which was a particular favorite, and emptied it into his food bowl. Raoul inhaled the cat food. The telephone rang, which made me jump. I looked at the solemnly ticking clock on the kitchen wall. It was 3 A.M.

I picked up the telephone, and a muffled voice said in my

ear, "I know you're up. I can see the light in the window." I stared wildly at the curtained kitchen window expecting to see a face pressed against it. "Next time I see you, you'll be alone." There was a click as the line was disconnected.

A spasm of fear ran through my body like a cold wind, and I leaped up and went to check that each window and door in the apartment was securely closed. The voice was unrecognizable. Dick Slattery was the first person I thought of, but could Lucille have another, violent side to her that I had not seen? For the first time since she confessed about how Teddy had set her up to steal the briefcase, I began to wonder just what Teddy was up to. He had been after that mysterious bankbook. Of course, I only had Lucille's word that there even was a bankbook, let alone three million dollars. If he and Lucille were involved in some kind of deception that included me, was I playing into their hands somehow? Had the caller been the same person who had hacked up Francesca Etheridge with her own ice axe? Whoever it was, that person was out there, close enough to see the light from my window.

After double-checking all the doors, I hustled back to the living room, where I felt most safe. It seemed to help, but I was still awake. I turned on the lights in there too.

Isadora Freechild's books were sitting on the coffee table. I found a relatively comfortable position with the help of an extra pillow. Raoul sauntered in and joined me on the sofa, licking his paw to groom himself, as he usually did after a meal. I started to read. It calmed me down although I could see why Ambrose might have found the fables disturbing. They did suggest that the male sex was irrelevant, and could be abolished, or possibly preserved in limited number for breeding purposes—with artificial insemination as a method of propagation, of course. I personally have a weakness for men, but I could understand Isadora's irritation with certain very popular male behaviors. I just didn't agree with the solution. Although I did like Cinderella running off with the fairy godmother, and skipping the ball entirely. The idea of dancing in glass slippers always struck me as unwise in the extreme.

Raoul settled in beside me, while I read on into the dawn.

When it was not too early to call, I dialed Ambrose's number and he answered on the first ring, in a hushed voice.

"How's Val?"

"He's sleeping. Just a minute, let me take this out on the balcony."

I had never pictured Ambrose's apartment as having a balcony. I wondered where he lived. "I want to look a little more closely at the Benedict family," I said when he came back on the line. "Where is that bookstore with the poster of Isadora?"

"You don't want to go there."

"Why?"

"Remember the woman in the bolo tie who was giving you that very nasty look when we left Isadora's place yesterday?"

"Right, the one who had been arm wrestling with Don Benedict."

"Well, she and her partner own the Yellow Brick Road Bookstore. You should let the rancor die down a bit before you go over there. But if you want to talk to an expert on the Hanged Man films, try Corey McQuade at Enter Screaming, over in the University District. Now let's talk about Val's apartment."

I told him I had a call in to Maxine, and I would get a professional locksmith to change all the locks.

"I'll set it up to change Val's locks. You're the owner, and I think you can be trusted to have a copy of his key just for emergencies. But whether or not Val intends to raise the issue, I've got a few words to say to Miz Maxine about endangering her tenants."

"I haven't been able to reach her since this whole thing happened."

"Jo."

"What?"

"Do you think she's okay?"

"You sound like Hope. She said Slattery was a convicted murderer, but I thought she might have been exaggerating."

Ambrose was silent for a second. "Get Mulligan to go with you and check."

"Okay. We'll check." After I hung up, I called Mulligan and met him in front of Maxine's apartment. We knocked and then I used my key to go in. We walked through the plant-bedecked apartment. It was tidy, with no half-read newspapers on the sofa, no unwashed dishes in the kitchen, no sign of where Maxine or Slattery had gone.

"The place seems empty without Groucho." I found myself almost whispering.

"Yeah, but nothing looks like it's been trashed," Mulligan said.

The glass-fronted cabinets full of china and photos of Maxine's ancestors still lined the walls. The jungle of plants still flourished, including the giant tropical creeper, which seemed to grow an inch a day, and now appeared to be nearing the door and freedom. But I kept expecting to hear a shriek and see that huge green tropical bird spreading his wings to attack. I led the way into the kitchen and opened the cupboard where Maxine kept the board with the keys to all the apartments hanging on it. All of the keys were in place.

"No way to tell if he made copies," Mulligan whispered in my ear, making me jump.

"Don't sneak up on me that way, you scared me."

We peeked in Maxine's bedroom and saw no signs of foul play.

We locked the place back up again and I followed Mulligan down to the basement, while we knocked at Hope's apartment. Groucho shrieked from within, but no one answered the door. I went through the whole routine of opening the door and glancing through Hope's smaller place for signs of violence. Nothing but an irritable macaw—unhappy to be alone in a space smaller than he was used to. Hope had put down newspapers all around Groucho's cage, but some of her furniture bore tell-tale traces of Groucho's unhousebroken outings.

Mulligan and I went our separate ways. We both agreed that we had done the prudent thing to check, but I felt slightly foolish—and a little uneasy that no one seemed to be home.

I looked in the yellow pages, and found that the store called Enter Screaming would not open till eleven o'clock, so I looked up the Benedicts on the Internet. Don Benedict's Snowcones Resorts had a website, but not much information. None of the resorts seemed to be up and running, except in a modified format attached to an existing resort. But there were opportunities for investors, and the site offered to send financial information to anyone who asked.

Brenda Benedict turned up in some news articles about Matt Gunther's campaign for the California legislature. She was also mentioned on some sites that centered on the Hanged Man movies. The local entertainment news had an article on a Hanged Man film getting an award at a Seattle film festival a few days earlier. I didn't find anything on Francesca. Isadora Freechild's books were listed on several bookstore websites, but that was all I could find on her. When I had bookmarked all the pages for future examination, enough time had poured into the Internet's bottomless maw for me to get up and stretch, and get ready to go out.

Enter Screaming had a deceptively small storefront, its windows filled months early with Halloween decorations. The store was a long, narrow space, and the aisles were crowded with plaster gargoyles, alien abduction night lights, and werewolf nun outfits. Halloween seemed to be not so much a season as a state of mind here. A gray-haired man in glasses and a heavy fisherman's sweater was crouching over a cash register behind the counter just inside the door.

"So, do people?"

He looked up in my general direction inquiringly, but didn't quite make eye contact.

"I mean do people enter screaming?"

"Okay, it was a bad idea." He had his eyes focused just slightly to my right, which made me glance around to see if someone was standing beside me. Nope. "But I already paid for the sign, okay? So I'm not going to change it. 'Scuse me." He turned away to answer the phone.

A few browsers flitted by like ghosts in the distant reaches of the store, which stretched backward for quite a long narrow way, and then branched off in a series of side aisles. Walls of books from floor to ceiling bordered the aisles, and oddities such as blow-up balloon Frankenstein monsters lurked at unexpected places along the way.

It was the kind of store that pulls you in to look at first one, then another curiosity. Before I knew it, I found myself at the end of the long straight center aisle, and turning into the maze of shelves at the end. It wouldn't hurt to buy a couple science fiction titles I'd heard about and a mystery or two.

When I tore myself away from the shelves, and went to the counter, the man behind it was chatting with a very tall man who was buying a Mothra lunchbox. "I didn't know Mothra had a lunchbox," I remarked, causing both of them to look at me in alarm. "I always thought Mothra was one of the lesser-loved Godzilla opponents."

"Not among entomologists," the lunchbox purchaser said, gathering the metal box to his chest as if to shield it from disapproval. "We love the big guy—he should have got more of his own pictures. So often they just threw him in with a bunch of other monsters. Giant moths just don't get no respect."

The proprietor nodded his agreement.

I couldn't resist asking, "Isn't Mothra a female? I seem to remember a cave with a lot of eggs."

"Technically, yes," the lunchbox man said in an aggrieved tone. "Mothra probably would be a female, but we'll never really know what went on in that cave." The bell on the door rang as he stepped past me and out into the street.

"Sorry, I didn't mean to—" I stopped because the man behind the counter didn't appear to be listening. He had taken my stack of books, and was noting their prices and titles, printing them with a ballpoint pen between the lines of an extremely low-tech sales slip with carbon paper.

"Are you Corey McQuade?" I asked.

"And if I am?"

"Someone told me you would be the one to ask about Don Benedict, and his involvement in the early Hanged Man movies."

"Well, I'm not the real expert," he said, putting down his pen but still looking at the stack of books as if talking to them. "There's a guy in LA who puts out the *Hanged Man Herald* from time to time for the real cult fans. But I know a lot about the movies—I keep the videos in stock, and they still sell."

"I met Don Benedict the other day, and he said he originated the part from a tarot card. Is that true?"

"That's right. Brenda Benedict is above all that now with her political husband. But Don Benedict was in town for the Ghoul Fest this past week, along with Wolf Lambert—the director—and the legend. Benedict played the part in the original Hanged Man picture, and the second one too. The tarot card story would seem to be true because when you look at the video, the credits even say, 'From an idea by Don Benedict.' I heard Wolf Lambert borrowed some money from Benedict and he gave him the monster part because he was kind of a jock, and he did his own stunts. But Lambert was stupid enough to give Don credit for his half-baked tarot card idea without realizing that he would be writing checks to him for as long as the film made a dime. Of course, none of them expected the picture to make any money. It did, but the third picture was where the Hanged Man series really took off, and it's well known that other actors were playing the part by then. Lambert took it as close to the mainstream as an idea like that could go. There was no way you could tell who the actor was."

"Why?"

"Because," he risked a glance up at me, as if to check who could be so ignorant, "in every picture, the killer wears the hood over his head with the hangman's knot—you know, a noose." He demonstrated with a sideways jerk of the head, and appropriate choking sounds. "He carries the coiled-up rope in one hand, and lassos or garrotes his victims, although in some of the later films he uses an axe."

"An *axe*?"

McQuade jumped and accidentally looked me square in the eye. He immediately flicked his eyes back down, and continued to converse with his order pad. "It does kind of dilute the whole point. I mean, was the guy hanged or beheaded? If he was supposed to be beheaded, he should be carrying his head rather than a rope. But there isn't much internal logic in the last several Hanged Man pictures. They kind of degenerated into teen-slashers in the eighties."

"I guess I missed all those movies."

"You can still rent them—or even buy the whole set. The first few with Brenda Benedict are the ones worth having. She plays the Hanged Man's loyal gun moll, who rescues him from the gallows, and hauls him off to the reanimator. Of course, she was an old hag of thirty by the time the films found their audience, and those teenagers wanted the Hanged Man to have a younger girlfriend—so off with her head."

"So the Brenda Benedict, who may be a senator's wife soon, started playing in horror films."

"She started there, and ended there. She retired after the Hanged Man series went another way. Okay, she did do some minor roles in a couple of other low-budget horror flicks. *Amazon Island of Cannibal Women* comes to mind. She also did a turn on a daytime television soap opera. I've got a couple of those tapes too—real collector's items. The soap opera took a flyer on a spooky plot line. They used Brenda to replace an actress they killed."

"An actress they killed?" I kept my voice down so as not to scare him again.

"They do that in soap operas. It's a way of getting rid of an actress they don't want, or someone who leaves the series. They just kill off the character. In this case they brought the character back from the dead with Brenda playing the part as a vampire. It never really took off, so they put a stake through her heart at the end of the season. Her career never rose again either."

"Well, she seems to have risen once more as a political wife. I met her the other day. Did you know that her daughter Francesca Benedict Etheridge died? She was a mountain climber, and she was supposed to be writing one of those Hollywood gossip–'I was raised by wolves' books."

"Oh, yeah, I heard about that one. Probably a lot of crying in her beer about her rotten childhood. Don't get me wrong, if people ask for it, I'll stock it. But my customers are interested in scary movies and books—period. Not scary families. Anybody can get that at home, right?"

I asked him how much material he had on the Hanged Man series, and he built a respectable pile by the cash register, including twelve videos, ten issues of comic books, an edition of the *Hanged Man Herald,* which he said was quite hard to come by, and a four-inch thick scholarly tome entitled *Symbolism and Splatter in the American Cinema of the 1970s and 80s.* This last had looked promising until I realized it was someone's doctoral dissertation, and filled with words like heuristic and symbiotic.

"It's autographed," the proprietor said.

"Uh-huh," I said. I leaned over my stack of purchases at McQuade. He only backed up a little, mellowed as he was by the triple digit dollar total on the receipt. "Thanks for all your help finding these. You know so much about these movies, I'm thinking of writing an article on Brenda Benedict, and how far she's come from those 1980s horror films. Who do you think I should talk with who would know the real scoop on the Benedict family?"

"Nobody this far north. A lot of people in Hollywood. There's Wolf Lambert, of course. Like I said, he was in town last week. Too bad you missed him. He's probably gone back home."

"Unless he stayed for Francesca's funeral."

"I guess that's possible," McQuade said, raising his eyebrows skeptically. "From what I've heard he's retired to his little private winery in Northern California, and he hardly ever comes out. If you ask me, a winery doesn't seem like the best hobby for a guy who practically has his own wing at the Betty Ford Clinic. Good luck talking to him."

The luck came at Francesca's funeral. My plan had been not to attend.

I wasn't sure where I wanted to be at 1 P.M. when the funeral started—I had it narrowed down to anyplace but there. But Griff called me in the morning to beg me to go.

"I could see why you don't want to, but it would help me a lot to have at least one friendly face there."

"Griff, the last thing you and I should be doing is getting together at Francesca's funeral—or anywhere else. Don't you realize the police are very suspicious of both of us? It makes a lot of sense for you to go, and no sense at all for me to be there. The worst thing of all would be for the two of us to be there chatting cheerfully."

"Well, that's not quite the worst thing. We could start necking during the services."

I laughed in spite of myself. "Okay, I think that's funny, but then I married you, so I've obviously got a warped sense of humor."

"Ouch."

"You're more than irreverent, Griff. I think you're dangerous, at least to yourself. You're acting like you're relieved that Francesca is dead. Don't you know how bad that looks?"

"Darling, if you only knew what a pleasure it is to have a sensible conversation with a woman. It's true that I'm relieved, but only to get away from her, and to be talking with you. I never wanted Fran dead. Her egotism and obsessive self-promotion was just driving me round the bend, that's all. Please come today. Seeing you there will help me get through it. I promise, I'll be good. I won't even talk to you—just the occasional longing glance."

"That's it! Now I know I really should stay away. You're almost as bad as Don Benedict. If you're not mooning after me, you'll be hitting on one of the other mourners—probably an undercover policewoman."

"A policewoman under the covers does sound intriguing."

"Griff!"

"Come on, Jo. You can shoot me nasty looks to keep me in a properly somber state of mind. If you want I'll let you hurt me. Fran introduced me to the wonderful world of masochism. Haven't you ever wanted to beat me up?"

"Griff, you can be irritating enough that every woman you've ever known has probably dearly wanted to slap you, but that is not funny."

"You're right, I shouldn't joke about it. She wasn't an honest, hardworking kitten with a whip, she was a cold-hearted bitch, and I'm glad she's dead." There was a serious note in his voice that I didn't know how to reply to.

"Are you okay, baby?" I said, regretting the endearment the moment I said it.

"You were too good for me, Jo. I didn't deserve you." He hung up the phone.

Great. I might have called him back because I was worried about him, but I didn't have the faintest idea where he was staying. Worse yet, I had a sinking feeling I wasn't going to be able to stay away from the funeral, despite every shred of common sense that told me not to. Griff had managed to offhandedly convince me that he would get himself in more trouble if I weren't there. I should have remembered that insane dynamic from our marriage. Worrying about just how much trouble Griff was in always clouded my judgment.

I started working on my report on the Women's Job Skill Center, but somehow it reminded me of something that seemed not to fit. I turned on the computer and looked at the websites I had marked. One of them showed a picture of Matt Gunther opening a day care center in his district. It was one of those photo opportunities that politicians love, because it featured Gunther talking to an African-American toddler, with Asian, Latino and Anglo children clustered around. The photographer had done an excellent job on a United Nations photo op. I knew photographers can find it a challenge to adjust the exposure, particularly when shooting black and white film of a wide range of very dark and very light skin tones. When I first looked at the photo, I had imagined Griff muttering about how really good fast film and computer imaging had made such pictures possible without darkroom headaches. When I looked at it again, I saw what I hadn't seen earlier. In the picture of the California event just behind Matt Gunther was Delores Patton. I printed a copy of the page and put it in a folder, in my file on the Women's Job Skill Center.

I stopped pretending I could ignore Griff's plea, put on my trusty black silk dress, and set off for the funeral. It wasn't cold, but the sky had clouded up to the point where I put a jacket over the dress, and a folding umbrella in my shoulder bag.

If I could get there just about the time it started, then I could observe from the fringes and leave early. But when I arrived at the funeral home, a slick modern place with beige carpeting and pale oak wood trim, it seemed deserted. The usher in the hallway informed me that the services for Francesca Etheridge were in the Sunrise Chapel. I breathed a sigh of relief when I saw that the casket was closed. On a stand in front of it was the huge color print of Francesca that had I had admired in her home, the shot Griff had taken showing her filling the frame, silhouetted against blue sky. Clinging to blue ice by the axes that had killed her. I wondered if anyone had thought of that when they selected the picture. I started toward the back to find a discreet place to sit, when Ambrose and Val came in, talking softly to the two women I had last seen in bolo tie and tank top, both now wearing muted pantsuits in blue and charcoal respectively. These were the owners of the Yellow Brick Road Bookstore.

Val had a few small Band-Aids on his chin, jaw and eyebrow. One eye was ringed with bruises. I heard him say something about "an ice-skating adventure that went wrong," when the woman who had arm wrestled Don Benedict exclaimed over his injuries.

Ambrose tipped me a wink, while Val and the two women pointedly ignored me. I sat down in a back pew and watched them talk in low tones. A short blond woman in a raincoat came in, and the muscular woman beckoned her over. A few other people I didn't recognize drifted in and then a rangy, elegantly attired gray-haired woman arrived, radiating impatience like a fever. She looked around and joined Ambrose, embracing the short woman in the raincoat who introduced her to the others.

Everyone found seats, but Ambrose came back to sit beside me. "The blonde is Karen Rhodes," he said without preamble. "She's the founder of Rainy Day Press. They publish Isadora's books."

"Excellent," I whispered admiringly. "You really do know everyone."

"Oh, I'm meeting new people all the time. The diva who just made an entrance is Fausta Green. Up until last week she was Francesca's literary agent. She is royally pissed off.

Francesca's tell-all had enough Hollywood gossip to get her booked on every television talk show going. Three networks were bidding for the TV movie rights. Then right in the middle of serious pre-publication publicity she withdrew the book."

"You mean, it wasn't because of her death that the publication was cancelled?"

"No. Fausta said her death gave everyone a way to save some face, but she withdrew the book a week ago. Her story was she had an attack of conscience and decided she didn't want to hurt her family."

"Could she do that—withdraw the book? I mean legally?" I asked in a whisper.

"I asked that too," Ambrose said. "Fausta told me she returned the advance." He smiled. "She also said that only someone who was very naïve or terminally honest would do something like that. Or someone who got a better offer. My guess is that Francesca Benedict Etheridge was not naïve, and I doubt if her cause of death was terminal honesty." The family began to file in, and Ambrose patted my shoulder and rose to go back to sit next to Val.

Isadora took a seat in the first row, looking weary and wearing what looked like the same black jeans, motorcycle boots and bomber jacket that she had worn every time I saw her. Juno and Darryl sat on either side of her. Juno was holding her hand.

Griff came in, and leaned down to say a few words to Isadora and put his hand briefly on her shoulder. She made some answer and did not move away from his touch. I wondered how they had got along. Griff nodded at me mournfully before taking a place in the row behind the family. Was that because the police and the family suspected him of the murder? Or are recently discarded consorts traditionally assigned to sit in the second row at such events?

Brenda Benedict made an entrance worthy of a film star. She was tastefully draped in black chiffon with a complicated small hat that managed to be covered with lace without obscuring her face or hair. Matt Gunther was by her side, and guided her into a seat with gentle concern. He didn't have a lot to do yet, but I was willing to bet he would end up making a speech.

It was hard to imagine anyone upstaging Brenda, but her ex-husband Don managed to provoke murmurs of surprise by walking in from the main entrance, down the aisle to the front row with a slender Asian woman in a black miniskirt on his arm. When I looked more closely, I realized the delicate figure was the transvestite whom Ambrose had identified as Anna May Wrong. The two women behind me recognized him as well. "It's Andrew Wong," one of them whispered. "Isadora's dad is still with him."

"Do you think they've been together since that night?"

"It wouldn't surprise me," the other voice whispered back. "You know, Andy's family is rich. Maybe Isadora's dad is hitting him up for investment money—she said he does that everywhere he goes."

"Andy's parents would never . . ." the first voice sank to a whisper and I couldn't hear more. Then the whispering stopped.

"Look," one of the women behind me hissed and we all turned to watch a short, stocky man with a Southern California tan, and a short-trimmed beard that still had as much dark brown as gray in it, walking briskly up the aisle from the back all the way to the front, casting his eyes from one side of the room to the other as if counting the house. "It's Wolf Lambert, the Hollywood director."

From this far back I could mostly see Lambert's head—also tanned, and bald except for a fringe of gray curls. Once in the front row, he embraced first Brenda Benedict, then Isadora. He wore a dark gray suit that looked expensive and quite proper, but with a certain flair to the tailoring. Isadora appeared to be introducing him to Darryl and Juno. Lambert exchanged warm handshakes with them, and with Matt Gunther. He went on down the front row to hug Don Benedict, and reached across him to take his Asian companion's hand, and raised it to his lips. Then he sat down in the front row next to Don, and Anna, a.k.a. Andy Wong.

The service began with a couple of fellow alpinists talking about Francesca's drive, and what a passion she had for living life to the fullest, climbing out on the edge. The words "death wish" were never spoken. Perhaps I was the only one who heard that subtext. When Matt Gunther got up to speak, I rose as quietly as I could, and left. I hated to leave Griff there. I saw Gonick and Tarrasch watching me go, but they stayed.

I had just realized who was missing. It may not be customary for a man to attend his ex-wife's funeral. But Teddy still had a key to her condo and had never managed to get a divorce. It would seem like simple good manners to pay his final respects at her funeral. But Teddy Etheridge was nowhere to be seen.

20

I felt ridiculous and vulnerable, standing in the corridor between the funeral home's Sunrise Room, and the Tranquil Garden Room. Was it more suspicious to leave the funeral early, or to stay until Griff came up to me afterward—because of course he would. Despite our divorce I still cared for him, in a cautious way. I felt certain he had not killed Francesca, but her family and the homicide detectives appeared to suspect him as much as they did me. Embracing Griff warmly at Francesca's funeral was a bad idea, but shoving him away would be even worse. It was time for me to go. But before I could leave, the door to the Sunrise Room opened and Griff came out, followed closely by Don Benedict. Don must have left Andy Wong back in the pew. Before the door whispered shut, I could hear Matt Gunther still speaking in gentle, comforting tones.

Benedict grabbed at Griff's sleeve. "You'd better hand over that book if you know what's good for you, man. Because when Brenda wants something, a minor detail like your life is nothing."

He fell silent when he saw me.

"Josephine!" Too late for escape. Griff pulled free of Benedict's grasp, covered the distance between us in a few strides and embraced me as if we were the last two survivors of some natural disaster. I gently pulled away as soon as I could.

Don Benedict followed Griff to stand a few feet away. He cleared his throat to get Griff's attention. "I mean it, Fuller. This is not something to joke about."

Griff turned to face him, but kept an arm around me. "Believe me, Don, this is a terrible time for anyone who cared about Fran. But we were breaking up and, even when we were together, I never paid attention to her stuff. That would have been the quickest way to end up carrying it. I told her she could bring anything she could haul under her own power. I've always been that way—ask my ex-wife."

Both men glanced at me. "That's true," I said.

"Fran had moved on, Don; I have no idea what she was up to the past few weeks."

"You can't say you weren't living at her place," Don said. "I saw a closet full of all your clothes and gear at her house."

So at least Don and possibly Brenda had been going through Fran's stuff very carefully.

"True, I left some of my things there. But I haven't even been back to pick anything up in nearly a month. She didn't mind keeping my gear for a while. She just lost interest in me personally."

"That's what you say." I had an idea that Benedict was a little lost without someone to write his lines for him.

"It's the truth, Don."

"If you weren't living with Fran, where were you living?" Don's eyes lit on me.

Griff laughed, "You don't understand, Don. I'm a nomad. I never live anywhere for long."

"He's been that way as long as I've known him," I told Don. "No fixed address beyond a post office box, and mail forwarding service."

"Excuse me now, Don. I have to talk to Josephine." With his arm still around my shoulder, Griff propelled me toward the door and outside.

Don Benedict did not follow. His brow was furrowed. He wasn't the only person to be mystified by Griff's lifestyle. My ex-husband's name opened doors for him and he knew so many people all over the world, that when he was between assignments with no client paying the bill, he would just make a couple of phone calls in any major city and spend a few weeks in someone's guest room, or in a pinch, in a sleeping bag on the floor. I had lived like that with him for six years. That kind of high-level homelessness had appealed to me in my twenties, probably a hangover from my childhood as a military-industrial brat.

"I shouldn't have come, Griff," I told him, standing just outside the funeral home. "Those two cops stared at me when they came in. I'd better go before they finish up in there."

He pulled me back for a quick hug and then released me. "Thanks for coming. You can't know how much it means to see you."

"Let me know if there's anything you need."

"Like bail?"

"Sure, Griff. If I don't get arrested as well. Give me a call and a few dozen of your friends will pass the hat. I hope it won't come to that."

"So do I." He looked at me with an abandoned puppy expression that caused me a pang of sadness I hadn't felt since we broke up.

"Anyway, I'd better go," I said. "I don't know how you can handle it, with everyone staring holes in your back."

"I had to say good-bye to Fran, poor kid. Even though I wish I'd never met her. I notice Teddy didn't even bother."

That reminded me. "Did you know Teddy told me he got my address from your Rolodex there?"

"Oh, yeah?" Griff didn't seem interested. "Well, the police have got my Rolodex now. I'm kicking myself for not taking it out of Fran's place when I took my duffel bag out a few weeks ago."

I kissed him on the cheek and quickly walked away.

On the way to my car, I passed a stretch limousine. It was cream-colored, possibly the same one that had pulled up in front of Teddy's place. I could never resist staring at the smoked glass of those vehicles, as if a proper squint would reveal the invisible interior. I was trying to be cool about that, but before I stopped my scrutiny someone bumped me sideways, and an arm went round my shoulders, this time from almost exactly my height. I turned to look into the designer sunglasses of Wolf Lambert. He smelled strongly of wine with an underlying scent of some woodsy aftershave.

"Hi, doll, are you blowing this place? Because I'd like to go wherever you're going. Or maybe you'd like to come with me—as you see, I've got the limo."

I recoiled instinctively from the wine fumes. "You're Wolf Lambert."

"At your service, dear. And you are?"

"Josephine Fuller."

"Okay. We can change that. I have heard your name though. I went to dinner with Fran's husband the other night—my God, I think it was actually the night she was killed. But in any event, Fran's husband was singing your praises and he scarcely did you justice. You are the most divine creature in the entire funeral home. Granted not a very sweeping selection, mostly tattooed dykes with military haircuts and those stick-thin girls. I don't mean to be forward, but—"

"That's very kind of you, but—"

"No, let me go first, I am making an entirely new kind of film now, and I'd like to take you to lunch, and explain just what kind, and how I can—" He stood back at arm's length and gazed at me. "I want to say this the right way. I don't want to turn you off."

I backed another foot away. The driver had gotten out of the car to see if this was a confrontation or a simple assignation brewing.

"Just give me a chance to explain before you say, 'no.' It might make you blush. On the other hand maybe it wouldn't. Could we go somewhere, talk about it? I'd like to see you blush."

I looked toward the funeral home, and saw that Griff noticed the encounter and decided to intervene. For some reason Lambert amused me. "Mr. Lambert . . ."

"Please call me Wolf, and your name again, dear?"

"Josephine."

"Right, we've got to change that, but go ahead."

"I do have some things I would like to ask you for an article I'm writing on the horror films of the nineteen-eighties. Are you going to be in Seattle much longer?"

"Alas, my dear, a friend's jet is waiting for me at the airport. Would you believe it? It's parked next to Matt Gunther's jet. Where did Brenda get that little mouse?"

"He seemed more like a squirrel to me—twitchy," I couldn't help but say.

Wolf raised his dark glasses and examined my face with a pair of very bloodshot blue eyes. "You're right. Squirrel would be the correct small mammal, not really a major meal for Brenda. Come back with me to Sonoma County? I guarantee there won't be any of this about to drizzle weather." He gestured to the sullen sky. "The sun will shine. We'll have some excellent cabernet. You can get your interview and we'll have a splendid time. You could bring—it's Griff, right?"

We both looked back at Griff who was halfway across the parking lot walking toward us.

"My ex-husband."

"I know, I know." He put his glasses back down over his eyes. "Here, I've got a business card somewhere." He patted in his pockets till he came up with one, and handed it to me. "Call me. My assistant's name is Thelma. Call her, call me. Call *on* me, let's talk." The driver helped him into the car.

The limo started up, and the window rolled down. "You might find my ideas intriguing," Wolf said, as the limo pulled away. "I give great hot tub."

I still couldn't get a good look at what was behind the tinted glass.

Griff arrived at my side too late to protect me from anything, but in time to hear Wolf's parting remark. "Great hot tub?" he said.

"Don't start with me," I said. But I had to echo his parting smile. My only consolation was that Mulligan wasn't here to see any of this.

I still had the address and directions to Teddy's place. I drove from the funeral home parking lot straight over to South Tacoma. No car or motorcycle was parked in the driveway. I went up to the window to peer in around the bushes that framed it. It was a little hard to tell because the place had clearly been rented furnished, but it looked deserted.

"He moved out yesterday," a woman's voice said from the end of the driveway. "We live across the way." I turned to see a gray haired woman in a heavy jacket standing on the sidewalk holding a leash that barely restrained a young golden retriever from running after—well, basically everything—the dog was so enthusiastic.

"What a beautiful dog," I said sincerely, holding out a tentative hand. "Is he friendly?"

"She. Oh, yes. She'll let you pet her," the woman said.

Sure enough the dog sniffed my hands and licked them, and proceeded to sniff me all over in true dog exploration fashion. "Did you happen to see if he was alone when he packed up and moved, or if he had someone with him?"

"I don't think he had much to move, but he went over to Mrs. Menson's house, she's the owner. She lives next door. She told me he was giving her the keys back when his girlfriend showed up, that big blonde who comes to visit sometimes. They had a loud fight."

"Could you hear what they fought about?"

"No, but she took off, and she wasn't alone. There was another man driving her."

"Really? Did you get a look at the man?"

"No. He stayed in the car, but when she came running out of the house all upset, he drove his car closer, and called out to her—it was clearly a man's voice. He must have opened the door because she got in so quickly, and they drove off."

"What kind of car?"

"It was one of those Japanese sedans, a fairly recent model, but small. That's why I couldn't really see him—the car was so small. I'll tell you, though, Mrs. Menson gave him back his deposit in a hurry. I think she was afraid."

The sound of a motorcycle interrupted us, and Isadora Freechild roared to a stop and parked her Harley. "Her, I've seen before," the old woman said, pulling her dog along, and walking away.

"Thanks for talking to me," I said to her retreating back.

The retriever was now straining in a different direction, and the old woman was out of earshot and working on keeping her footing without getting dragged along like a sled.

Isadora came up the walkway. "He's gone, isn't he?"

"That neighbor was telling me he moved out yesterday after a big fight of some kind with a woman who sounds a lot like Lucille."

"So you've met Lucille?"

"Yes, I have."

"Teddy seems to like you a lot. I haven't figured out why yet."

"Did you and Teddy always get along?"

"Maybe because we're both crazy writers. I've always liked

Teddy. He's funny, and a hell of a lot easier to be around than my sister. He stayed in touch with her after they broke up. He and I talked more after that than when they were together."

"That's why I was surprised Teddy wasn't at the funeral."

"Me too. That's why I came here, to see if he was dead or something." For the first time, she looked distinctly uneasy.

"Do you feel threatened after what happened to your sister?"

"What the hell kind of question is that?" she said. Her eyes flicked back to her motorcycle, but she didn't move. "Wouldn't you feel threatened? Wouldn't you wonder if you were next?"

"Maybe. But Fran was hard to get along with."

"You think I'm not?"

"Judging from all your friends and admirers, you have a support network that your sister didn't."

Isadora looked me over carefully and took a deep breath. "Teddy seems to trust you. I haven't eaten all day. You want to buy me lunch?"

"Sure."

I followed Isadora to a Chinese restaurant with sparkling white tablecloths and pine paneling. "This place isn't totally vegetarian," she said after we were seated, sipping tea, and looking out a window at a parking lot framed with large bushes. "But I've met the chef, and I trust that his kitchen is pretty clean. They have some very good stuff on the menu."

"I appreciate your talking to me. I know we kind of got off on the wrong foot."

"You think so?" She grinned mischievously for an instant. Then a wave of sadness and weariness passed over her face like a cloud.

We both studied our menus. Isadora recommended the pancakes with green onions and peanut sauce, vegetarian spring rolls and spicy bean curd with green beans. I opted for hot and sour soup and kung pao tofu. I was paying, I could have ordered from the carnivorous side of the menu, but I wanted to be able to share everything and I wasn't about to put her off by ordering something she couldn't or wouldn't eat.

The soup arrived and then the green onion pancakes. After she had eaten something, Isadora began to relax.

"That's better," she said. "I couldn't stand more than tea for breakfast and I've been just drinking Gatorade all day."

"I overheard your father ask Griff about a book they can't find at Fran's place. But her agent was saying the book was withdrawn even before your sister died."

"That's right," Isadora said. "Fausta Greene was there, and she was mad enough to spit nails. She gave my own mother and little Andy Wong a real run for their money in the queen derby. That's the closest I'll ever get to a high-powered agent. Even at my own sister's funeral she made it a point to say how she conveyed her deepest *personal* condolences. It's just as well Ted wasn't there." Isadora sipped tea, and tackled some steamed rice and green beans.

"Why is that?"

"Oh, Ted used to travel in higher circles. The big publishing house he was with dropped him, so he's with Rainy Day Press now. That's my publisher. They're great over there, but no money, no perks, no respect. Seeing Fausta Greene like that and knowing my sister withdrew her book and turned all that down would have rubbed him totally raw." She shook her head and poured herself more tea.

"It seems odd to me that your sister withdrew the book after going so far. Someone said there was a movie deal in the works."

"I'm sure she still liked the idea of it, and she wasn't past threatening someone with it, even if it wasn't a real threat. Just throwing it in someone's face would have been fun for Fran."

"Did she talk to you about the book?"

"Not a word." Isadora picked up a green bean with her chopsticks but put it back down again. "Teddy knew about it. He asked if I would help him talk her out of withdrawing it. That surprised me. Maybe he thought that if she trashed him in the book at least it would get his name out there again. He said she was a fool—which was not news to me. He said she had no idea what she was giving up, that people have gotten sued for less. He said we should get together at Fran's and maybe talk some sense into her. I thought it was sweet that he wanted to keep her from screwing up, I didn't care either way. But Ted was right that we should make sure Fran understood that she was throwing away something the rest of us poor slobs never had a chance of getting. I didn't expect her to listen to me. We probably would have got in a fight. But that was okay. The only time we talked was when we were yelling at each other. I didn't know Ted still had keys to her place though."

"Did that seem odd to you?"

"Guess not. He and Fran kept in touch."

"If Teddy hadn't called, would you have picked that day to visit?"

"Probably not. After what happened with Sandy, up on Denali, I usually tried to have another person there when I talked to my sister, just to keep me from hauling off and slapping that smug expression off her face."

"Did you?"

"Did I what?" Isadora looked up from contemplating her rapidly cooling plate.

"Did you hit her?"

"Not since we were kids. Felt like it a lot. But never did anymore."

"Were you worried about what she might say about you in her book?"

"Why should I be? I haven't been in the closet about anything since I was thirteen."

"And you were never tempted to write your own tell-all book?"

Isadora smiled. "All my books are tell-all books. But I'm just preaching to the choir and the occasional convert. Gossip could have been a gold mine for Fran, but not for me. Dykes on bikes are scary. Mountain climbing breeder girls are sexy—particularly if they have an axe to grind." She shook her head. "Gee, I can't believe I said that." When I met her eyes I saw that they were nearly overflowing with tears. "You know what I meant."

"Yes. I do." I rummaged around in my purse and came up with a packet of tissues, which I put on the table tactfully. She took one and dabbed her eyes and sniffed.

I gave her a few breaths to settle down. "Why do you think your sister had a change of heart, after she went to all the trouble to write it, and then market it? Why throw it all away?"

"That's where you're wrong. My sister never threw anything away that might benefit her. The bottom line was, someone must have made it more than worth her while."

"So you don't think someone killed her to stop the book?"

"Only if they didn't know she withdrew it. The book would have been dead when she died because the whole point would be for Fran to go on a million television talk shows and play the wounded child of a Hollywood mom."

"You don't think there might have been something so explosive in the book that someone wanted to get all the copies before anyone read them and leaked the information?"

Isadora shrugged. "Nothing I know about. Unless Fran made up something really juicy." She took a few more bites of kung pao tofu. "Our mother didn't treat us all that badly growing up. She just kept forgetting we existed. As if Fran and I were part of a movie she was in a few years back. She had forgotten the lines, and she was more excited about the part she was playing now. We were old news to our mother."

"What about your father? Aren't those Snowcone Resorts he's promoting aimed at the family crowd?"

"Dad was a little better. He had custody of us, and he had a procession of 'aunts' who sometimes even tried to take care of us. Fran dealt with it by doing everything they expected, and more so. She isn't—" Isadora gulped, "she *wasn't* all that good of an athlete. I could beat her at most everything growing up. I had to. If you were a little girl going on a camping trip with our father, you'd better keep up or he might just leave you there."

"He was violent?"

"No, but it never occurred to him to try to go slower because we were kids or to allow in any way for the fact that it wasn't all about him. He's a very stupid, selfish man, but he means no harm. It didn't help when I hit my teens, and realized I like girls not boys. Fran had been driving the boys crazy ever since puberty. So for the longest time no one realized I was even sexual at all. Good old Dad still doesn't really believe I like girls. But you know what? One of his girlfriends was bisexual, and she was my first lover. She helped me a lot. Because she knew my father, she understood what I had to deal with. Dad even said that because Fran was so popular that I was probably too scared to compete with her for boys." Isadora threw back her head and laughed. "Hell, yeah, I could compete—I even took his girlfriend—and you know what? She liked me better. Not that he really noticed, he uses women like napkins at a restaurant. You're thinking a psychiatrist could have a field day with this, aren't you?"

"I'll plead the Fifth on that one." She must have read my face correctly because she snickered. "Okay," I said, "I'll ask. I noticed he's still with Andy Wong. Could he be bisexual as well?"

"Hmmm." She considered the idea and put down her chopsticks. "I wouldn't count on it. My bet is that he's hitting Andy Wong up for money. But he could be using him for sex as well. What can I say? My dad's a whore."

There was a brief silence while I contemplated what to say. I hated to return to the question, but I couldn't help it.

"What about that guy at the funeral today, Wolf Lambert?"

"Uncle Wolf is an old family friend." Isadora smiled a little. "I've heard he's a chubby chaser, if you're interested."

"What?" I wasn't sure if I had just been insulted. Lambert had demonstrated his interest in at least my own full figure very decidedly. The term "chubby chaser" I'd heard before, but it had been used as a put-down.

"Uncle Wolf—he's really not our uncle—technically speaking he's our godfather—anyway he's retired from Hollywood. He was here last weekend because there was a film festival in the U District. He and Mom and Dad all got some kind of awards, press coverage. Just like the old days. But Wolf hasn't made a real movie in years." Now she was smiling more broadly. "I hear he makes fetish films now."

"By fetish films, you mean videos where some guy has a gripping relationship with a spike-heeled shoe?"

"Um, sorta like that." There was a twinkle in her eye, as she took a sip of tea. "*Any*way, no matter what Uncle Wolf is doing these days, the films he made with my parents were straight horror flicks."

Our conversation hit another snag and we both picked

through the rest of the green beans and tofu for any last pieces of interest. I sensed great weariness in the way Isadora moved her chopsticks.

"So what is it that your father was asking Griff about, if it wasn't Fran's autobiography?"

"Some bankbook. Typical Mom. She doesn't need the money but she accused me of taking Fran's bankbook. She would have left right after the funeral if she had it. But she's staying another day to look. My father is looking around too, so she must have offered him a piece of it."

"If your father needs money, do you think he might have taken this bankbook and tried to blame someone else? He seems to be afraid of your mother."

Isadora smiled wearily, and raised her eyebrows. "He's smart enough to know that. Her handouts have been paying his rent most of his adult life. But it doesn't pay for his new business ideas. If my father had got the money he needs for his new resort or whatever, he'd be there now, not here. When he has enough for whatever he wants to do, he goes off and does it. Believe me I know."

"You think your sister had some kind of hidden assets that your mother knew about?"

"I think my mother and Matt paid her off to drop the book, and probably quite handsomely. Now that she's dead, they want their money back—and it's gone."

Ted and Lucille were gone too. According to Wolf Lambert he had gone to dinner with Ted the night Fran died. That sounded like an alibi for Ted. I was going to need to talk to this Wolf Lambert.

Isadora put down her chopsticks. "I'm starting to get very tired," she said, standing up, and shrugging into her leather jacket.

"I'm sorry to bother you with so many questions," I said,

feeling like a complete jerk. "Are you going to be okay riding home? I could drive you."

"I'll be okay if I go now."

I gave her my card and got one of hers in return, which was unexpectedly in raised lavender letters on rainbow-edged paper.

"Good-bye," I started to say, but she had already put on her helmet, and was heading for the door. She looked unexpectedly small and frail, despite the helmet, jacket and boots.

I was about to look back down at the check the waiter had just put in front of me when I noticed a blue Geo Metro drive past, following Isadora's motorcycle. The driver was the red-haired Juno, the passenger her former husband Darryl. The parents of Sandy, Isadora's late lover. She didn't seem to notice they were following her. I asked the waiter to wrap up the leftovers. What the heck. One less meal to cook.

I drove home from the restaurant, and went reluctantly up to the apartment. Mulligan wasn't home yet, and I didn't know if I should be bothering him, even when he did come home.

Raoul came to the door to greet me, and led me through the apartment to the kitchen. He stood expectantly by the back door. "Okay, okay." I watched him scamper downstairs with the agility that even twenty-pound cats seem to be able to muster.

I wasn't sure what to do next. I was supposed to go in to the police department and make a statement, but somehow I didn't want to do that right after running into Gonick and Tarrasch at the funeral.

The telephone rang. It was Ambrose. "Val and I are just finishing up with the locksmith, would you like to come down?"

I went down one floor and paid the locksmith who had just changed Val's locks. Val and Ambrose were standing outside the door, still in the suits they had worn to the funeral. I hadn't seen Val's new décor and at this rate I probably never would.

The cuts on Val's face had begun to heal, but he looked pale and drained. I wanted to ask him to lecture me about some vegetarian matter, or get him to criticize my drapes—

anything to lift his spirits. Ambrose was still very solemn. He asked Val if he minded my having a key, or if he would rather Ambrose himself kept it, and Val mumbled something I craned my neck to hear but couldn't make out.

Then all three of us froze as Dick Slattery sauntered out of the apartment across the hall from Val's—the vacant one that had just been painted.

He stopped in front of Val and looked up at his injuries. "Sorry I had to do that to you pal, but you made a pass at me, and I don't go that way."

Val took a deep breath, but Ambrose stepped in front of him and looked down at Slattery, who was nearly a foot shorter.

"Honey, don't flatter yourself. Val may pick up some trashy young men on the streets, but he's not desperate enough to resort to someone like yourself. You're on parole. I would think you'd have at least enough sense to be more careful, if you don't want to wind up back in prison."

Slattery glared up at Ambrose. "I could hurt you." The threat would have been more impressive if he hadn't had to crane his neck to make eye contact.

"Would it surprise you to know that I have already spoken to Mr. Durslag, your parole officer? Val may or may not file charges. I personally think he should. But don't think for one second that I would hesitate to put your scruffy ass back in prison if you even breathed on me the wrong way."

Slattery spat on the carpet, very close to, but not quite on, Ambrose's highly polished loafer, and turned and walked down the stairs. When his footsteps died away all three of us took a deep breath.

"Come on, Val, let's go up to Jo's for a minute." Before either Val or I could protest, he was walking up the stairs to my apartment, waiting while I opened the door. Both men walked in and Ambrose waited while Val looked around. He had passed through the room just after Slattery's attack, but clearly it hadn't registered that time. "You just moved in?"

"No it's been like this for months," Ambrose said.

"I see." Val went over to the wall and started examining the places where Nina's pictures had been taken down, leaving a sort of patchwork effect in the overall wall design.

"Jo, what did Maxine say?"

"I haven't been able to get through to her," I said. "I did leave two messages, but she hasn't called back. And yes, Mulligan and I looked in her apartment and there was no sign that anything had happened to her."

"But did you tell her about this?" Ambrose swept his hand to indicate Val.

Val turned around. "Excuse me. I get a couple of black eyes and a cut lip and suddenly I've sunk to the status of '*this.*'"

"You know that I meant the attack."

"I'll call Maxine again," I said. "I'll call from the kitchen. I'll be right back."

"Tell her to come up here if you reach her," Ambrose said, before turning back to face Val who had a few more choice words for him.

Maxine answered her phone, for which I breathed a prayer of thanks. I asked her to come up, and five minutes later she knocked on the door. She looked relaxed and mellow, wearing a purple sweatshirt and pants.

Val paused in berating Ambrose to greet Maxine. She took one look at his face and hugged him. "Poor baby!" she said. "What happened to you?"

Val didn't say anything.

"He interrupted Dick Slattery burglarizing his apartment. Slattery beat him up," Ambrose said.

Maxine stood stock-still and her nostrils actually flared like a woodland creature testing the air for predators. "No."

"It's true, Maxine," I said. "I saw him. If Lucille hadn't yelled at him to stop, he might have hurt Val seriously."

Maxine turned her large blue eyes on me. "Who is Lucille?"

"It's a long story. She's a woman who came to talk to me."

"She's a big blonde," Val said. "She was in the backyard when I ran out the back door calling for help. She was coming up to pull him off me when Slattery ran away. He didn't tell you any of this?"

"No." Maxine looked at Ambrose and me and then back to Val.

"He'll tell you I tried to make a pass at him, Maxine," Val said. "But, honestly, I never—"

"Have you got anything to drink?" Maxine asked.

"I second that motion," Val said.

"Come on, I'll open a bottle of wine."

Ambrose opened the wine while I got out some glasses and we all sat down at Nina's table. "How long have you two been seeing each other?" Ambrose asked.

"Since the first week of August." Maxine had gulped down the first glass of wine as soon as it was poured and held her glass out for another.

"How did you meet?" Ambrose easily stepped into the interrogation role.

"He delivered some flowers to me by accident and we got to talking. He insisted I keep them. He said he'd heard the bird shrieking all the way out on the sidewalk. He asked to see Groucho. He was nice and funny, so I invited him in, and one thing led to another. He was always totally honest about his prison record."

"He acted like he was proud of it," I said.

Maxine looked at me blankly, and Ambrose shook his head very slightly. I shut up.

"Maxine, did he have access to the tenant's keys?"

"Oh my God." Maxine put her hand to her mouth.

"Is he down in your apartment now?"

"No. He went out. He's been going out evenings. He's got a job on the night shift downtown."

"I'm just worried about your safety," Ambrose said. "I'm worried about all the tenants' safety."

Maxine put her glass down so hard it rang on the table. She stood up, scraping her chair. "Maybe you should worry about his safety."

"We are going to have to change the locks, though," I said to her retreating back.

The door to the apartment slammed.

"That went well," Val said into the silence.

"Jo, have you considered a career in diplomacy?" Ambrose asked.

The two men left soon after. I went out onto the back stairs with the magical can of cat food, summoned Raoul back up to the apartment and closed him in against the vast world of danger out there.

Raoul vanished into one of his hiding places and I sat next to the phone and thought about what might be happening. Lucille had the bankbook with a couple million dollars and all the information needed to withdraw the money. I couldn't see Griff getting involved with that. I had never known him to bother with deception when it didn't concern his love life. Lucille hadn't said whether she was carrying the bankbook. She might have given it to Ted. To complicate matters further, Lucille had been seen with another man. She could be anywhere. Ted could also be anywhere.

I wondered if Lucille might have touched base with her

family, perhaps even gone back to stay with or near them. I pulled out the picture of Delores Patton at the day care center opening with the candidate and his ex-movie star wife. I called the Women's Job Skill Center.

I wasn't really surprised that Delores accepted my call—she couldn't very well turn down a possible grant for her non-profit.

"I don't know if you've been following the news lately, but Francesca Etheridge died a few days ago. You know, the woman who wrote that complaining letter you showed me."

"Oh, really?" Her tone remained Teflon smooth, so that I couldn't tell whether this was information she was just getting or had heard about all along.

"I'm not sure how any of this is going to affect our inquiry into the center quite yet, but I wondered if you were aware that Francesca's mother was Brenda Benedict. The actress? Her husband is running for office in California."

"I'm sorry, I can't keep track of politics in other states."

"Well, now you see that's the thing. I have a news photo that shows you at a day care center opening in Orange County, California with Brenda Benedict and Matt Gunther."

Delores laughed. "I'm sorry, but I go to so many openings of community service organizations, they all blur together. I used to live in California, so I've been to many there."

I was impressed. If I hadn't seen her in person, I might have imagined her as a hardworking, but slightly disorganized person.

"Do you have some time tomorrow? I just need to show you the photo and ask a few of questions about it. I won't take more than a few minutes of your time. But I need to have all the information for my report. My immediate supervisor at the foundation is a stickler on accuracy. If I don't get all the facts, my report isn't worth anything."

She agreed to meet me at the Women's Job Skill Center at eleven o'clock.

While I was putting my things together to get up and go to Bremerton the next morning, I took a moment and looked up the restaurants. Sure enough there was a Meeker Family Cafe in the telephone book. There was even a Meeker home address. I called Mulligan.

"Jo, I heard you went to Francesca Benedict's funeral. Are you out of your mind?"

"How did you find that out?" I asked, startled.

"Gonick came by to talk to me at work. He mentioned that you had been seen hugging your ex-husband at the funeral."

"Great."

"Are you trying to get the police to think you are involved in this? Because it's working. Gonick's a nice guy, and he appreciates that you have been of some help to him last May. He came by to ask me if I could talk some sense into you."

"And incidentally to see if he could drive a wedge between us. Which appears to have worked, not that—" I shut up.

"What?"

"Nothing. Never mind." I felt like crying.

"Jo—Sorry, I went off on you like that. It was probably appropriate to hug your ex-husband, and it's not really my business anyway, I guess."

"Okay."

"You called me. What's going on?"

I told him I was going to go to Bremerton. Before I could ask, he volunteered to take care of Raoul. That was the end of the conversation. No mention of sharing a meal, which was just as well. The whole day had given me a bit of a queasy feeling.

That night the anxiety I felt in the apartment was even stronger. I managed to sleep in the living room toward dawn.

Raoul frequently slept with me on the sofa but I was so restless that he moved over to one of the armchairs. The next morning I dropped him off at Mulligan's apartment for day care and he immediately headed for the bedroom. Much as I wanted to do the same, I headed for my car and the ferry to Bremerton.

It was mid-morning when I loaded my car onto the Bremerton Ferry from Pier 52. The ferry began to churn through the waters of the Sound. The long, green presence of the Olympic National Forest across the way soothed my nerves, although the tight knot of anxiety in my solar plexus never quite untangled. I found the Meeker Family Cafe easily. It was doing a brisk business, and the teenager behind the counter told me that none of the Meekers were working today. They were at home. Fortunately, the local telephone book listed their street address.

It was getting close to eleven, so I parked and walked into the Women's Job Skill Center. I didn't recognize the woman behind the desk, but before I had a chance to tell her about my appointment, Delores herself came out and hustled me into her office. Once the door was safely closed, she gestured me to a seat and went behind her desk. Another chair had been placed at an angle to the desk and that chair was occupied by a silver-haired, well-tanned man in a three-piece suit.

"I assume you are a lawyer," I said.

"Yes, Ms. Fuller, you can call me Mr. Cavendish," he said with a minimal smile.

"What happened, Delores? Couldn't find a woman or a minority lawyer?"

"I try not to discriminate in these matters," Delores said.

"All this fuss over one picture." I opened up my briefcase and put the picture I had printed off the web page on the desk. "It's a matter of public record."

Mr. Cavendish glanced at the picture as if noting the web address printed at the top. "Not anymore," he said. "I think you'll find there is no such picture posted on any website now."

"Okay," I said. "And you don't want to explain what your involvement with this day care center has to do with Brenda Benedict or Matt Gunther."

"The short answer is nothing," Delores said. "I attended on opening, to support a community facility in a community where I have relatives."

"Uh-huh." I put the picture back in my briefcase. "Well, thanks for your time." I started to rise, but Mr. Cavendish gestured me back to my seat.

"Ms. Fuller, I just want to make one thing clear here. We will not tolerate any harassment, either by you or by any of your associates."

I stood up. "Gee, Mr. Cavendish, who am I harassing? Ms. Patton, or you, or maybe Matt Gunther?"

"Leave it alone, Ms. Fuller. Don't overestimate your skills or intelligence. That sort of mistake can be fatal."

"If he's the new counselor, Delores, I've got to say he's not very empowering." I opened the door to go. "But heck, maybe he's real fun at parties."

Mr. Cavendish lazily watched me depart without moving a muscle, but he gave the impression that if he snapped his fingers, several capable henchmen would be dogging my every step. I didn't see anyone following me. Of course, I might have been overestimating my skills and intelligence again like the man said.

The Meeker home was in a modest neighborhood a few miles from downtown. I drove past some spectacular views of the water on the way but then the streets led inland to a tract of older, smaller homes with tidy little lawns like green handkerchiefs.

A couple of children rode past on bikes. The neighborhood had a quiet, wholesome feel to it like a child's first reader.

I knocked on the door, and it was opened by a tall, very broad man, with the slight stoop of a grizzly bear. I told him I was a friend of Ted Etheridge who had met Lucille through him, and that I was trying to get in touch with Lucille now. He gave me what amounted to a pitying look, and invited me in. He called over his shoulder, "Abby, there's a lady here who's looking for Lucille." Then he gestured to me to have a seat, and he sat down next to a boy, who looked to be eleven or twelve.

The room was small. Both father and son had that grizzly bear size, and they pretty much filled up the sofa. The television was a large screen variety, stacked with video and stereo equipment. The room wasn't meant to hold much more than that. There wasn't a book in evidence, or even a magazine. My heart went out to the boy who looked fat enough to be teased at school. I could tell by the way he steadfastly refused to look away from the television screen that he wouldn't be surprised to be harassed or lectured by anyone who walked through the door. My guess was that almost everyone talked that way to him—even, I suspected, the television. The advantage was that he could turn the television off, or like now, use the television to turn off the other people in the room.

Abby Meeker came bustling out of the kitchen drying her hands on a dishtowel. She had the same green eyes, and beautiful gold-blond hair as her daughter, but she was petite—a small-framed deer next to her bear-like husband and son. I instantly sympathized even more keenly with Lucille.

Mrs. Meeker's mouth had pulled down into a suspicious frown that appeared to be permanent. I introduced myself, and explained that I was trying to reach Lucille. It was just as well that I didn't make up a cover story. Mrs. Meeker had already heard of me.

"You're that fat-girl friend of Teddy Etheridge. I have no patience with you. Just because Lucille had the willpower to lose her weight, you want to try to find her, and make her get heavy again. What is wrong with you? You've got to try to spoil things for other people, just because you couldn't stick to a diet yourself? Can't you be happy for her?"

"That's not it at all, Mrs. Meeker. I met Lucille the other day, she's a beautiful woman. I hope she does stay exactly the way she is."

"Don't even think that! She'll get even thinner. She's got to. She can do it. If I can do it, she can do it. She's got a nice doctor now who gives her pills. She's just picked up a few pounds the last month now, but it's just the plateau thing."

I sighed. "I notice you're very thin yourself, Mrs. Meeker. Are you on a diet?"

"I have to be. I've never been really big, like Lucille. But I could be ten pounds heavier easy if I didn't watch every scrap."

I could see this dialogue was going downhill—and would become subterranean shortly. Mrs. Meeker clearly worshipped at the shrine of Our Lady of Perpetual Anorexia. Her mind was set in stone. Anyone who disagreed was branded a heretic, and anyone who failed at dieting was revealed as an unrepentant sinner.

When I didn't say anything, she volunteered, "I don't know where Lucille is, but if I did I wouldn't tell you or that Teddy

Etheridge. She can do better than him. That doctor she sees even told her she could be as pretty as a movie star if she lost a little more. She's a beautiful girl."

"I agree," I said, but my words were lost in hers.

"Don't tell me about that Teddy. What kind of name is that for a grown-up? That man has never held a responsible job. He has no insurance or pension."

"He did have six books published that sold quite well."

"So what? Does he have a house? No. Does he have a car? No. Just that damn motorcycle. She's better off without that man. He was only using our Lucille. Did you know he didn't even have an apartment, just a room? Of course he'd move in with her, first chance he got. She said he paid his way, but so what? She's got a chance to meet a man who will really take care of her, if she can just lose that last bit of the weight."

From the way she said it, I realized that from her mother's viewpoint "the weight" was a ball and chain Lucille must have dragged her whole life. That wasn't an unusual viewpoint. My own relatives had felt that way about my size when I was young. They had the good grace to politely whisper about it behind my back. Unlike Lucille's mother, who hit her in the face with it every day of her life. I glanced at the husband and son, but they were steadfastly ignoring her. Perhaps that was safest.

"I'll tell you, just like I told Teddy," Mrs. Meeker concluded, "go bother someone else."

I left, but as I was getting into my car I noticed that the boy had followed me, "Hey," he said.

"Hey."

"I know where to find Lucille."

"Where?"

He smiled slyly. I reached for my wallet, wondering what kind of bribe children required these days. He accepted ten dollars but kept his hand out. I added another twenty. "And a ride to my friend's house."

"Is this okay with your parents?"

"Hang on a sec—" He darted across the yard—very nimbly despite his size—opened the door, and yelled in, "Mom, Dad, I got a ride to the Gibsons'."

I didn't hear any reply but no one came running out of the house to inquire further. The kid got in the passenger side of the car. I started the engine.

"What's your name?"

"Archie."

"Where do you want to go, Archie?"

"Go up to the end of the block and turn left. It's a couple of miles."

"How will you get home?"

"Mrs. Gibson will take me. She's a nice lady."

"So where is Lucille?"

"She's in Seattle at her friend's place. She has a new boyfriend. I think he's like—a criminal."

"What makes you say that?"

"I heard her talking to him on the phone. She said she wouldn't do what he asked because it was illegal, but she would go with him if he wanted to leave the country."

"When was this?"

"Yesterday."

"She was at your parent's house yesterday?"

"Yeah. But she went back to Seattle now. At her friend Cammy's house. She gave me the number, in case I decide to run away from home or something." He told me where to turn off, and when we got to our destination, he took a wallet with a Velcro fastener out of his pocket and let me look at a folded-up sheet of what looked like the same blue paper Ted had shown me with Lucille's note on it. The name Cammy was written on it, along with a telephone number and address. I copied down the number and the address was near Seattle, in Kent.

"If she left the country, Cammy would know. You can drop me here. Thanks."

"Wait, I have to make sure—" Before I could finish the sentence he yelled out, "Deke!" Another boy around his own age opened the door, and they both went in.

I stayed in the doorway, and called out, "Hello!"

A harried looking woman came out, and looked startled. "Oh, hello. I knew Archie was coming over but I'm afraid I . . ."

I introduced myself, and explained that I just wanted to make sure an adult knew where Archie was.

"Oh, I know that all right. They'll be holed up in Deke's room for the next several hours playing video games and surfing the Net."

"Oh, okay."

When I drove off the ferry, I was tired enough that I almost didn't make the trek down to Kent, but I decided to check it out. The house at the address Archie had given me was at the end of a dead end street. The windows were dark in the twilight. There was no answer at the door, no vehicles in the driveway, and several newspapers stacked up on the doorstep. A dead end in more ways than one.

Sitting at the end of the driveway, I used my cell phone to call Wolf Lambert's assistant Thelma in Sonoma to make an appointment to see him. I was a little surprised when she said he was expecting my call and could see me the next afternoon. I had somehow thought it would be a little more difficult to see a famous director.

Then I called Ambrose. He indulged in a moment of silence as his method of conveying that he disapproved of my action. But he said he would field any inquiries with the appropriate cover story, and he hoped the results would be worth the time and trouble. I hesitated a minute, then I told him about my encounter with Delores and Mr. Cavendish. Just saying his name made me want to look over my shoulder to see if someone was stalking me.

"If this guy made you that nervous, watch your back, Jo. I'll look into it. But call me if you see anything unusual or anybody who seems to be following you."

When I got home, I knocked on Mulligan's door, and asked if he could take Raoul one more day. The cat wound around his legs, trying to get out and Mulligan picked him up and hugged him. I petted him too. Raoul, cheerfully stretched out in Mulligan's arms to provide the maximum pettable surface, said his own name in his self-absorbed fashion, and then settled down to purr and accept affection from two humans at once. "Why don't I just keep him tonight so that we don't have to shuffle him back and forth in the morning?"

"Okay, thanks." I stood there for an awkward moment until I realized I was waiting for him to invite me in. By the time I muttered good night and stumbled upstairs I realized I was tired enough to be greatly relieved that he hadn't asked. When I got up to the apartment the familiar anxiousness set in, and I thought how much I was going to miss the cat. I did manage to sleep eventually.

Leaving the building I kept an eye out for signs of surveillance. Not finding any didn't set my mind at ease, because I kept wondering if someone really skillful might be following me. By early afternoon, when I started to relax, I was on the airport shuttle bus from San Francisco Airport to Santa Rosa. I rented a car there, and drove to Wolf Lambert's vanity winery down the country roads winding through vineyards just outside of Baronsville.

It was Indian Summer in Sonoma County, although not quite time for the harvest. I pulled the car over to the side of the quiet two-lane road that wound among fields of grapes, and got out to take a deep breath. I took off my jacket, and folded it on the seat beside me. It was clear, sunny, nearly eighty degrees outside—about ten degrees warmer than the warm summer day in Seattle. The air was hot but not oppressively humid. The prospect of the grape harvest seemed to hang in the air like a promise. I could see why someone who had made a fortune and developed a taste for the finer things would want to retire here.

The winery had more of a family farm look about it than a rich man's toy, although when I turned off the two-lane road onto a gravel drive, I had to speak into a black box with a security camera mounted above it. The whole setup would have been more impressive if anyone had ever bothered to clean the pigeon droppings from the plastic housing around the box. The wrought iron gates were topped with an elaborate "Lambert's Lair Winery" sign. A woman's voice said something too garbled to decipher, but the gates buzzed open, and then closed behind me with a tinny clang. I toiled uphill in the rental car to a house under shade trees. A few outbuildings sat behind the house, where the fields of grapes rose on gently rolling hills.

I parked between a pickup truck and a sport utility vehicle on a little patch of cement in front of the house. A thicket of rosebushes and a chain link fence shielded most of the house from view, but at one end a couple of wine barrels planted with geraniums framed a door with glass panes. A carved wooden sign that read "Welcome" hung from two hooks in front of the door, but a hand-lettered piece of cardboard taped below it advised that "Tastings have been suspended until after the harvest—call the number below for the new schedule." I walked between the geraniums, and rang the bell.

The door sprang open, and I jumped back before realizing it was remote controlled. A melodious woman's voice called out, "Come in. I'm back here." I stepped over the threshold into a room that was cool and beautifully paneled but not large. A counter at one end held several wine glasses on a tray. Wine racks behind the counter held examples of the winery's vintages. Several framed labels with a distinctive logo of a wolf and a lamb cuddling up hung on the wall, a couple of them with ribbons that indicated awards they had won. The room was quiet, and lacked the invitingly convivial air of most wine tasting rooms. There was also no sign of the corkscrews, T-shirts or postcards aimed at tourists that I'd seen when Griff and I had gone through several Sonoma County wineries in the past.

"Hello," I called out.

"Come on back here. Go around the counter, and past the wine racks. I'm in the office." It was a woman's voice.

Behind the wall of wine racks I found an office that was at least as spacious as the tasting room I had just left. At the desk facing the door, sitting in a red upholstered office chair, was the largest woman I have ever seen.

"Hi, I'm Josephine Fuller," I said, a little embarrassed by the fact that suddenly seeing her had shocked me. I realized, looking at her, that I was experiencing some of the discomfort that I often provoke in people who simply don't know how to respond to a woman over two hundred pounds who looks back at them, and expects to be respected. This woman was easily double my weight, and probably closer to three times. She also had a heart-shaped face atop several chins, and eyes that were a rare shade of pastel blue. Her face was framed by a cascade of stunningly red hair.

"I'm Thelma, Wolf's bookkeeper. This week I'm all the office help he's got. Please sit down, he'll be back soon. Normally his secretary would talk to you, but that foolish man has gone and lost another one. Is there something I can help you with while you're waiting?"

I gulped, and realized I'd been staring. "Honestly, I'm jealous of your chair, where did you find it? It looks great."

She smiled an enchanting smile. Perhaps she had been fearing the "such a pretty face" lecture. Fat women can be the worst culprits at giving each other that kind of grief—as if criticizing another woman's body will somehow make things better for both. It's a sick variation on the "I hate my body too, let's be friends" female bonding ritual that makes me crazy.

Thelma brought out a catalog. I sat down in an armless visitor's chair beside the desk, and we talked office furniture.

I wrote down the 800 number, realizing that I was going to need to get some furniture for the apartment in Seattle. The idea of putting together my own home office suddenly intrigued me.

"What was it you wanted to talk to Wolf about?" She asked with a meaningful glance, as if I might be here under false pretenses.

"I'm hoping he can shed some light on some people he knew."

"Would you like to be more specific? Maybe I can pull together some information for you while we're waiting."

"It's about Don and Brenda Benedict. Have you ever met them?"

"Oh, from the Hanged Man films. That was before my time. From Wolf's other life. He doesn't have much to do with those Hollywood types now. He's retired, and pursuing his new career as a dirty old man."

"Now Thelma, don't talk behind my back." I turned to see Wolf Lambert looking just a little less drunk than he had in the funeral home parking lot. Today he was wearing a lightweight sports shirt and khaki shorts. His eyes were concealed behind sunglasses. He was carrying a bottle of white wine and a couple of glasses. He put them down on Thelma's desk.

"I remember you," he said, snapping his fingers. "What was it, Hortense? Winifred?"

"Josephine."

"Right. Right. We'll change that," he said, enveloping my hand in a firm grip, while he backed off at arm's length, and looked me up and down. "Very nice, very nice. I believe I mentioned that I heard great things about you from Francesca's husband."

So Teddy was still singing my praises. "Tell me again—when did you have dinner with him?"

Wolf sighed, "You know, dear, I believe we were having dinner the night Francesca was killed. We invited her along, but she was busy with some business. Who knows? If she had put up with us, she might be alive today."

"Are you sure you were out with him the night she died?"

"Darling, you can check with the limo driver. We were out carousing from dusk till dawn. He's a great storyteller with a few drinks in him. Better yet, check with the hotel staff. Fran's husband ended up passed out in the other bed in my hotel room. Not my choice of companions, but we were both too drunk at that point to do more than pass out. I woke up briefly when he left, but it was well after dawn. The front desk would know—the bastard ordered room service breakfast and put it on my tab."

"Did you tell the police this?"

I extricated my hand from his grip, but he was so close now that it didn't make much difference.

"They never asked."

"It would take some of the suspicion off him if you told them he couldn't have done it and the limo driver bears you out."

"The poor boy may not have my number, I thought I gave it to him. He would have found it eventually. Isadora or her parents would have told him." Wolf turned to Thelma and snapped his fingers. "Make a note for me to call the police later, dear."

"I'm sure that will make him feel a lot easier in his mind."

"Always glad to do that. So—you interested in a little nudity?"

I and smiled politely. "Oh gosh, no thanks. I just wanted a few minutes of your time to talk about Don and Brenda Benedict."

"So you said in your message. You're supposedly doing

research for an article in some kind of feminist film history. Which I don't believe for a moment, by the way. You're not the type. But your employer has got enough clout that it really doesn't matter if you're simply scratching some private itch. You're attractive enough to scratch my itch anytime. I can spare half an hour—but I'm going to spend it in the hot tub. You can join me or not as you please, it's through there. Thelma are you coming?"

"In a minute. I think I may have to scrape Josephine here off the floor."

He chuckled raucously, and headed for the back door of the office, where I could see through the glass panes a hot tub steaming on a back deck, with a magnificent view of the slopes of the vineyards.

"If he acts like that all the time, I could see why he might have trouble keeping secretaries," I remarked to Thelma, who appeared to be enjoying my thunderstruck expression.

"Oh that. It's not what you think. Wolf always picks pretty, thin girls for his secretaries. I think he does it to put his business visitors at ease, because he's not a closet case in any other way. He never makes passes at them. Couldn't you tell, or didn't anyone warn you about Wolf? He's a notorious FA."

"Huh?"

"Fat admirer. In fact, that's the kind of movies he makes now."

"Oh, that's what Isadora meant about fetish movies."

A frown came over Thelma's cheerful face. "Well, if you want to believe that someone would have to be a deviant to be attracted to someone like me—or in point of fact to someone like you—it's your business."

"I see what you mean," I said, a little startled. "I'm sorry, Thelma. Please, I meant no offense."

Thelma smiled, as if the sun had come out from behind a cloud. "I'm sure you didn't. It's a limited but very passionate market. Wolf would never lay a hand on a skinny girl, and he's so happy not to have to make films with anorexic actresses anymore. He's got plenty of the kind of girls he does like. There's no shortage of lusty fat girls."

"Uh, I guess not," I stammered, literally not knowing what to say. "If he doesn't make passes at his secretaries, why are they always quitting?"

Thelma's smile became rueful. "Like I said, Wolf gets pretty little local girls to handle wine tastings and reception, and type the occasional letter. The girls he picks come in two flavors—the conservative ones who can't handle it when they find out he makes adult films, and the star-struck ones who can't believe that he's making films and not asking them to the party. Sometimes he has to fire them, because some of the prettiest ones have had everything handed to them on a plate their whole life. He's always surprised when they don't know how to do anything but smile. It never occurs to him that if they're too stupid to breathe, they're not going to be very good at office work."

"How'd he get you?"

"He had to get lucky sometime. Besides, to balance the books, you have to know how to add and subtract. He sat me down, and told me what kind of films he made, and I was intrigued. He was turned on that I wasn't horrified. So he decided to make me a star. And here I am." She smiled, and opened her massive arms as if embracing and demonstrating the status quo all at once.

"Okay," I said. I took a deep breath because it seemed to demand more comment. "Good. Okay," was the best I could do.

"Wolf likes you, that's a big plus. When you walked in, and I saw you were a big gal, I was going to ask if you came to audition for one of his films."

"Uh, no." I could see she was enjoying shocking me.

"You do seem awfully shy to do that kind of film. Let's go out to the hot tub, and you can ask your questions. Come on, you don't have to strip—I'm going to keep on my sports bra and thong."

My jaw dropped a little as she stood up and pulled off her skirt and draped it over the back of the office chair. She led the way toward the back, moving slowly because she had a lot of mass to move, unbuttoning her blouse as she went. I followed even slower. Once out on the back deck Thelma folded her blouse, and laid it carefully on a redwood bench beside the hot tub. She patted the bench. "You can sit here if you're certain you don't want to come in."

Mercifully Wolf was already in the hot tub, which was sunken low enough that Thelma had no trouble slipping her abundant body into the water, where her belly immediately floated up.

"You're dressed!" Wolf said with some disappointment, reaching out to her.

"Josephine is very shy," she said, nudging his hand away. "Come on, you can be good for half an hour."

"Oh, all right." He turned back to me. "You're really missing something because Thelma is a natural redhead, but you can see for yourself in the films. We'll send you a catalog. Help yourself to some wine."

"Thanks, but I'll be driving soon." I sat on the bench and took out my notebook, trying not to look down into the hot tub at Wolf. Thinking back to Dick Slattery, I decided that the gods of irony were working overtime this week—I managed to have two men I wasn't interested in exposing themselves, while Mulligan whom I was interested in, managed to remain resolutely zipped up.

I still didn't quite know how to look at Thelma, who was

demurely pouring herself a glass of wine. I took a deep breath, "Okay so Mr. Lambert—"

"Wolf, please."

"Wolf, I understand you and Don Benedict were college roommates; where was that?"

"What? You think I look older than Don? Well, you're right. We had an apartment together in West LA, I was a grad student in film at UCLA, and he was a physical education major—he minored in theater arts, but he was a sensible guy. With the PE major he could teach high school if he never got a big break in movies."

"So you were still in school when you made the first Hanged Man movie?"

"I got hold of my aunt's American Express card, and never looked back."

"The story is that Don suggested the title character from the tarot cards."

"Yes, that's true. But we just went with the idea of a Hanged Man. In the tarot cards the guy is taking a leap of faith." He chuckled. "We were taking a leap all right, but our Hanged Man was a killer who refused to die even after he was hanged. Don went through a lot on that film, he let us hang him, and burn him up—our special effects were pretty primitive, but the picture had a certain vitality. He was a jock so he knew how to move, even with a hood over his head."

"How could he see with a hood over his head?"

"It was an interesting technical problem. It looked opaque, but he could actually see through it. I just did an interview with a cinema buff who wanted to know all the gory technical details, and some of them were pretty gory. But you don't really care, do you?"

"Uh—"

"Never mind. Anyway, on the later films we decided it was too much of a pain, so we got the Hanged Man a job working as an executioner; that way he could wear a black hood with eye holes."

Thelma appeared to hang on his every word. Either he didn't tell these stories often, or she was a very good listener.

"Why did you stop using Don Benedict?"

"Have you ever met Don Benedict?"

"Yes."

"Then you should be able to answer that question. The man's a moron. I mean, I make adult films now for God's sake, and I have a better sense of decorum. I'm not saying he didn't think he was serious about what he called his acting, but any bozo in a hood could have done the part just as well."

"A minute ago you said that because he was an athlete he moved well."

"Correction—he was an athlete who moved well, whom I didn't have to pay because he was my roommate. He even put a little of his paltry savings from his job as a lifeguard into the film. An investment which has paid off handsomely for him, I might add. Then, too, Don always bought donuts for the rest of the cast. He was a nice guy but it's not exactly a challenge to find an athletic actor in Hollywood. Not that Don was bad. He was happy to wear the hood. He was thrilled when we did the second one, and he got some money for it. But Brenda started to make a name for herself, and she asked us to get rid of him."

"His wife wanted to get rid of him? Why? Was he cheating on her?"

"Only every chance he got. But it wasn't that. It was more that he was an embarrassment to her. Their two daughters were getting in the way of her career. She wanted to dump him for someone with power but first she wanted him out of the pictures. So we gave him a little stipend that amounted to child support, and sent him off with the little girls to live the wholesome life in Montana or wherever the hell he ended up."

"They divorced?"

"Not at first. Don didn't care so long as he could ski in the winter and boat in the summer. He didn't have to work, and there were enough naïve women at the resorts where he lived that he kept himself amused. Brenda divorced him as soon as she found a suitable replacement."

"That was before Matt Gunther's time, I take it."

"Oh, years before. Her second husband was a director. Third one was a very wealthy businessman. Matt is number four. He's just using her to open doors for him with the media. But she's using him as the architect of her latest performance. It works out well for them."

"What about the kids?"

"They're messed up, so what?"

"Correction—Isadora is messed up. Francesca was messed up, but now she's dead. How well did you know the girls?"

Wolf sipped his wine, and stared at the cloudless fall sky. I concentrated on his wine glass so as not to look down into the hot tub. I noticed that Thelma had one plump hand on his shoulder—her fingernails were long and scarlet.

"Francesca was the older daughter," Wolf said. "I think she inherited Don's stupidity, and Brenda's looks and drive. The younger girl, Isadora, was more athletic, and too damn smart. I always wondered if maybe Don wasn't the younger girl's father, but he took them in the divorce. I have never heard from Isadora. Francesca would call—when she wanted a favor. The last time was a year ago when she was putting together some kind of all-female mountaineering expedition with her sister, and she wanted it filmed. I think she wanted me to fund the filming, but I turned her down. Gave her some names to drop at film schools. Told her to get some young female jock who's looking for a feminist project. I told Francesca she should get some money from some women. She said, 'Uncle Wolf, you know women don't have any money.' "

Thelma giggled. I gave her a look that should have turned her wine to hot vinegar. I didn't think it was very funny. She smiled benignly at my scowl.

"Was this a little over a year ago?"

"That sounds about right."

"Probably that was the film expedition to Mt. McKinley," I said.

"If you say so. There was a gay tie-in because the sister was tagging along with her lover to reaffirm their vows on some mountaintop—blah-blah-blah. When I heard that I suggested some gay filmmakers I knew who might be able to help her network."

"You hadn't heard whether she found someone to film it?"

"Nope. Haven't thought of it since I hung up the phone. I never heard back from Fran. I figured she'd call next time she wanted something."

"You hadn't heard that Isadora's lover died up there?"

"No."

"Would you mind telling me who you referred Francesca to?"

"I'll have Thelma send you a list. You can do that, can't you sweetie?"

Thelma nodded. She made eye contact with me, and winked.

"I don't know that she even contacted any of them," Wolf said, holding out his wine glass for a refill. "She was very driven as an individual athlete but when it came to things that involved other people, she preferred letting them do the work."

"Did most people give her what she asked for?"

"She was a beautiful woman. Not my type. But a lot of

men, and women for that matter, would give her things in expectation of her favors. Now you'd be more likely to get a favor out of me than a skinny little thing like Franny. But she was Don and Brenda's daughter, so I indulged her within reason for old time's sake."

"Is that the only connection—you never, for example, had an affair with Brenda?"

Wolf threw back his head and roared with laughter, which set off Thelma to the point where that the water in the hot tub sloshed back and forth.

"I know you don't get it, honey. Brenda has a very lovely face, but she's much too thin to interest me. I've never been to bed with a woman much under two hundred pounds. That was useful in Hollywood, believe it or not. Most of the actresses working there didn't interest me in the slightest. Sad ladies some of them. I worked in show business long enough to know what kind of black hole hides in the heart of a woman like Brenda Benedict. She'll let herself be carved up by a plastic surgeon, happily exercise three hours a day, starve herself and then inject her breasts with silicone. Because breasts are made of fat, honey. When girls starve, the breasts are the first to go."

He put his wine glass down to free his hand to grope Thelma, who reached up to hold his hand. "Screwing Brenda would be like going at it with one of those carnivorous insects. She'd bite your head off, suck out your life and step over your body to the next victim." He shuddered, setting off waves in the hot tub. "Besides, it's a major waste of energy to spend time with a girl who needs to be adored in order to get out of bed in the morning. Very hard work."

I cleared my throat, keeping my eyes on Wolf's face.

"Fran took after her mother," he said. "Although she's a jock rather than an actress. I'm surprised she lasted with

Teddy Etheridge as long as she did. She must have fainted when she saw how much a best-selling humorist really makes. I think she planned on him to bankroll her climbing career. That poor schlump couldn't even bankroll a car with four wheels. She probably kept him on as long as she did because he convinced her she was getting a free publicist. Then he ended up running errands for her."

"And she cheated on him."

"Honey, is it cheating to be unfaithful to the guy who fetches your coffee? She left a humorist and moved on to a photographer. What would be next, a jazz musician?" Wolf laughed again, and sloshed around in the tub, which caused Thelma to giggle some more. I didn't look to see exactly what he was doing to cause that. "Poor Fran didn't have a clue about marrying for money."

"Well, Griff was always broke, but she got some very fine portraits out of the relationship."

"Right, right, great stuff. Saw them at the funeral parlor. If I were a proper godfather, I would have sat that girl down and had a serious talk about economics, maybe introduced her to a nice nerdy millionaire."

"Why didn't you?"

"Fran never came to me for advice, only money. I never gave it to her, but she asked from time to time, just to keep in practice. If I'd talked to her, would she have listened to me? Who knows? She never lived that long." His face grew sad. "She died so young. That's the sad part. She was only twenty-five. At that age they know everything."

"Can you think of anyone she might have offended? Anyone who might have wanted her dead?"

"Anyone aside from you?" He smiled, and raised his glass. "I did hear about how she took your husband away from you, Ms. Josephine Fuller."

"Obviously, if I were involved myself, I'd be staying away from anyone who knew Fran instead of coming around asking questions."

"My dear, I try to stay out of real-world dramatics, and I do believe that what goes round comes round. But if I were trying to find out what went wrong in the Benedict family, I'd follow the money. There never is enough for any of them, and if they get a little, they're not about to let go of it without a struggle."

"I'll keep that in mind."

"Look, Thelma, she's playing detective. I like it. It turns me on."

"Oh, it does, Wolfie, it really does!" Thelma exclaimed with a Marilyn Monroe–style breathlessness.

I made it a point to keep my eyes on their faces.

"Hand me the microcassette, dear. I feel inspired."

Thelma reached up to retrieve a small microcassette recorder, which had been in the pocket of the blouse folded on the bench. She clicked it on, and handed it to Wolf. He spoke into it rapidly, never taking his eyes from me. "The voluptuous visitor drops her clipboard, abandons her questions, and her clothes. Except for the gun in a shoulder holster—are you wearing a gun, honey?"

I shook my head.

"I'll take that as a 'no.' The girl in our movie has a gun though. She'll take off everything but the shoulder holster, and the gun. Wait, I've got it! She can force the men to service her at gunpoint."

"I love it!" Thelma cried out, with a throaty laugh.

"You sure you don't want to play the part, doll?" Wolf asked.

I stood up to go. I started to thank him for seeing me on such short notice, but Wolf was spinning out more pornographic plot twists. I turned on my heel, and walked out. "You're still welcome to join us, sweetie, last chance," Thelma called out.

I didn't look back but I heard a bra strap snap, and Wolf began to sing, "T for Texas, T for Tennessee. T for Thelma, who made a wreck out of me!"

On the way back to the airport, I stopped at a real winery and bought several bottles of wine to be shipped to Seattle, and had two packed to go in my luggage.

I got back home late in the evening. Raoul was only mildly interested in my reappearance. Mulligan had dropped him off in Nina's apartment with a note taped to the cans of cat food to inform me that no matter how the cat might beg, he had been fed. I called to let Mulligan know I was back, and spoke to his answering machine. Rather than unpack, I simply stripped off my traveling clothes, and went straight to sleep on the sofa. Raoul was happy to curl back up with me. Whatever it was that scared me about the apartment usually bothered me more at night, but I was too tired to be anxious.

The next thing I knew it was early morning. I tried to sleep more, but ended up surrendering to the day. I fed Raoul, drank some coffee and turned on my computer to catch up on my email.

It was mid-morning by the time I unpacked one of the wine bottles and went down to knock at Maxine's door. I wasn't looking forward to seeing Dick Slattery but I had to talk to Maxine. If necessary, I would bring her upstairs for a private talk.

But Maxine answered the door alone, wearing her lavender terry cloth bathrobe. Her face was swollen.

"My God! Did he hit you?"

She shook her head and moved aside to let me come in.

"Did you ask him about the keys?"

"Never had a chance." Her voice, like her face, was swollen with tears.

"He left, didn't he?"

Maxine seemed to be using her cane more than I remembered. She looked ten years older than the last time I saw her. "Left with a girl half his age," she muttered in her husky voice. She stared at the gift-wrapped bottle in my hand.

"I was in the California wine country yesterday," I explained. "I brought you this." I held it out.

"Maybe later," Maxine said. "Let's go in the kitchen."

We walked past the cage. Groucho was back in his customary perch in the corner. The macaw shifted from foot to foot in a very subdued mood, hunching his green feathered shoulders as if embarrassed. He extended his wings when I walked past the cage, but he even waited till we had gone into the kitchen before letting loose with his ear-splitting screech. The bird appeared to sense that Maxine was in a precarious mental state. She stood a moment gripping the back of the chair.

"Maxine. I need to talk but I don't want to . . ." I ground to a halt. I didn't know what I didn't want to do. She fumbled her way into the chair, and looked at me dully. "Maxine, I'm so sorry, but if he could do that to you, you're better off without him."

"I know," she said, resting her elbows on the table and putting her face in her hands. "The worst of it is, he met his new girlfriend here in the building."

"A tenant here?" I was startled. There were only eight units in the building, and aside from Maxine, her daughter Hope, and myself, the only other unattached female in the building was Beth Kent, who was an extremely savvy company executive. I couldn't imagine her falling for Dick Slattery.

"It's not someone who lives here. He said she was just passing through. I didn't ask him for details. It was bad enough what he did tell me. He said that she was young and blond and fun. He said I was too old for him. I suppose everyone else in the world knew he was just using me."

I put the wine on the counter, worried about her now. "What did Hope say?"

"Hope is thrilled. Of course she also wants to kick his butt. She never was real great at consistency. She's my daughter, and I love her, but if she says, 'I told you so' one more goddamn time, I'm going to slap her silly."

I gulped. Maxine had never seemed to be the violent type, but she sounded quite sincere. "I'm sorry it hasn't worked out but maybe . . ."

"What would you know? When you're my age—" She grabbed a tissue and wiped her eyes and nose, already reddened with tears. "When you meet a man, you always wonder if this will be the last one who will ever look at you."

"I know it's no consolation, but I always feel that way too. I don't even think it's about being fat, exactly, I think it's about being alone. It just seems like you've always been alone, and always will be."

"Yeah, well, nothing personal, but at sixty-something the odds are against me in a way they weren't when I was just barely thirty, like you."

"You just never know," I said.

"So things aren't going well with you and Mulligan either, huh?"

For the first time since I'd walked in, Maxine seemed to buck up a little. My initial instinct was to say nothing. But, after all, I had wanted to talk to her, so I ended up telling her about how Mulligan and I had somehow stalled after the first night.

Maxine nodded. "I thought it looked like you and Mulligan weren't on the same page."

I winced at that description, but managed to say, "We may not even be reading the same kind of book. Sorry to burden you with my problems when you're not feeling well yourself."

"No, no, other people's problems cheer me up." I could tell that. In fact, I was getting a little irritated seeing how my problems had revitalized Maxine.

"I'll get a handle on it, I just haven't yet," I said. Then, anxious to change the subject, I told her how I was unaccountably afraid of Nina's apartment. The minute her eyes lit up, I realized I had probably made a major mistake.

"Let us help you, Josie. The women's group is here for you too. They planned to come over tomorrow night. Why don't you let us come up to the apartment? Nina meant so much to us. Maybe all of us being there together for an evening might help."

"Nina was a lot more into groups than I am," I said, massively understating the case. The idea of having a group of people I scarcely knew invading my space en masse and poking into my deepest fears triggered a sudden urge to head for the airport and take the first flight in any direction.

"True, Nina was more of a people person," Maxine remarked, growing calmer by the minute as I got more distressed. "Scar's psychic sister was coming to clear up any negative energy Slattery might have left on me, but getting your apartment cleared might help you tremendously."

"I don't know." I hesitated. I actually liked the women in the group.

"How about tomorrow night at seven?"

I cast around for a plausible excuse. Nothing surfaced. "I haven't been cooking much, what do you—"

"Don't worry, we always bring pot luck. Thank you, Jo." Maxine put her hand on mine, and squeezed briefly. "This really takes my mind off that jerk, Slattery. I'm sure we can help."

I didn't share her confidence. I did give her a copy of my new key and she promised to have all the tenants' locks changed and notify them today. When I left, Maxine was calling Hope, and I winced again when I heard her describing how I was having trouble sleeping in the apartment. I already regretted having mentioned what was happening with Mulligan. I hoped Maxine wouldn't tell all those women about that.

The idea of laying out all my deepest fears made me queasy. Even if Maxine didn't tell all of them, they would figure out something was up if they noticed how much I had been camping out in one room. Mulligan had figured it out, and never said a word to anyone else about it. This was different.

I felt like a total idiot. I went back upstairs. To my dismay, the anxiousness came over me like a fog as I approached the apartment. Whatever it was usually left me alone in the daylight—usually. Was it was getting worse? Maybe it wouldn't hurt to have the women's group up here Saturday. At least I wouldn't be afraid while they were around—or if I were, I would have company.

I decided to stave off my fears by typing up my notes. The phone rang when I was printing off a short summary of my conclusions, which boiled down to: I didn't know what was happening and mistrusted everyone.

I answered. There was music playing in the background

and a man's voice said, "I've got your blond friend. Give me that bankbook and you can have her back alive."

"Listen, Dick—" I assumed it was Dick Slattery, but either way the name seemed appropriate. "I don't have any bankbook."

"Bullshit. She had it when she went in. She don't have it now. It's in your apartment and I'll get it one way or the other. Say bye-bye to Blondie." A muffled cry and then a woman's scream, and then a hang up, and a dial tone.

My hands were shaking when I took out my cell phone and called Gonick. I told him about the call. Coming on the heels of what Slattery had told Maxine about his blonde friend, I was terrified for Lucille.

"It might be a crank call. But turn your answering machine to record your incoming calls. If this guy calls again a tape might help to find out where he is located. If it's Slattery, he's violated his parole, so we can pick him up if we can find him. Keep me posted."

I put a call in to Mulligan, but he was at work. I left a message on his machine.

Staring at the phone as if I might need to jump back if it started to bite me, I dialed *69 and a recorded voice told me that service was not available to this number. Okay.

Then I called Ambrose.

"Put your answering machine on," he said, "and it will do as much as Gonick told you to do. Come over, I'll cook dinner."

I was surprised to be invited. I had never been in Ambrose's apartment, it was only in the past few months of our year and a half of acquaintance that I had gotten to know him well enough to imagine sharing a meal.

He gave me the address, and I was surprised to find it was

only a short drive. His condominium on Queen Anne Hill was far enough up the hill to offer a view of Puget Sound from its deck. Ambrose took the bottle of wine I had brought when he ushered me in. He took my jacket as well. He hung up the jacket, and brought the wine into the kitchen. It wasn't a very large room, but it was dominated by a large, cream-colored antique gas stove, complete with folding hood over the burners and a complicated system of bread warmer, ovens and grill that framed the burners.

"So how was your trip to the wine country? Mrs. Madrone is in San Francisco now, and I'm planning to meet her there next week."

I watched him stir a pan on the stove. "The weather was beautiful—the information was uncertain. What are you cooking?"

"Remember those lentils we talked about at the grocery store? This is the soup."

"Your influence is insidious, Ambrose," I said. "I bought all that lentil soup stuff but I have to admit that I've never met a lentil I ever liked."

"Try it." He dished a couple of bowls full of the stew, which did smell good. He put out bread and butter. He poured the wine into glasses.

I was surprised. "It's very good—texture, taste everything. Where did you get the recipe?"

"It's really simple, it came from an older man I met at the GLTS Celebration. Have you heard of the Gay, Lesbian, Transgendered Seniors?"

"I have now. Tell me about the recipe."

"Not a lot I can tell," he said with a red-haired, six-foot-two-inch-tall version of a Mona Lisa smile. "Suffice it to say, he shared it with me as part of our oral tradition. But feel free to write it down later. I'll recite the ingredients."

After dinner Ambrose cleared the table. I offered to help.

"Let me tell you about another woman of my acquaintance who insisted on doing the dishes after I cooked for her. I let her do it because she wouldn't take no for an answer, but then I had to wash them again properly after she had left. So, why don't we just let me do it right once?"

"That works for me."

"Tell me about your investigation while I work."

So I sat at the table, watched him wash dishes, and explained as much as I knew about Delores and the Women's Job Skill Center. Her possible ties to the Benedicts. Teddy and Lucille's snatching of the laptop computer and the missing bankbook.

"I'm sure that call was from Dick Slattery," I said. "It really did sound like a woman screaming in the background."

"Unless it was someone who was playing along with Slattery. Pretending to be hurt."

"I never thought of that. But he might do that. I also don't know where Ted Etheridge has gone to. Isadora thought Don Benedict would have left town if he'd had the money."

"My, my, you and Isadora got chummy. I asked someone who knows Anna May Wrong, and I understand Don is still camping out, if you'll excuse the expression, at her place. And Miz Brenda Benedict is still in town too—at least according to the society column. She's winding up her daughter's affairs."

"I wonder if she's staying at the townhouse."

"If she's looking for something as small as a bankbook, she's probably pried up half the floorboards and unscrewed all the lighting fixtures."

"And for all we know the bankbook has already left town with Ted."

"Perhaps you should let this alone, Jo. Do you think the Women's Job Skill Center might be involved?"

I described visiting Delores to ask her about the picture with Matt Gunther and encountering Mr. Cavendish.

"Goodness, an Ivy League thug. That doesn't sound so innocent, does it?"

"No. But I still haven't found whatever it is they don't want me to find."

"That doesn't sound good. They aren't even concerned about losing a possible grant. So maybe you should just let Mrs. Madrone know that they're questionable and move on. The purpose of the exercise is to decide whether to recommend grants to do-gooders, not to chase down evil-doers."

"I know, I know. But there's the little problem that the police still suspect me of being involved in Francesca's murder."

"Did they tell you that?"

"No."

"They haven't arrested you."

"You'd be the first to know if they did."

"That is a delightful prospect I hope to avoid. You know, Jo, the police might be a lot less suspicious of you if you'd just drop the whole thing."

"But what about Griff? They really do suspect him."

Ambrose finished up with the dishes, and came to sit across the table from me. "A lot of people would be delighted to have their ex-spouses under police scrutiny."

"I still like Griff. I think he's a good person, just not a good person to be married to."

"Are you totally sure the police aren't right?"

"As sure as anyone can be about another person."

"Jo, if one of these people killed an ex-wife or blood relative for this bankbook, think what they'd do to a total stranger."

"I just don't want the police to think Griff did it."

"Or you did it."

"That too."

"Why don't you give it the weekend? Can I tell Mrs. Madrone you'll have the report on Monday?"

"Okay. That seems reasonable."

"Jo, you might have to face the fact that there just isn't anything there that can be found."

"Maybe."

I went back to the apartment and found that Raoul was waiting for me. And so was the anxiousness that seemed to envelope me like a fog whenever I entered the place. I decided to do some work at the desk Nina kept in one corner of the living room. I turned on the computer and stared at the screen.

If I just said, "Not recommended" and why, the Women's Job Skill Center report could be finished in an hour. But if I was going to do that, I had all weekend, so I decided to do it some other hour.

Instead I went online to look at Ted Etheridge's website. I was pretty sure he would have one, and he did. Was I being as naïve about Ted as I would be in imagining that Griffin Fuller was a noble soul simply by looking at his sweeping photographs of the Himalayas?

Griff had a dark side—well, at least, he had a lying, cheating side. I wondered about Ted.

Lucille had told me Ted had suggested she use the Women's Job Skill Center as a cover. So he hadn't just wandered in there at random. There were a lot of things Ted hadn't told me. But there was no denying Wolf Lambert's alibi. He had said that the night Fran was murdered he and Ted had been out carousing till dawn. I couldn't see Wolf lying to protect Ted or anyone. Even if his passengers were too drunk to pay attention to details, the limo driver and the hotel staff would have recorded their comings and goings and room service orders.

Alibi or no, I wondered if Ted's website would give some clue as to his whereabouts. It was as funny as Ted himself. He had employed a cartoonist to create a small bumbling cartoon image of Ted meandering all over a cartoon of the globe, and pointing out short essays on travel topics.

Isadora had mentioned that Ted's publisher had changed. The only indication of it on the website was in the "Upcoming Bumbles" section, which informed the web-reading world that his next book, *Bumbling in the Rain—Travels around the Pacific Northwest,* would be published by Rainy Day Press right here in Seattle. He had a link to their web page. I went there to see a press release about Teddy's upcoming book, and how thrilled Rainy Day was to have such a class act as Teddy. I noted that they were having a weekday Rainy Day authors event tomorrow at Yellow Brick Road Books at 6 P.M. Ted was scheduled to attend.

I sent both Ted and Rainy Day Press emails saying I had come across something of Ted's that I wanted to return, and I would try to catch up to him at the book signing. Of course, for all I knew, Ted might have his hands on the missing bankbook at this very moment, have transferred the money to his own account and settled down to sun himself on a beach in some tax-free haven—where it might take him weeks to check his email.

I closed down the computer and decided to contact Griff. Easier said than done, but my address book still contained a list of some of the riff-raff who might be counted upon to let Griff stay there while he was in Seattle. The second call to Paddy Fernandez paid off. Paddy was a fellow photographer whose darkroom Griff often used both for making prints and—occasionally—for sleeping on the floor.

"Yeah, sure he's right here—oops, you're an ex now, Jo, I better ask him if he wants to talk to you, sorry."

"No problem."

Griff came on the line with alacrity. I didn't give him the whole story about the bankbook—I wasn't yet sure what his part in any of it was. But I did say I hadn't been able to find Teddy for a while. "Do you know where he might be?"

"No idea. He might be staying in town to fight with the Benedicts over her stuff."

"Why would he do that?"

"Well, he and Francesca never formally divorced. That might mean some money for Ted. One of the things that gave living with Fran that extra, added air of spice was the fact that she always expected Ted to come and demand that she return to him."

"But he never did?"

"Not that I'm aware of. As you pointed out, he had a key, maybe he liked things the way they were. Personally I prefer a more stable arrangement."

"Like a nice stable wife you can cheat on?"

"That's the ticket! Want to give it another go?"

I had to laugh, he was so incorrigible. "So are you going to be at Paddy's a little longer?"

"Unless you decide to rent me a place or let me stay there."

"I'll let Paddy do the honors."

27

The next day was Thursday, and I had penciled in Teddy's book signing at six. No one replied to my email.

I called Maxine to see if the women's group would want to reschedule, since I might not get back from Teddy's signing by seven. I might have known that they had no problem meeting me at seven-thirty or eight or even later. It was still early enough that I could cook something and reheat it for the coven. No, that was being unkind. They were coming to help me. I just needed to do a little mild, self-defensive hostess work. I pushed the boxes up against the walls and tidied up the stacks of paper that I accumulate somehow whenever I am not traveling. The sheet of paper on top of the stack was the recipe from Ambrose. I had all the ingredients for that. Clearly this was fate, that sort of thing didn't happen to me all the time.

I took it into the kitchen and looked at my purchases from the other day:

1 package dry lentils—check.

Best possible beef bouillon—check. I had bought the expensive kind Ambrose got, so this was not strictly vegetarian, unless I was going to take his "don't tell them what they don't want to know" strategy.

Package of frozen spinach—check. Ambrose had said I

could use fresh spinach, but he looked at me so sternly when he suggested how thoroughly I would need to wash it, that I decided life was too short to wash fresh spinach according to Ambrose's standards.

Can of tomato paste—check.

Onions and garlic—check. Ambrose said these were optional, but I was used to using them for spaghetti, so why not?

Wash lentils and cook in bouillon until tender. When the lentils were happily simmering away, I looked at the sheet again.

Sauté onions and garlic until transparent.

So I happily chopped and sautéed, and put the onions and garlic aside and looked at the sheet of paper, which now had a blot of olive oil on it. I was going to have to put it in a plastic sleeve or something, but I could do that later.

Add onions and garlic to spinach and tomato paste several minutes before serving.

I could do all that just before the exorcising ladies arrived, or maybe before I left for Teddy's book signing. At least I could let the spinach defrost in the meantime.

I reached into the freezer compartment and pulled out a package of frozen spinach. A second package of spinach flew out on the floor. Something was stuck to the surface. Something that didn't belong in a freezer, Nina's or mine. It was a small leather pouch wrapped in plastic, and secured with a rubber band.

I sat down at the table, and opened it up. There was a checking account drawn on a local Washington State bank with a balance of around five hundred dollars, a savings account with about twice that amount, and a much newer bankbook on a Grand Cayman Island bank that contained only one entry—a receipt dated last week for a deposit of three million dollars. The personal ID information was thoughtfully, or perhaps stupidly, noted in ink on the envelope that the book had come in as PIN and MMN—which must mean mother's maiden name because it was followed by the word Oglethorpe. That might be a very noble surname, but I could see why Brenda Benedict was so anxious to take Don Benedict's name, and keep it. I kept the last name Fuller, even after I divorced Griff, because I felt the same way about my maiden name of O'Toole.

There was also a passport with, of course, a stunningly attractive passport photo of Francesca, a birth certificate, social security card and a handwritten document: "I, Francesca Benedict Etheridge, give and bequeath all my earthly possessions to my beloved husband Theodore Etheridge." The date was five years earlier, before Francesca met Griff. It was a handwritten will. Unless there was another copy, she could have voided it at any point by simply tearing it up but she hadn't. There was also a small sad packet of pictures of Francesca and Isadora with their parents—a handsome young family with seemingly endless happiness in their faces. Then there were pictures of the girls with their father. As the girls got older the pictures were of just the two girls together, and at last each one separately.

The phone rang, and I jumped as if someone had zapped me with a cattle prod. It was Ambrose and his tone was urgent. "Mrs. Madrone needs to see you now. We're at the airport." He gave me explicit directions to the terminal. "Mention her name and ask for the VIP lounge. And bring everything you've got on that Job Skill Center and the Benedicts."

I wrapped everything but the Grand Cayman bankbook in its original plastic wrapper and put them back in the refrigerator. Then I put the bankbook in a Ziplock bag and put that in another and buried it underneath the litter in Raoul's litterbox, which was an elaborate model with a privacy shield that appeared to be more for human than feline benefit.

I made it to the airport in a little over an hour, thanking the wardrobe goddesses that I had set out the dress and accessories I had meant to wear the next week to make my report to Mrs. Madrone. Dropping her name worked its magic and I found myself in a plush airport VIP lounge I hadn't known existed. Ambrose met me and ushered me down a passageway into an even more exclusive room. Mrs. Madrone looked elegant, with a thick cashmere wool coat and pantsuit the color of champagne shielding her thin frame from the slightest breeze. Her pewter colored hair was tightly coiled under an elegant asymmetrical hat with a feather that gave her a roguish air. She sat in her travel wheelchair, conferring with a man who might have been Mr. Cavendish's older, taller brother—for all I know he was. He had seated himself on one of the armchairs so as not force her to look up, but Mrs. Madrone saw me and wheeled over. The Cavendish clone followed a pace or two behind.

"Josephine." No one introduced me.

"Hi, Mrs. Madrone. I take it this is about Delores Patton and Mr. Cavendish?" I said. No sense bothering with formalities, she never did.

"Judging from the phone calls I'm getting this morning, you've met Cromwell Cavendish?"

"He was in Delores Patton's office yesterday when I went to ask her what the center's connection was with Matt Gunther. I have a picture of her at a day care center opening in California with him and Brenda Benedict. That seemed odd, since Brenda Benedict's daughter was threatening the Women's Job Skill Center with legal action. If Delores knew the family, why not just pick up the phone when the daughter made threats? No one had said anything about the center or Delores Patton being connected to the Benedict family or to the Gunther campaign."

"Have you found anything to connect them?" she asked.

"So far not directly. That's where Mr. Cavendish comes in. He suggested that whatever evidence there might be, like the picture I found on the Internet, it would disappear shortly, and it would be dangerous for me to pursue it."

"Did you mention the Madrone Foundation?"

"No. But they might have figured it out when I said they were under consideration for a grant. I'd run out of options to get more information by volunteering there. Also, Teddy Etheridge came in and made a pest of himself and got me, um, ousted."

I didn't want to use the "F" word in front of my boss. No sense tempting fate.

"From a volunteer job," Ambrose murmured.

"All right, all right," I said. "I apologize for Teddy being involved. It was an accident, and I did go to lunch with him, which might have been unwise. He's involved somehow with the Benedict family. Before I say much more I should find out if this gentleman is someone I should talk in front of."

"This is Prescott Sloan. He might be useful to you as a trial attorney."

Sloan stepped forward. "Anything you say will come under attorney-client privilege." His voice was as dry as his handshake. "I'd appreciate it if you didn't confess to murder. If you did it, I can still defend you, I just don't want to hear it," he said, and then moved back to Mrs. Madrone's side.

"Don't worry Mr. Sloan, I haven't killed anyone. Although the day is yet young."

No one laughed. It was a tough crowd. I gave them a brief rundown of what I had found out to date. I included the discovery of the bankbook. Mrs. Madrone looked at her watch.

"I must go. These gentlemen will go back to the apartment with you. I think we'd all be much more comfortable if that bankbook was in safe hands."

I looked at all of them uncertainly. "You realize that whoever has that bankbook essentially has three million dollars at his or her disposal. I mean, I'm not a total idiot, but I feel somewhat responsible because it landed in my freezer." I took a deep breath. "What do you plan to do with it?"

"Josephine." Mrs. Madrone wheeled close enough to put a cold hand on mine. "Your freezer is not a safe-deposit box. I trusted you with a million dollars of my money, not that long ago. My trust was rewarded. Can't you trust me? After all, this is not money that belongs to any of us."

"Yeah, but I only just met this guy."

"But you do trust Ambrose."

I looked at Ambrose. "Yes. I do."

"And you trust me." It wasn't a question, but she raised one pale eyebrow.

"Yes, ma'am."

"There might be someone with access to your building searching it at this very moment, might there not?"

She was right, we hadn't changed the front door locks. Dick Slattery could be picking the new lock at this very moment. "Okay. Let's go."

Mrs. Madrone signaled the conclusion of the interview by gesturing for her nurse Constancia to come wheel her to her next destination.

Sloan, Ambrose and I set off in our respective cars to my apartment. Ambrose led the way in his black Taurus, I followed and Sloan tracked us calmly in a Mercedes.

Sloan glanced in dismay when we came into the apartment. "It's always like this," Ambrose said to him, earning me an eloquent look from Sloan. I went straight to the litter box. I took off the removable "privacy" hood and proceeded to run the scoop through the litter. No plastic-wrapped bankbook surfaced. It didn't look as if Raoul had been in the box—he usually piled all the litter into one corner and then tried to scratch down the sides and the wall outside the box as well. He was very good at covering things up. I didn't really see him as absconding with a bankbook though. I picked up the entire litter pan and looked under it and all around it. No sign of a bankbook. So much for my great hiding place.

"I wonder if they took the stuff out of the freezer."

We went into the kitchen. I washed my hands at the sink. They waited patiently. When I opened the freezer door, the plastic-wrapped parcel was still there. I spread it out on the table and Sloan and Ambrose looked at each item thoroughly.

"Who did you give the key to, after you changed the locks?" Ambrose asked.

"I haven't given one to Maxine yet, so Slattery couldn't have gotten one from her. Once her locks are changed it should be safe to let her have the tenants' keys. She's the manager," I explained to Sloan, who just nodded. After witnessing my housekeeping, any atrocity was possible. This guy was not getting an invitation for lentil soup. Although after watching me rake through the litter box, I doubted if he could have unpried his lips to permit a spoon to enter.

"I'll explain later," Ambrose said.

"That's fine," Sloan said heartily. "This will be enough to convince the people I'll be talking to that more threats would be unwise."

He led the way back to the front door.

"Could it be in one of the other boxes?" Ambrose asked,

as we passed the stacks of bankers boxes that lined the wall in the front room.

Sloan looked at him in horror. I figured with his billable hourly rate, for him to spend hours looking through the contents of stacks of boxes must be the equivalent of hiring a neurosurgeon to paint your kitchen.

"That doesn't make sense," I said. "If someone took it out of the place where I hid it—which they would have had to do in the last two hours, incidentally—why hide it here again? Why not just take it?"

"Why not indeed?" Sloan turned to Ambrose. "They were watching the apartment. I'd suggest getting someone in to sweep it for bugs, Terrell, but there's nothing left to steal. Nice to meet you, Ms. Fuller."

"Thanks for stopping by." I held the door for him.

He turned on his heel and started down the stairs.

Ambrose leaned close to me as he went through the door. "Call Mulligan," he hissed. "Make sure he doesn't have this. Let me know."

The door closed behind them and I went back to the pot with the lentil soup and stirred it. The spinach was almost melted but not quite yet. I called Mulligan and got his machine. I left a message asking if he had noticed anything odd when cleaning out Raoul's litter box.

The bookstore where the event was held was near Francesca's townhouse. I still had time before the signing so I decided to drop by and see if Brenda Benedict was still there. I suppose I rang her doorbell because I didn't expect her to talk to me. I half expected the door to be answered by one of the bodyguards who had been escorting Matt Gunther.

I rang the doorbell again. When a woman's voice answered, I explained who I was and said that we had met at Teddy Etheridge's place. She didn't ask why I wanted to talk to her, but she did buzz me in. I wondered if she would slam the door in my face once she recognized me, but she waved when I rounded the glass trophy case at the head of the stairs. All the athletic trophies had been removed and now it stood open, its contents spread out on the floor around it.

I paused, astounded at the edge of the room.

I have never been a tidy person, but I had to grant that Brenda Benedict had created a howling wilderness from what had been an extraordinarily neat and almost sterile apartment. The table that had been draped with a drop cloth for Francesca to organize her climbing equipment was now stacked with towering piles of miscellaneous stuff. Papers, clothes and electronic equipment leaned on one another in unsteady piles.

I always enjoyed meeting someone who was an even worse housekeeper than me.

Most of the furniture had been unceremoniously pushed to one side and the gleaming hardwood floor was littered with take-out Styrofoam containers and undiscarded coffee cups.

"Sorry about the mess," Brenda said, gracefully indicating the chaos around her as if it were a minor inconvenience. "Matt's people helped while they were here, but they went back with him to California. I've been trying to sort out Fran's things."

I smiled, thinking how popular Brenda must be with Matt's bodyguards if picking up after her was included in the job description. Then it hit me. "Too bad there's no one to help." She didn't have any "people" of her own—which must be the equivalent of living on the corner in a cardboard box to some people. "I hadn't realized that Fran had so much—stuff," I said, unable to keep the astonishment out of my voice.

Brenda examined me for a moment, perhaps wondering if she was going to try to enlist my aid. My clutter-level was about a tenth of what I was looking at, but she had still picked the wrong person if she wanted organizational or tidying help.

She moved closer. I found myself taking a step backward.

"It's true then." Brenda's voice grew slightly throaty as if she were suddenly aroused to total interest. "You were here in my daughter's apartment, the day she died."

I looked at her with alarm and then realized that the suddenly husky voice indicated that Brenda was about to start to seduce someone into something they didn't want to do. I was the designated someone, but I didn't think it had to do with housecleaning.

A direct attack was my only hope. "You didn't find it, did you?"

"It?"

"The bankbook that contains the money you paid Francesca not to publish the book she'd written about you."

"That's ridiculous!" she said a little too quickly. The small, delicate woman stared at me in consternation. "Where did you ever hear such nonsense?" I could see why her acting career had stalled—she was a rotten liar. Maybe she was better when she wasn't rattled, but my words had frightened her.

"I had it in my hands earlier this morning."

She shifted gears from indignation to kittenish flirtation instantly. "Did you? Where is it now?"

I smiled and said nothing.

"What do you want?"

"What have you got to offer?"

"If you have my daughter's personal papers, they would be worth getting back." Another instant gearshift and now she was hard as nails. "I don't have a lot of money on me, but I could get some. I'm assuming you wouldn't take a check."

"Would you?"

"No." Brenda Benedict smiled, and I could see why Wolf compared her to an insect who devours her mate—but did she eat her young as well? "I need to be sure you're going to keep it confidential. It's no one's business but my own."

"In other words, the funds in that bank account are illegal."

"It was a private matter. I gave my daughter some money. She's dead now. She can't use it, I want it back."

"Except that you can't find where she put it."

She threw up her hands, indicating the chaos around her, and sighed gustily. "No," she said.

"Are you staying here?"

"Yes," she said grimly. "Until I find what I need to find."

"I'll call you." I got the number from her and left her standing among the piles of things. I heard a tremendous crash as I started down the stairs. My guess was she had just toppled one of those leaning piles of clutter in a fit of pique. As I neared the bottom of the stairs, I looked up to see Brenda Benedict at the top of the stairwell, hands on her hips, regarding me with a cold, hard stare that made the hairs prickle on the back of my neck.

A man came up behind her and said something softly to her. I reached out and gripped the railing to keep from falling because my knees gave way under me.

The man whispering in Brenda Benedict's ear was Dick Slattery.

I forced myself to keep walking and just before the door shut behind me I looked over my shoulder in the earnest hope that I was mistaken, maybe that wasn't really him. But he met my eyes and smiled. If he was the one who made that phone call, could Brenda have been playing the horror film actress and screaming in the background? Or worst of all, did they have Lucille hidden somewhere and in dire trouble? I couldn't think of any evidence of possible foul play to warrant asking the police to intervene. For all I knew Gonick was right and it was a prank.

I had planned to stop for a sandwich somewhere before the book signing, but the encounter with Brenda Benedict had taken away my appetite. I ended up getting to Yellow Brick Road Books early. It turned out to be an unexpectedly calm haven. The store specialized in lesbian and gay books (if Ambrose were around I would have included "transgendered" in that list—although I didn't actually see any books addressing that group I'm sure they were there). But another area of interest for the owners were all things outdoor and natural. The Rainy Day Press authors fit right in. Teddy Etheridge was there. He waved and I started to approach him, but before I could get across the crowded room, the event had begun.

Tables and seating for the event had been set up at the back of the large, square bookstore. People who had been milling around all found seats and the event began. Rainy Day Press books all had a homemade, local, folksy quality. Isadora Freechild read some meditations on nurturing the inner child and followed it up with a recipe for a date and almond confection, which one of her supporters had brought along on a large plate. A local Native American poet read some of his poems while accompanying himself on a drum. The author of *How Green Is Your Money?*, a book on ecologically-friendly investing, offered those who bought a book a raffle ticket for a chance to win a free financial consultation. Teddy finished up the presentation by reading from his *Bumbling in the Rain* and reducing everyone to hysterical laughter.

After the readings, each author moved to a station behind a stack of books and waited for those who bought them to bring them to be signed. There was a little flurry of getting books and signing and a buzz of conversation as this process began.

Isadora Freechild had several followers grouped around her table lending moral support. Most of them looked as if they had come directly from the great outdoors. I noticed Juno and Darryl standing at the edge of the crowd and looking at the poster of Isadora and her late lover, Sandy. The picture had been taken during a climb—I wondered if it was the one that claimed Sandy's life. Darryl and Juno seemed to be communing with their dead daughter.

A woman stuck a plate of almond-studded dates under my nose. I took one. It wasn't bad. The woman who had brought them showed me the recipe in Isadora's cookbook. I bit the bullet, or rather the almond-date mixture, and bought a copy of *Finding Your Vegetarian Inner Child*. It was worth buying a book to sample a few. I decided I would test out that recipe.

Isadora appeared to vaguely remember me, but she seemed a little glazed. I wondered if she was on some kind of tranquilizer. To come out to perform at an event after the death of a relative must be like sandpaper on a raw wound. She didn't even seem to really see me until I put the book in front of her and then her eyes fastened on me as if I were the answer to some private prayer.

"Thanks for coming," she said hoarsely. I had noticed when she read from her book that her voice was unusually husky. Suddenly I wondered if it could have been her making the threatening calls.

"It looks like you picked up a cold," I said.

"Like you care," she whispered, signing the book and pushing it back to me.

"We all care, Dora," said a voice behind me. It was Juno. She and Darryl had come up to stand nearby. The protective note in Juno's voice made me wonder, with a thrill of fear, whether many of Isadora's circle felt that I was a threat to her. If they felt strongly enough about taking care of her, Isadora herself would not have to do anything. If Juno and Darryl had been following Isadora the day we had lunch, someone might have followed me as well and found out where I lived.

"Thank you," I said, taking the book and moving on to the next table.

There wasn't much of a crowd around Teddy's table. I picked up a copy of his new book. He beamed at me with that extremely grateful look that I recognized from having been to book signings in the past.

"Jo, it's so good to see you here. Thanks for coming."

"I saw from your website that you had changed publishers, and you would be here."

He managed a sigh. "Yes. They're very nice to me." He glanced around to see if anyone from Rainy Day Press was in earshot, and lowered his voice, "Unfortunately they're almost as broke as I am."

"I've got my fingers crossed for you," I said.

"Dear Jo, thanks." He stared at me fondly. "You're a sweet kid, and I'd keep my fingers crossed too, but then I wouldn't be able to sign the book for you. Do you want it inscribed?"

I said, "Yes, please." But all I could think of was whether his voice was the one that had frightened me at three in the morning. First Isadora, now Ted—I would have suspected Juno or Darryl but I was pretty sure they didn't have my number.

I watched while he thought, wrote and then signed with a large flourish. "Teddy, I didn't know you had moved. I was afraid you might have left town."

"No such luck. I found a less expensive place. No sense keeping that one bedroom if there was no chance Lucille would be back to share it."

"Right, your neighbor said she saw her drive off with another man."

"The woman with the golden retriever, I'll bet anything. I wouldn't take her too seriously. That must be the best-walked dog in North America."

"The only reason is that I've had a couple of weird phone calls."

"That's not good. Did you tell the police?" Teddy seemed concerned. If he was the threatening caller he was a good liar.

"I did talk to the police, but they can't do much unless they call again and I get it on tape. They thought it might be a crank, but it's the second one I've gotten. The reason I mention that Lucille might be involved with someone else is that the last call seemed to be threatening her."

"What!" He leaped to his feet. Isadora, Juno and Darryl were leaning close to listen and most of the customers in the store had turned to stare. Ted looked around and sat down and leaned forward to whisper. "I need to talk to you, Jo, but I can't leave here for another hour. I don't want to offend anyone."

"Can you give me a number to call you, Ted? I've got people coming to my place in an hour, so I would have to call you tomorrow. Lucille came by my place yesterday and, you're right, there are a couple of things we should talk about."

"She left it with you didn't she?" He looked at me sharply. "Don't pretend, she told me she did."

"So she has been in touch?"

"Yes. She called."

"When did you last talk to her?"

"Yesterday afternoon, why?"

"Because the threatening phone call was this morning."

"I don't have a number you can reach me at. Can I call you this evening?"

"After nine, I have some people coming by. Gotta go."

I left with my purchases, feeling vaguely uneasy. Well, of course I would, I was on my way to an exorcism.

The book signing had taken longer than expected and I arrived a few minutes after eight to find Maxine waiting in the hall outside the apartment with three other women. It must have felt odd to all of them to wait outside. Maxine, as the manager, did have a key. "Josie, you remember Joan, Patrice and Cora."

"Sure, hi." They had all been at Nina's apartment a month or so earlier, and had helped go through her belongings, taking as mementos things that meant something to them. I opened the door, and they came in.

Joan Leti, who was Samoan, and substantially larger than I, possessed the mellowest temperament of anyone I had ever met. Today, she wore an embroidered top that was almost long enough to qualify as a dress. I was happy to see she had brought one of her legendary casseroles. "Beth couldn't come—she has auditors," Joan said.

"Talk about a fun weekend," said Patrice, who was an almost equally large African-American woman, with an attitude at the volcanic opposite end of the mellowness scale. Her clothing was usually as hot as the homemade salsa and chips she brought. Today she was dressed in a neon green sweater and leggings with gold dangling earrings.

Cora, who was incredibly quiet, brought a salad and came

dressed in her usual gray sweatsuit, as if to conceal her lush, hourglass figure. I noticed that the rest of the women in the group treated her as if she were a pre-school child. I guessed it must be her extreme shyness.

"She said to let her know more in advance next time we get together," Maxine said. Hope trailed after her mother carrying the cheese and crackers they had brought. Everyone trooped in and headed for the kitchen.

Maxine was filling the kettle for tea by the time I got there. "Scar is coming soon with her sister, the psychic," she said.

Patrice was opening up a cupboard to bring out glasses. They knew the place better than I did. These women were like one of those pit crews at the auto races. I stood back and let them organize it.

Joan was getting out dishes for her casserole. "There's something on the stove, Jo."

"Oh, my God the lentil soup."

Joan lifted the lid, inspected it and gave it a quick stir. "It looks good, Jo. Why don't you reheat it for your lunch tomorrow; we've brought enough for tonight."

"Uh, okay," I said a little dubiously. "I really appreciate you all coming, but, uh, what exactly did you have in mind?"

"We'll start with some coffee and tea," Maxine said.

"Oh, sorry. I haven't had many visitors in—well, hardly ever . . ." I trailed behind them into the kitchen. These women had been in the apartment visiting Nina there every other week or so for years. They had organized chips, homemade dip, cheese and crackers, Joan's casserole and salad onto trays and brought it into the front room with plates, silverware and napkins.

"I'm taking that king-sized armchair," Patrice called, out, heading for that very comfortable wing chair.

"Do you need anything?" Joan asked, hovering over the sofa.

"No thanks, just make yourselves comfortable," I said. Hope sat on the floor, and Cora followed me back into the kitchen to get a chair.

"Maybe I should bring two chairs," Cora said.

"Okay," I said, checking the burner under the kettle. "I'll be in there in a minute." I got out some tea and coffee, and even found an unopened box of Girl Scout cookies—somehow that seemed appropriate. When the water boiled I poured it out, and brought the tray in. The women were joking among themselves, and I watched them at a loss for words. I went back and got the other two kitchen chairs and sat on one. They talked about mundane things. Being a loner came naturally, so sitting with these people, Nina's friends, felt strange. I did notice, however, that at least with them in the apartment I wasn't afraid.

Of course, we hadn't gone into the bedroom where Nina died. I wondered if that was Maxine's plan, or Scar's-sister-the-psychic's plan. The doorbell rang.

"I'll get it," Maxine said. A moment later she ushered two very thin women into the living room.

The younger one was Hope's friend Scar. She was rail thin as I had remembered, she still had a dark rinse over her brown hair, and she wore the leather jacket I'd always seen her wear before. The woman with her bore a family resemblance in the thinness and pale face, but her hair was brown with gray streaks, and she wore a long skirt and a black turtleneck sweater. She carried a box that resembled a cardboard pet carrier.

"This is my sister, Melanie the psychic," Scar said a little shyly. I remembered that Scar was short for Scarlett, and guessed their mother must be a serious *Gone with the Wind* fan.

Melanie lightened the mood a little by punching her sister

on the arm. "I do have an actual last name, Scar." She turned to us good-humoredly. "It's Paulson."

Maxine introduced everyone, and we all shook hands. I poured cups of tea for everyone, but noticed no one was touching any of the food, and barely sipping the tea. With all these people around, I wasn't afraid. But I did feel tense. If nothing else, Maxine appeared to have totally put aside her anguish over Dick Slattery. If it didn't help me, at least it was distracting her.

"Shall we do this first and eat later?" Melanie asked.

"Where do you want to start?" Maxine asked.

Melanie turned to me. "Maxine said you feel uneasy in the apartment. Is there a room where you feel the most comfortable?"

"Here in the living room." I knew Maxine had told her, and probably everyone, what I was going through, but I felt foolish and a little ashamed. If I had been a stronger person, I wouldn't have been afraid.

"We'll start here," Melanie said. "Do you mind if I light some candles?"

"I have electric light. But sure."

She lit candles more or less in all four corners of the room, and then turned off the lamps I had turned on against the evening gloom. All the women watched her with interest. No one said anything.

We settled into a rough circle with the sofa and the chairs at either end and the kitchen chairs facing them. Scar sat on the floor but Melanie sat next to me. "Maxine, pull your chair over so you can touch Jo, and I can reach your hand."

The three of us ended up in an awkward triangle of kitchen chairs. Everyone else leaned forward to watch.

"We're going to ask your mind-body what it's afraid of,"

Melanie said companionably. "Maxine will answer for it by hand testing."

"Uh . . ." I didn't have the faintest idea what they were talking about, but I said, "Okay."

"Don't worry," Melanie said, "her body can pick up on what your body knows. I'll show you. Maxine hold out your hand, now say, 'yes.' "

Maxine complied.

"Now say, 'no.' Did you see how her hand stayed steady when she said *yes*, and dipped down when she said *no*?"

"I think I did," I said, not totally clear.

"We're going to ask your mind-body yes or no questions, and see if it can tell us what's happening here."

"Okay. But I already know that I don't know what's happening here."

"That's your conscious mind. If your conscious mind knew what the problem was, you'd be telling us, right?"

"Okay, that makes sense."

She proceeded to ask if it was okay to do this work.

The answer was *yes*. I thought it was nice that my mind-body, whatever that was, had decided to be cooperative. It wasn't like it wanted me to be anxious, right?

There were several health questions, and then she asked if this fear of the apartment was due to Nina's death.

The answer was *no*.

We all got more interested. "Is it something that happened in the apartment?"

Again, *no*.

"Is it something that happened in the building?"

Yes.

We all leaned forward. "Is it something that happened around the time Nina died?"

The answer was, *Maybe yes, maybe no.*

"Was it something that happened on this floor of the building?"

No.

That was puzzling. She asked again if it was something in the building. *Yes.*

"Something that happened in Maxine's apartment?"

When Melanie asked the question, I immediately thought of Slattery, but the answer was, *no.*

"Something that happened in the basement?"

Now I thought of Mulligan; Hope's boyfriend, now in prison; and the bloody axe stuck in my packing box. But the answer was, *no.*

"Ask if it was something that happened in the apartment beneath this one?" Maxine asked.

Yes.

"Eric." Maxine, Hope and I all said the name at once. The very name sent a chill down my spine.

"Is it something to do with Eric?" Melanie asked.

Yes.

"Isn't he in jail awaiting trial?" I asked.

"Well, his body may be in jail but—" Before Melanie could finish there was a knock at the door.

We all looked at each other, and I realized that the anxiety I had felt was now shared by everyone in the room. I took a deep breath, and went to answer the door, fully expecting, for no rational reason, that it would be Eric.

It was Mulligan. He looked at the women in a circle, the darkened apartment and the flickering candles. "I think I've just stumbled into every man's worst nightmare," he said with an uncertain grin.

Everyone laughed. "No, no, come in, come in," Maxine

said, glancing at Melanie who shrugged. "We were just about to do a ritual sacrifice of the male visitor."

"That's it—I'm outta here."

"No, really it's okay," Hope said.

"You're welcome to join, if you want," Melanie said.

Mulligan came in. "So what *are* you doing?"

Hope was eager to explain. "This is Scar's sister Melanie, the psychic. She's going to exorcise whatever it is that's scaring Josephine."

I felt everyone looking at me, and began to blush. "I don't know if it will work," I said.

"Hey, if it works, that's great," Mulligan said unexpectedly. "Is it for women only or can I sit in?"

"Please," Joan gestured to a place next to her on the sofa, and Mulligan went to sit there. I remembered that Joan had always been interested in Mulligan in a romantic way. I hadn't thought it was possible to feel even more alone and miserable, but that certainly added to my hopeless feeling.

"Don't let me stop you—go ahead," Mulligan said.

"She just asked if it was in the apartment below this one, and it said *yes*," Hope said, bringing him up to date.

Mulligan raised his eyebrows. "It?"

"Josephine's mind-body, Melanie is asking it what's she's scared of," Hope said.

"Shhh," Maxine said fiercely.

"So whatever is bothering Josephine is in the apartment below this one?" Melanie asked.

Yes.

"Is it something that is in the building now?"

Yes.

"Is it in the apartment below this one now?"

Yes.

"Should we go down to that apartment to purify it?"

Yes.

"Well, I guess we'd better go down there," Melanie said. "Do you have keys?"

"Yes," both Maxine and I answered at once.

"But there's no heat or electricity down there," Maxine said. "They just finished painting Thursday."

I found that I was starting to shudder just a little at the thought of going down there in the cold, dark apartment that had once been Eric's.

"Do you have any more candles?" Melanie asked. "I probably have enough, but just to make sure."

"I've got some utility candles in the kitchen," I said.

"That's good," Melanie said. "If you don't have holders for them bring tin foil, and we can improvise."

"Didn't Nina used to have some decorative candles in the bedroom?" Mulligan said helpfully.

I was irritated by the faint pause. Certain that every woman in the room was absorbing the fact that although he had been going out with me, he hadn't been in the bedroom recently enough to know if there were candles there.

"I don't know," I said. "That room freaks me out a little." Now I was starting to flush with anger rather than embarrassment, and it drove out the fear.

"I'll check," said Hope, leaping up to do so.

No one but me was afraid of that bedroom. Hope came out with three beautiful layered wax candles. I fetched the box of utility candles and the tin foil from the kitchen. We set off to go one floor down although it seemed like a much longer journey.

We trooped downstairs, keeping close together. I wasn't the only one unsettled by the proceedings. Maxine, who had a key ring with all the apartment keys on it, opened the apartment below. The hall was bright because the hall lights had come on for the night. Everyone looked at Melanie once Maxine had unlocked the door. It was very dark inside. Melanie put her carrier down, pulled out a candle, and lit it with a wooden match. Then she led the way into the apartment. It smelled of recently dried paint.

"Everyone take a candle," Melanie said, and we each took one of Nina's large, decorative candles, or one of the utility candles. We each lit our candle from hers. Our candles illuminated the empty apartment and cast flickering shadows. Our footsteps echoed on the freshly-waxed hardwood. We all looked at the floor.

"I am not sitting on that floor," Patrice said.

"I could sit on the floor," Joan said gently, "but getting back up again might be a problem."

"How about if I go get some chairs from upstairs? I think Nina even had a couple of folding chairs," Mulligan suggested.

"I'll go too," I said with alacrity. "I can carry a chair or two."

"Okay. Go ahead. Meantime I'll light more candles. We won't start till you get back."

"I'll go too," Hope said.

I realized as we went back out into the brightly lit hall that I had been shivering in that apartment, not just from cold. Whatever fear I had felt in Nina's apartment had been doubled in the place where Eric had lived. Mulligan must have noticed because he put his arm around my shoulders, and squeezed me close.

"That apartment hasn't been heated in a couple months," he said. "Let's get you a sweater or something—most of this is just cold."

I nodded. "Yeah. But some of it isn't," I said. "Did you get my message? We have to talk," I whispered.

"Later," he said.

"Okay."

We went back upstairs and I opened the door to the apartment. I got another heavy sweater and put it on over the one I was wearing. Mulligan found three folding chairs, and gave them to Hope to carry. She went ahead, while he and I each carried two kitchen chairs. By the time we got back downstairs, Hope had already gone in, and was setting up the folding chairs.

Maxine held the door open for us. "Ladies and gentlemen, circle the wagons. I mean, the chairs." She was recuperating from her heartbreak over Slattery in record time.

We went back in. The place didn't seem quite as cold with the sweater, but I was still trembling a little. The last time I had been here, it had been dark, lit only by flickering computer screens, and Eric had had a knife.

Melanie had unpacked her case a little more, and closed it back up to use it as an improvised tabletop to set up more candles, matches and various bundles. She finished making a little candleholder out of a square of tinfoil crumpled into a flat base at the bottom of a utility candle. All the candles were now on the case. As Melanie instructed, we pulled the chairs into a circle around the flickering candles.

"Nine people and seven chairs," I pointed out.

"I can stand," Mulligan volunteered.

"Someone can have my chair," Melanie said, "I'll be walking around most of the time."

"No, no," Scar said, sinking down to sit cross-legged, "I'd rather sit on the floor."

"Me too," Hope said, joining her friend on the floor.

Then Melanie lit the last four new candles, and began to talk as she lit them. I wasn't able to follow a lot of what she said. Something about stationing candles in the four directions. She consulted a compass on a cord around her neck to determine north, south, east and west. She continued to talk about the properties of each direction, and protection of elemental forces in drawing a circle around the space. Her words were soothing, perhaps hypnotic, and the shaking I had felt began to die down.

Then Melanie lit a small bundle of what proved to be white sage, wrapped up with twine, and blew on it. It burned for an instant, and then began to smoke. It was a pleasant smell, which was good because she waved it over each of us in turn, and then went round the perimeter waving smoke around the edges of the invisible circle she had described.

Then she stood for a moment at the center of the circle in a mediative stance. "The force I am feeling is the energy of an unhappy young man. He's not a ghost, he's still alive, but imprisoned."

"If it's Eric, he's in the county jail awaiting trial," Maxine said gruffly.

"That would explain why he's so unhappy," Melanie said.

"He loved this place. He wants to be here. But he did great wrong, and he must not come back here. He lives in fear of the people around him. His only joy is gone, so he visits this place in his mind constantly. That's why you feel his presence."

"His only joy," I said, surprised to find myself speaking. "That must be computers. They probably don't have computers in the county jail."

"That, and—he loved the woman in the apartment above this. He is grieving for her."

"Nina," Patrice breathed out the word.

"Yes. He loved her. And—" Melanie turned to me suddenly, causing me to jump slightly on the folding chair when she focused on me. "He hates you."

"Oh," was all I could say. I was glad that Mulligan was sitting next to me. I didn't touch his shoulder. But he reached out, and took my hand, for which I was pathetically grateful in a way that had nothing to do with any romantic bonding.

"I am asking his mind-body if it knows that this hatred destroys him as well as others," Melanie said, cocking her head as if listening for an answer. "I'm getting a *no*."

"*No*, he doesn't know it? Or *no* he doesn't believe it?" I asked.

Melanie asked each question aloud, and reported back, "Doesn't know it, doesn't believe it."

She asked if he realized he was hurting himself. *Yes*.

"Do you want to hurt yourself?" *Yes*.

"Is it because you hurt other people?" *No*.

"Is it because you hate yourself?" *Yes*.

"Would you like me to heal that in you?" Melanie paused for a moment. "He doesn't seem to know. May I try?" She wasn't asking us. No one made a sound. Melanie paused again, and appeared to be listening to something none of the rest of us could hear. "*Maybe yes, maybe no*. I'm going to try."

She put the sage bundle down on in an abalone shell on top of her case. A trickle of smoke ran up from the bundle. For the next few moments she murmured to herself about clearing meridians and running energy, while she made passes through the air that appeared to have a purpose I could not fathom. At last she said, "I think I cleared him. He's sleeping now, and although I don't have any way of proving that, I'll bet he really is. But I have to tell his mind-body he can't come back here. What's his name—Eric?"

We all nodded.

"He's a sick puppy. Eric, you need to stay in your body, and concentrate on where you are right now. You are in a dangerous place. You want out, but you have no choice but to stay there for now. If you send your energy to scare Jo here, it will bounce back, and pull danger to you. So—don't—do—it. I am going to seal this space with salt. You will not come back." She took out a shaker of sea salt, and carried it into each corner of the room, poured a small amount into her hand, and from there into the corner.

Soon afterward she closed down the circle—she was using much more poetic language than that, but I didn't grasp the sense of it beyond that concept. She took up her sage and salt, and gestured for us to follow her from room to room while she circled the other rooms in the apartment, fanned sage smoke along the perimeter, and poured salt in the corners.

"Now, let's go upstairs, we can bring the chairs later. This won't take long," Melanie instructed. We trooped upstairs carrying candles in the brightly lit hallway, and went into Nina's apartment, where Melanie repeated the same sage and salt routine with each room. I caught my breath when she led us down that short hall, which always seemed too long to me, and we entered the room where Nina had been murdered. We turned on the lights, but left the candles burning.

"I don't sense any presence here," Melanie said, after standing a moment near where the bed had been. "I think the problem was from below." She indicated the apartment below. "He really cared about her, and resented you. I think that's the root of it. But, Jo, you have to let go of your guilt. That's the chink in your armor that let him in. You are not responsible for Nina's death. You had no part in it. Do you want to contact her spirit?"

I realized, standing in the room where my best friend had died, that tears were streaming down my face. Mulligan had taken my hand again, and I gripped his as if it were a lifeline. I couldn't say anything.

"Yes," Mulligan said.

"Jo?" Melanie prompted me.

"Okay," I said. My nose was running, and Maxine pulled a pack of tissues out of her sweater pocket and handed me one. I let go of Mulligan's hand to take it. I wasn't about to put down the candle in my other hand.

"She has moved on, but she can come back for a moment. Does she have a message to you? Yes, all she has to say is that she has paid her karmic debts for this life, and moved on. You need to live your lives now, and not worry about her. That's all." Melanie looked at me kindly.

"Does that make sense to you?"

"Yes," I said, sniffling into the tissue again.

"Are you still afraid?"

I took a shaky breath and considered. "No." I shook my head, marveling at the fact that the absence of fear, like the absence of pain, was so clear. "I don't think so. Sad, but not afraid."

One of the other women sniffled and Maxine handed round more tissues.

"Good. I put a seal around this room, just to make sure we don't have any more problems, but I think our work here is done. We can go back in the living room now, and finish up."

Melanie concluded the ceremony, ritual—whatever it was—and snuffed out each of the candles. Then we helped her pack up her implements, went down, and brought the chairs back up. Then we followed her down to Maxine's place as if unwilling to let her go.

Everyone hugged everyone before Melanie and Scar left. Joan, Patrice and Cora said goodnight to her, but almost immediately afterward they left as well. Mulligan and I were left standing in Maxine's apartment.

"Jo, I want to rent that apartment below yours. Is it okay?" Mulligan said, tentatively.

"Yes," I said slowly, as if testing the word.

"Well, that's great," Maxine said, gruffly. "If that's what you kids want. Let me just get the keys and rental agreements." She went into her spare bedroom, which was also her office. We followed her as far as the doorway, but the message light was blinking on her answering machine.

"Just a minute, I've got a message." Mulligan and I backed out of the room to give her privacy.

"You sure you're okay with this?" Mulligan asked, while we waited. "It would be better for Raoul too, he could go between apartments through the back stairs."

"You guys are crazy," Hope said. "Everything is for the cat."

Maxine came back out of the room with a key and a rental agreement. "That was Dick Slattery," she said. "He didn't leave a message except to say he would call back shortly."

"Mom is just upset because that jerk left her for some young blonde he met here in the building," Hope said, with the cheerfulness of one whose dearest hopes have been realized.

Mulligan snorted, "A young blonde. You mean that big, strapping girl who saved Val from getting beat up by Slattery."

"I can't imagine his getting involved with Lucille Meeker," I said. "I do remember that Lucille was supposed to have a new boyfriend, but it couldn't be Slattery."

"You know her?" Maxine said. "You brought her into the building?"

"Now, Mom, if he hadn't left with that blonde he would have left with someone else sooner or later."

"Let Josephine answer my question," Maxine persisted.

"It's a very complicated situation. As far as I know Lucille and Slattery have never spoken beyond her yelling at him to stop hitting Val."

Maxine rubbed her eyes. "God, what a monster I brought on us all."

"Um, one other thing, Maxine." I told them about the phone call I had gotten threatening a blonde and ending with a scream.

"Hope is blond now," Maxine pointed out. "Maybe you should stay up here."

"I'll be okay, Mom," Hope said. "Frankly it's a relief to have my place to myself without the bird. I'm going to go down and check my locks though." But they both hugged as if departing on a long journey.

"I'll walk you down and make sure everything is secure," Mulligan said. "I'll be back in a few minutes to fill out that rental application, okay?"

Before they could leave the phone rang. This time all three of us crowded into the doorway to watch Maxine answer. "It's him," Maxine mouthed silently.

We waited. "My God! Are you sure? Where? What's the address?" She scrambled for a pen and paper and wrote down an address. "Dick, where are you—hello?"

Maxine came into the front room holding the pad of paper, her face pale. "He's killed his new girlfriend. He just told me where her body was. Will you go with me?"

31

We took my rental car because Mulligan's truck would not have held us comfortably, and Maxine's old Dodge Dart was not totally reliable. The neighborhood we were going to, out by the airport, was not the best place to be stranded with a stalled engine.

"We should call the police," Mulligan said.

"Here, use my cell phone," I told him. "Do you have Gonick's card? You could start with him."

"Maybe we should see if there is even a body. Maybe he's just jerking me around. That's why I appreciate you all coming along with me. Hell, he may just be trying to get me alone, and rob me."

I refrained from saying that he had had ample opportunity to rob her while he was living with her. Dick Slattery could have robbed all of us. I was kicking myself for not thinking of that much earlier. Before Val got hurt. Now someone might be dead.

"I'll just tell Gonick where we are," Mulligan said reasonably. "That in itself is a kind of back up." He spoke to Gonick who said he was willing to meet us at the address Slattery had given Maxine. "He said he'd like to talk to Slattery anyway."

We got to the address, and found a grimy studio apartment, converted from an old-fashioned garage behind a large old house that looked like it was being torn down from within by disgruntled renters.

"He said the body was in the front room just inside the front window," Maxine whispered, although there was no one around but Hope, Mulligan and me to hear her.

"Well, that's good to know, because I am not about to break into a house to see if there is a body in it." We all tiptoed up to the front window, and looked in, expecting a burst of shotgun fire or a yell from the neighborhood watch committee at any moment.

We gasped in unison instinctively. The flood of blond hair was just inside the window a few inches from our noses. The woman had a curtain cord wrapped several times around her neck, the ligature only partly hidden by her long mane of blond hair, her body and neck tipped at an odd angle no living person could endure. Her red, swollen face was turned slightly away from the window, and shaded by that beautiful golden hair and a white embroidered scarf that had been draped over her nose and mouth like a mask, as she hung by the neck, suspended from the curtain cord. I recognized the rain clouds and rainbows on the scarf. I felt a tremendous rush of sadness that Lucille should have died by hanging with her favorite scarf around her neck.

32

Gonick and Tarrasch arrived a few minutes later, looked in the window and made their own calls. Maxine wearily explained her connection with Slattery, and the police, with extreme delicacy, asked if they could interview her at more length, at her home the following day. I explained my encounters with Lucille, and how I recognized her scarf. They took down Lucille's parents' name and number. I was relieved that we left before they arrived.

Once we got back home, we separated in the front hallway, and went in separate directions with the alacrity of the truly exhausted. I didn't realize till I got home and stared at the wall for several minutes that I had totally forgotten to ask Mulligan whether he had found the bankbook. Only he and Maxine had the key to my place now. I called his number but got his machine again. Could he have gone back out?

Whatever Melanie did, it must have worked because the apartment didn't scare me. I didn't bother to look in the front bedroom, but I did walk into Nina's room, look around and walk out again. There was no question of sleeping there at the moment—no bed. I had no fear, but I was possessed by the kind of nervous energy that drives some people to wash and wax all their floors and reorganize their silverware drawers till all hours. There wasn't much danger of my doing that.

I tidied up the food everyone had brought, some of which my guests had kindly left, although none of them had eaten much of it. I had a few bites of everything as a kind of late supper—casserole, salad, chips, dip and Girl Scout cookies. Not bad really.

The message light was blinking and I played the message back. Mulligan's voice informed me that he had to see me right away. I had just parted from Mulligan, and the call couldn't have come in while I was there, so he must have called before Melanie did her séance or exorcism or whatever the heck it was, and I just hadn't retrieved the message.

The doorbell rang while I was listening to the second message. I let Teddy in as I heard Griff thanking me for having Wolf Lambert get in touch with him. He appreciated the alibi, even though he had to explain to Wolf that he wasn't actually married to Fran.

It took me a minute to work out that if it was Griff who had been out drinking all night with Wolf Lambert, Teddy Etheridge didn't have an alibi at all. It was too late to close the door on him, he was already inside.

"Hi, Jo, I'm sorry to bother you, but I wanted to get that thing you were telling me about before tomorrow. I'm leaving town very early, and I didn't want to wake you." He pushed past me in a way that worried me. Suddenly I noticed for the first time in a while just how big and burly he was. He could easily have overpowered me. Tiny Francesca, for all her athletic ability, wouldn't have had a chance.

"I can make some tea or would you like wine? There's something I need to tell you."

Teddy followed me into the kitchen.

My purse was on the table. "Just let me make one call before we talk." I took my cell phone out of my purse, and started dialing.

"No." Teddy took it out of my hands, and disconnected before I even heard it ring Mulligan's number. I looked at him, startled, and suddenly terrified. "Let's talk first."

"Okay, sit down Teddy." He sat on the kitchen chair within arm's reach, and I sat down as well. "It's about Lucille."

"Have you seen her?"

"Yes. Just now."

"Where is she?"

"I'm sorry to have to tell you this, but she's dead, Teddy. It seems like she was abducted by a man who killed her."

"What? How do you know this?"

"The man who killed her knows Maxine. He called and told her what he had done. We went over there. We saw the body."

"You saw Lucille's body?"

"We looked in through the window. We saw her, with that beautiful blond hair, and she was wearing that rain cloud and rainbow scarf."

For a moment a thrill of fear went through me and I wondered if Ted could have killed Lucille. No. That was impossible—Dick Slattery had almost bragged about it. Teddy sat at the table in stunned silence for several seconds, then he began to cry. "I gave her that scarf. I wanted to make it right for her. I never could make enough money to make Lucille feel secure. When Fran told me she wanted to cash in on her parents by writing a book, I helped her. But I did it for Lucille."

"You wrote Fran's book?"

He nodded, tears pouring down his cheeks. "She never even bothered to read it. The woman could barely write a grocery list. She told me the most sordid stories from her childhood and we came up with juicy exaggerations. Nothing her relatives could prove or disprove because there was a shred of truth in every yarn. She could have made a fortune and dined out on those stories for the rest of her life. We never had a contract. I did it in strictest secrecy—it was supposed to be her book. But then I didn't even own my own words." A flush of anger began to replace tears.

"I spent months on that damn book. It was a big gamble, but my Bumble series was dying. Going with Rainy Day Press was like putting it on life support. They operate on a shoestring, and pay in postage stamps. Papers were dropping my columns. This was my last chance at a nest egg."

He turned his tear-stained face to me. "You should have read it, Jo. I wrote the book Fran might have written if she'd had two brain cells to rub together. I gave her voice—reinvented her as the beautiful victim, climbing out of the wreckage of a rotten childhood and up to the heights of the tallest mountains in the world. She could have been a myth. You can't buy that kind of image. But I ran into the reality of what she was. She was a greedy little con artist and she didn't want to share."

"I understand."

"I doubt that you do. You said you have something of mine—you mean Fran's bank papers, and the will?"

"If I did?"

"Don't toy with me, Jo. My life was over the day Lucille found that bankbook in Fran's briefcase. I knew Fran had already met with her mother, but she wouldn't tell me what happened. I suggested to her that she get the book indexed. That was when she told me her mother was paying her off to withdraw the book. She didn't say she wasn't going to share the money with me, but I started to wonder. So I told her there was an even better reason to get the book indexed quickly so she could show it to some other important people we had trashed in case they might want to pay to stop it from coming out. Only she'd better do it immediately before the news got out that the book was cancelled. Fran liked that idea a lot, it appealed to her greedy nature. I told her I'd get a secretary who could work quick and cheap. I asked Lucille to set up the assignment as if it was from that Women's Job Skill Center.

"I knew Fran kept all her papers in that briefcase with her laptop. So I asked Lucille to borrow the whole thing so I could check for evidence of a pay-off. She took it, but instead of bringing it to me, she read the book, and looked at the papers. She called and told me about the bankbook. She wouldn't bring it to me. She said that wasn't right and she was taking it back to Fran. That was when I realized Fran had already been paid off and wasn't even going to tell me, let alone pay me for the months I spent writing the book.

"Ever since Lucille wrote to me that she'd been going to the Women's Job Skill Center, I'd been watching it, hoping for a glimpse of her. Instead I saw you, so I tried to get you to contact Lucille for me. I needed that bankbook. You couldn't help me, so I went to Fran and bluffed and told her I knew Brenda had paid her off and I wanted my share. But Fran just said thanks for reminding her. She picked up the phone to call the bank and tell them her papers had been stolen and get a new set. I was just another expendable stepping stone. I couldn't expose her—I was as guilty as she was."

I licked my lips. "What happened?"

"She told me to stop wasting her time. She laughed at me, and told me my books weren't funny!"

I looked at Teddy and stifled a hysterical giggle at what he had said.

"I picked up her climbing rope," he said, moving toward me as he spoke. I involuntarily took a step backward.

"She grabbed one of her ice axes and started to swing it at me, yelling at me to put her stuff down. I took the rope and wrapped it around her neck while she was yelling. She flailed at me with the axe, but she was so small, she never even touched me. I took it away. I had the rope around her neck and the axe in one hand. She kept yelling, so I tightened the rope to make her shut up. She did and I felt better. She even stopped struggling. I dropped her down on the floor but then she started clawing her way up my leg and grabbing at my crotch. I clipped her with the axe. I think I'd even forgotten it was in my hand, but when I saw her fall back on the floor I picked up the other axe." He looked at the floor and shuddered. "You saw what I did.

"Tell me I'm not funny now, bitch," he muttered.

I gulped, but didn't say a word.

"I left one axe in her chest. I put on my gloves and used her shirt to wipe the axe handle in her chest for fingerprints. Then I dipped the other axe in her blood. I wrapped it up in a plastic bag, and took it away. I was going to leave it somewhere to point at someone else."

"Why me?"

"You showed up when I came back several hours later. I arranged to meet Isadora there because I didn't want to be alone when I discovered the body. When I saw you, I thought you would be a likely candidate, and you probably had an alibi. All I needed was enough time to get the money and get away to a place with no extradition treaty. So I put it in your backyard."

"It turned up in my storage unit."

"I don't know how it got there. I left it in the trash in the backyard still wrapped in a plastic bag."

"I put it there." Both of us turned to see Dick Slattery coming into the kitchen. He was carrying a large, silver handgun. "I saw you leave the axe in the trash and I checked it out. It was too good to waste."

"Where did you come from?"

"I've been in the front bedroom since you came in."

"How did you get in?"

"I picked the lock. I had lots of time to search the place while you and Maxine and that big hulking boyfriend of yours were visiting Blondie."

Teddy clenched his fists. "You killed Lucille."

"I never caught her name, man. But yeah, I grabbed her in the parking lot and knocked her out with a lead pipe. I wanted some time with her before I killed her. Once I told Maxine, I watched you all go out. That gave me plenty of time to search your apartment. I knew you put the papers in the fridge."

"How did you know that?"

He laughed. "I heard you. The apartment below this one already had holes drilled in the ceiling, so whoever lived there could listen up here. I just enlarged them and put in a microphone—made tapes of everything. Brenda-baby gave me a credit card to buy whatever I needed in surveillance toys."

"I saw you with Brenda today, but what possible connection could you have with her?"

"She's family," Slattery said with his feral grin. "Matt Gunther is my cousin. Got me out of prison and he found me work. I think I make a good detective, don't you?" He nodded at Ted. "When Matt heard from Delores that you were watching her office, they both flipped out. Then Delores told him there was this suspicious volunteer asking all these questions. Matt started twitching like he was in the 'lectric chair. He was sure the Feds were onto the dirty campaign money he was laundering through all Delores's nonprofits. I poked around and found out she's got a couple dozen of 'em. Pity I could never get a detective license with my record."

He leered at me companionably. "I followed you back to

Seattle and got in with Maxine—which took about two seconds."

The thought of this sleazy character listening to everything that went on in my apartment made me nauseous and profoundly grateful that Mulligan and I had never given him anything really hot to listen to.

"Once I got in with Maxine, I had all the keys, so I could search your place. Never found anything official, so I'm guessing there wasn't anything to find. Still, I've got a feeling my cousin is going down soon and I better get the money and go. So hand over the bankbook."

"I gave it to the cops."

"I don't believe you."

Slattery had the gun trained on me, when Teddy rushed at him. He swung it round and pulled the trigger. The explosion was deafening in the small kitchen and I leaped for the back door before I even knew I was moving. I got to it, and was scrabbling at the chain lock when Slattery grabbed me from behind. I glanced back and saw that Teddy was down on the floor bleeding.

"Oh, my God, Ted?" I managed to get the chain off the door when I heard the sirens.

"Dick, the police are coming. It can't be the gun shot, they must have seen you."

"Give me your car keys, bitch."

"Let go of me and I will," I said, pulling free from his grip. He kept the gun trained on me while I walked past Ted, who had both arms folded across his chest. Blood was on his shirt and he was panting. I couldn't look. I took my purse, dug out the keys and handed them to Dick.

He took them, threw the back door open and slammed face-first into a trash can lid held up by Lucille.

"Lucille?"

Slattery screamed when the aluminum lid hit him. He backpedaled up as Lucille stuffed the trash can lid in his face, and charged through the door. Slattery slipped and went over backward. His gun went flying and Lucille threw herself on top of him, pressing the lid over his face and putting a knee on each arm. I scrambled to grab the gun and looked wildly around for a place to hide it. I took the lid off the lentil soup, threw it in and covered it again.

"Lucille!" Teddy and I both yelled.

Lucille looked up and saw that Ted was bleeding. "Oh, my God, Teddy, did he shoot you?"

"Here, Lucille, let me help." I put both hands on the trash can lid and carefully took her place, straddling Dick Slattery's chest with one knee pinning each arm. I was much heavier than Lucille, which brought a muffled scream from Slattery. It was an oddly intimate posture, yet totally nonsexual. He tried to thrash upward and I thought I heard a joint pop. I wondered if I was damaging him permanently. He whimpered and lay still.

Lucille went to put her arms around Teddy, who stared at her in wonderment. "You said she was dead," he said.

"I thought she was." I turned to Lucille. "This guy said he

killed you. I saw a body—someone your size, with hair like yours and your scarf—couldn't see the face."

This brought an undecipherable explosion of noise from Slattery, which we all ignored.

"Yeah, I know," Lucille said, stroking Ted's hair. "You gave the cops my parents' number, and they called them up to come identify my body. They totally fell apart, but then my brother suggested they call Cammy's place where I was staying to double check. Boy, if you think my parents hated you before—they really hate you now." Lucille said with a kind of admiration in her voice.

"You weren't with him?" I nodded my head toward the trash can lid, which I was holding with both hands. I wasn't about to let go.

"Hell, no. He did steal my scarf though, when I left your place. He jumped out and grabbed my scarf, and wouldn't let go. Then I heard the police coming out on the back stairs, so I just let go of the scarf and ran."

Teddy tried to get up, bracing himself on Lucille's protective arm. "Forget all that," he said urgently. "Lucille, if you help me, I can walk. Let's go now. I know people who have boats. We could sail out tonight. I can't bear to lose you again. I think it would kill me."

"I listened at the door, Teddy. I heard what you told Jo about killing your wife. It's not right what you did. I can't live with blood money, even if was legally yours."

"I don't care about the money. We'll live somehow."

"Don't you see, Teddy? What you did can't be wiped away. I won't stop caring about you, but I can't run away with you."

"Is it because—before you told me you met someone new."

"The doctor who prescribed the diet pills was nice to me for a while," she sighed. "Until he found out I was starting to gain weight again. Then he started talking like my mother, and wanted me to take more pills and maybe get surgery. I dumped him."

She gently stroked his hair. "I still love you."

"You want me to turn myself in?"

"Yes, baby. You know it's the right thing to do. I'll stick with you."

They were still embracing when the uniformed police officers came through the door with service revolvers drawn. They yelled at us to put our hands up, and I slowly released my hold on the trash can lid, which rolled to one side. Slattery had lost consciousness.

One policeman went to look at Teddy's wound.

"Where's the gun?"

I nodded toward the pot of soup and one of them went to look.

He started to laugh and said something to one of the other policemen about my cooking.

Mulligan came in as one of the policemen was helping me get up off Slattery's unconscious form.

"Josephine, is there something you wanted to tell me?"

"Shut up."

Teddy went to the hospital, under police escort.

The paramedics didn't seem to think that Dick Slattery had suffered any permanent damage, but they took him in for X-rays because he was convinced there was some.

The policemen were scrupulously polite, and clearly amused.

I heard one of them say as he led Dick Slattery away, "Sir, if you want to press charges against these two ladies for assaulting you and taking away your gun after you shot their friend, you are free to do so. But I'm not sure I'd want that story widely broadcast around jailhouse circles if I were you."

The rest of us ended up going down to the police station for an orgy of statements that lasted till dawn. Lucille, Mulligan and I left about the same time. We wound up at a restaurant near the apartment. It was early enough that there were only a few other customers. Lucille cast a sympathetic eye at the waitress.

"Are you going to be okay?" I asked her.

"I don't know. I'm more worried about Teddy at this point."

"They say his wound isn't life threatening. I could be wrong, Lucille, but he does seem to care about you."

Lucille sighed. "He's a good guy, and I do care about him.

He just lost it. His wife really was a bitch, but—I just don't know."

"Encourage him to write about it. It's what he does. That's the best way for him to cope."

Lucille shook her head. "It was writing that got us all in this trouble. Teddy got in trouble writing that book for his ex. I wrote him a letter about the Women's Job Skill Center that gave him the idea of how to steal Fran's briefcase. And all that money. I left it in your refrigerator."

"I know."

"And I found it in Raoul's kitty litter," Mulligan said.

"Okay, so I moved it. The police have it now," I said. "I wonder what will happen to it."

Mulligan stretched, and we all started to get ready to go home. "I'll bet that they'll treat it as Francesca's property. It couldn't go to Teddy, because you can't inherit from someone you murdered. Probably to her family as if she hadn't left a will."

I wondered if Isadora would get some portion of the money under the inheritance laws. Matt and Brenda were going to have major legal bills defending themselves against money laundering charges for their irregular campaign contributions. Lucille drove off to her friend Cammy's house. She said she would come back to visit Teddy, and asked if she could come over and talk. I realized that there was a lot to talk about.

Mulligan went up to the apartment with me. "Are you okay here now?" he asked.

"I probably won't move into the bedroom for another few days, but I feel okay." And I did. "I do have a rather high-tech infestation problem." I explained about Slattery's listening devices.

"I'll bring some bug-sweeping equipment this weekend. We should look for the video stuff too," Mulligan said. "It's probably in the smoke detector, the VCR or the clock, if it's got a power source. If it's battery operated, it might be a lot of different places. We'll find them, don't worry. They're also going to run out of tape without him to change it, if that's any consolation."

"Sort of a consolation. Thanks. Are you still sure you want to move into the apartment below?"

"Jo, I promise you, I will repair all those holes in the ceiling and get rid of the listening devices down there."

"I trust you, Mulligan." I stopped before I said something I would regret.

He went back downstairs and Raoul looked up sleepily from the sofa. I fetched my blankets and pillow, which I had tidied away the day before. It seemed to have been another century now, even another lifetime.

Mulligan moved into the apartment under me over the next few days. He was typically efficient about it, moving most of his furniture with the help of a couple of buddies from work. I heard him banging and hammering. I assumed he was setting up shelves, but I didn't go down and ask and he didn't come up to tell me. He did come up with some science fiction style equipment and swept the place for bugs. He had already taken up the microphones Slattery had installed in the floor from the apartment below, and he found a few more and a video camera in a potted plant opposite the sofa. I got a chill up my spine thinking of that creep watching me sleep, but it didn't turn into the kind of fear that had gripped me in the apartment before. The memory of kneeling on Dick Slattery's arms and totally immobilizing him had a certain power. It was the first time I could remember my weight offering a distinct advantage.

I spent the week researching just what nonprofits Delores Patton was involved with, what her ties were to Matt Gunther, and putting into a report just why I could not recommend a grant to the Women's Job Skill Center in Bremerton.

Finally I went down to a furniture store and bought a bed, which the store delivery people installed in what had been Nina's bedroom. I slept in the bed, in the bedroom. True, I did leave all the doors open, and snuggled in with Raoul for company. But I was not afraid—it was hard to remember how it had felt to be afraid, not that I wanted any reminders. Not being afraid suited me fine.

Mulligan invited me to come for dinner the following weekend. Because I had last seen the place darkened and empty, I didn't recognize it with Mulligan's furniture there. He was cooking something that smelled good when I came in.

"Are you still going to open up the window so Raoul can come and go as he pleases?" I asked.

Mulligan smiled. "I intend to do that. It will expand Raoul's turf. But I have a confession to make."

"Okay," I said cautiously. "Go ahead."

"There's a lady I want you to meet—my new roommate."

My heart sank, but I realized he was pointing under the table. There was a cardboard cat carrier under the table. The top was open but no occupant was visible. I stuck my head under the table, and directly over the box. In the darkness of the box, a pair of round, orange eyes, appeared to belong to an invisible cat. Then a small black-whiskered nose poked out the opening at the top of the carrier, and a tiny black fluffy kitten popped her head out.

"Oh my God, what a seriously adorable kitten," I said.

"I'm calling her La Niña. You think Raoul will like her?"

"Who wouldn't? So Raoul hasn't met her yet?"

"I'm sure he knows she's here, I caught him sniffing around the back door earlier today. But I thought I'd let her get used to the place first. I'm not about to let her out in the cold cruel world till she's had her operation, so the window will stay shut for a while. But we could bring Raoul down, and bring her up to let them meet, and get used to each other."

"This encounter, I have to see."

"Well, then you'll have to stick around for a while, won't you?"

There was no way around it, I would.